DON'T TELL ME WHO TO LOVE

EMMA NICHOLS

First published in 2022 by:

J'Adore Les Books

www.emmanicholsauthor.com

Copyright © 2022 by Emma Nichols

ISBN: 9798804958542 (pbk)

Also available in digital format

Other books by Emma Nichols

Other books by Emma Nichols...

The Vincenti Series:
Finding You
Remember Us
The Hangover

Duckton-by-Dale Series:
Summer Fate
Blind Faith
Christmas Bizarre

Forbidden
This Is Me (Novella)
Ariana
Madeleine
Cosa Nostra
Cosa Nostra II
Elodie
Rock My Heart

To keep in touch with the latest news from Emma Nichols and her writing please visit:

www.emmanicholsauthor.com
www.facebook.com/EmmaNicholsAuthor
https://twitter.com/ENichols_Author

Thanks

Without the assistance, advice, support and love of the following people, this book would not have been possible.

Bev. Thank you for your immense contribution, for working studiously through chapter by chapter, multiple times throughout the course of writing this book, and kicking my backside when I needed it.
Gill and Anne. Thank you for your feedback.
Claire, and Ana. Thank you for your Spanish expertise.
Mu. Thank you for this brilliant cover.

Thank you to my editor at Global Wordsmiths, Nicci Robinson. It is a pleasure to work with you and your team to get
the best out of my writing.

To my wonderful readers and avid followers.
Thank you for continuing to read the stories I write.
I hope you enjoy this one as much as the rest.

If you enjoy my stories, please do me the honour of leaving a review on Amazon or Goodreads as this helps with visibility so that other readers may discover my stories too.
You can also subscribe to my website at
www.emmanicholsauthor.com
for updates on my book releases.

With love, Emma x

Dedication

To those who have had to make difficult
choices to be with those they love.

Emma x

Author's Note

I have endeavoured to keep the writing of this story authentic to the location and culture in which it is set, Granada, Spain. To that end there are a few simple words spelt in Spanish throughout the text.

I have discovered that the Spanish language is one of the most widely spoken languages across the world, and that also means some words are spelt differently from place to place, a bit like English versus American.

Having consulted with native Spanish speakers and a specialist in linguistics, I have stuck with the European Spanish spellings. I am aware that Mio cariño will in some parts of the world be spelt with an 'a', as in, mia cariña. In Spain this term of endearment is gender free and picks up the 'o' spelling rather than the 'a'. Cariña, I am told is in fact not a word other than in Galicia in another language.

I hope you enjoy Don't Tell Me Who To Love.

1.

Devon, England, April 1995.

THE THUDDNG INSIDE GABI'S head this morning, like every morning, had a regular beat. It held her attention, like when she used to watch the pendulum of her nana's grandfather clock as a young child. Tick, not knowing, and tock, waiting to find out. She would ignore her papa's raised voice coming from behind closed doors and fantasise about girl pirates battling against each other on majestic ships in search of treasure. She would become one of them, and the ticking clock served as the clash of pirates' blades.

Hypnotised by the rhythm, she drifted in and out of a hazy sleep, with no care for the time or day. The weight across her chest came from the arm of the woman she'd brought home, who now lay too close for comfort. There was a foggy memory of who she was. Her search through her half-awakened brain for any recollection of the previous evening revealed a blank. *It had been fun though, hadn't it?* She couldn't recall anything to justify her optimism.

She forced her eyes open. Even with the blinding pain, this woman looked sweet and thankfully, not familiar. Women who clung on like they'd won first prize because she'd spent the night with them were a total turn off. Clingy women reminded her too much of the part of herself that she hated. She'd avoided being that way with her policy of one-time-only fucking that she'd adopted after Shay had left her. Shay hadn't been clingy. Shay had been perfect.

Until she'd told Gabi she didn't love her.

What's her name? Her head screamed for relief from the constant battering and the strain of trying to think. She needed to extract herself from the human clamp that pinned her to the bed and go to the loo. That last tequila shot had been the killer. The woman taking up two thirds of her bed was a Capricorn. Gabi had listened to her promoting the merits of being guided by star signs for the best chance at a relationship while being guided by the best part of a bottle of vodka at the bar. Capricorn was single and totally into horror-scopes, as Gabi called them, and the irony of Capricorn's personal situation hadn't been lost on Gabi. Despite her disbelief, Gabi knew quite a bit about star signs from watching the daily horoscopes on early morning TV, which was fascinatingly addictive. She'd told the woman she was a Taurus because that would make them totally compatible. Gabi hadn't deliberately misled her, she'd just told Capricorn what she'd wanted to hear, as she always did. She'd known the sex between them would be fiery. Sex was about all an Aries had in common with a Capricorn, so it had been a safe lie because Capricorn would leave in the morning feeling great. Though her justifications didn't stop the sober truth gripping, and self-disgust leaving a bitter taste in her mouth. This wasn't who she was; it was who she had become since Shay.

The thumping in her head demanded she take some pills. She picked up her phone and stared at the blurred screen until the numbers finally registered. Ten-thirty. "Shit."

It took effort to prise Capricorn off so Gabi could slip from the bed. Judging by the array of clothes scattered across the floor, it must have been a hell of a night. Gabi cleared her throat because she still couldn't recall the woman's name—maybe she'd never asked her—and hoped the noise would wake her. She continued to sleep like the dead. Shit, her head hurt, and still there was nothing that resembled a waking sign from Sleeping Beauty.

Gabi stripped the covers off the bed and revealed the woman's slender body. Her breasts were the kind she could bury her face in, though she couldn't recall doing that. The woman's beautifully shaped nipples stood out against her paler skin. "Nice legs." A twinge of early morning desire stirred, but she wouldn't go there and prolong the inevitable that would just encourage something more than she really wanted to offer. Besides, she had more important things to do. She nudged the woman's shoulder. "Come on, sleepy head. I've got to work."

Capricorn yawned and opened her eyes. "Hey, lover."

Gabi laughed. "Yeah, right. Come on, baby girl. Get your sweet ass up and out of here so I can get going."

The woman huffed and lowered her eyes. She blinked rapidly and rolled her tongue around her bottom lip. Gabi couldn't be drawn into her sulk-for-sex appeal because it might lead to a misunderstanding with respect to the one-night-only policy. She chucked the woman's clothes at her and quickly dressed herself. She would shower after Capricorn had left just in case the woman decided to act on the desire that, judging by the way she looked Gabi up and down, was clearly streaming salacious thoughts through her mind.

"There's juice in the fridge," Gabi said, putting on her trainers.

"Any coffee?"

She had coffee, but she didn't have time for it to brew and them to sit around chatting. She had Nana's birthday bash to get to, and she had to finish the gifts she'd made before heading to Nana's house. She wrinkled her nose at the thought of letting Capricorn down. One time or not, it was always hard to boot a woman out of her bed the next morning. It would be so much easier if they just upped and left, and she didn't have to engage with them. "Can't. I'm running late."

Capricorn shimmered towards her and stroked her cheek. The smell of sex lingered on her fingers. In the thundering of her hangover and the ache in her heart that reminded her that this wasn't what she really wanted, Capricorn was quickly becoming less appealing, while Gabi's self-disgust gained momentum. It was starting to feel all a little too familiar—too claustrophobic. Gabi ushered her down the stairs.

"Spoilsport." She pouted and headed out the door. She wiggled her backside as she walked down the communal hallway.

Gabi closed the door. She leaned her head back against the wood, inhaled deeply, and savoured the lighter feeling that replaced the tension of having a stranger in her home. She didn't really pick the women she slept with. They approached her at the bar where she worked. She rarely turned them down, because spending the night with someone was preferable to spending it alone. But even with the attention, she was lonely.

Pills. Where were the pills? Coffee, strong and hot, then a shower. The shower gel that gave off a great menthol hit when the water was roasting hot would do the trick.

By the time Gabi sat down to work on the gifts, the fog in her mind had lifted a little, though her hands still trembled and made it a challenge to embroider her nana's name, Estrella, onto the white cotton handkerchief. She polished the silver

4

butterfly brooch she'd made to make sure it was perfectly clean, set it in a presentation box, and wrapped it in the finest gold-coloured paper she'd acquired from the card shop in town. Her heart swelled as she imagined the joy in Nana's eyes and her big smile of appreciation.

It was a short walk from her place to Nana's, and although the wind always whipped across the fields no matter what the season, the breeze, the pills, and the warmth of the sun combined to lift the last of her hangover.

Nana and Grandpa had bought their farmhouse when they arrived in England in 1939, and other than the occasional lick of paint, its appearance hadn't been altered over the years. The sandstone was her favourite stone, and its large glass windows drew in the sun, making it bright and warm inside. It had a quaint thatched roof that gave it a quirky character, and a slightly musky smell in Gabi's old bedroom that she'd become accustomed to. She loved the farmhouse, because it was a part of Nana, and Nana was a part of it. It was where Gabi had spent her childhood because her dad had been away sailing the seas. The farmhouse would always be home to her, something she'd never managed to achieve with the flat she rented. Sometimes, she wished she'd never moved out, but independence had won the day back then, when she'd started seeing women.

The wraparound garden always had something new going on. The rose bushes Nana had planted recently had lots of tiny buds on them that would ease themselves into full bloom for the summer. The lavender scent gave way to a floral aroma from the early spring flowers as she reached the open front door and, hovering at the threshold, Gabi got a whiff of the freshly baked sweetened bread.

5

"Cariño, Gabriela, come in, come in. I have to rescue the torta before it cremates."

Nana had set her white mop of hair, though Gabi wondered what the point was given she'd managed to cover herself in flour and heaven knows what else she'd got splattered on her face and red blouse.

"Happy birthday, Nana." She put the gifts on the only clear space she could see.

Nana plonked the hot flan onto the kitchen surface, shut the oven door, dumped the oven mittens on the surface, and stepped towards Gabi with open arms. The twinkle in her eyes hadn't faded with the years. She looked better than ever, as though she'd been given a new lease of life.

"Come here, Gabriela," she said.

Gabi enjoyed the warm hug and the tenderness in Nana's tone. She released a deep breath. "So, how's the birthday girl?"

"Getting older and wiser, cariño," She kissed Gabi's cheeks and stared at her. "You look tired. You need a proper holiday."

"I can't afford one."

"I'll pay for you."

"I'm not taking your money, Nana, you know that."

She looked at Gabi, pinched her lips together, and mumbled something in Spanish that Gabi couldn't make sense of.

She picked up a dish of food from the worktop. "Help me take the buffet to the table, Gabriela."

Gabi traipsed back and forth until she'd shifted the tapas dishes from the kitchen to the dining room. It all smelled delicious. There was only one downside to this family event, and he'd just stepped through the front door. "Dad."

"Gabi."

She didn't expect any more conversation from him, and he wouldn't be getting any from her either. It was just the way it was. No love was lost between them because there had never been any to lose. He'd been more like a boring old uncle, and it'd been irritating when he'd tried to assert the fatherly rights he believed he had over her whenever he returned home. He'd bring her gifts from the places he'd visited and yet, didn't ask her what she'd been doing at school or play games with her in the garden. Later, he'd talk to Nana behind closed doors, sometimes raising his voice, sometimes leaving without much of a goodbye. She'd always known him to be as distant as the shores he travelled to for his Naval career, and she didn't expect that scenario to change just because he had retired.

Nana always said it was just who he was and that he loved her. Gabi hadn't been bothered since Nana always arranged for Gabi's friends to come around and play with her whenever he was home, and that had been more fun than being with her dad. By the time she'd grown into a teenager, she had more interesting things to think about than him. He was as much of a stranger to Nana as he was to her, and Gabi wondered how Nana felt about that. She seemed unaffected. But that was Nana all over. Accepting and loving, and fiercely defensive of those she loved.

"Hugo. How nice of you to come."

Gabi bit her lip to stop a smirk.

"Happy birthday, Mother."

He pulled a small box from his coat pocket and handed it to Nana. It looked as though it had been professionally wrapped, and Gabi wondered whether he knew what was in the box or whether he'd asked someone else to purchase it on his behalf.

Nana smiled. "You shouldn't have, Hugo." She put the present on the dressing table. "Come, let's eat before it gets cold."

Her dad picked up a plate and loaded it like he'd not eaten for a month. "You had something you wanted to tell us," he said, while chewing on a mouthful of Nana's homemade pisto con huevos, small bits of which fell from his mouth.

Given his privileged upbringing, he should have at least swallowed before speaking.

Nana cleared her throat. "Yes, I do, Hugo." She stayed still and quiet for the time it took him to draw his attention from his plate.

"Well, what is it?"

Gabi would have liked to think that his impatience was down to his concern for Nana's wellbeing, and that maybe he expected some bad news that he didn't want to hear. But his irritation hadn't affected his appetite and that suggested otherwise. He'd become even more up his own arse since he'd settled in London, though how he'd managed to get worse was a mystery.

"I'm going to Spain," Nana said.

He lifted his chin. "Ah, right. One week or two?"

"I haven't decided."

Gabi popped the cork on the chilled Cava and poured them each a glass. "Nice one, Nana."

Nana took the drink from Gabi and sipped. She turned to Hugo. "I might not come back."

It was a good job he'd already swallowed, because if he hadn't, Nana would have felt the full force of any remaining pisto that he was now doing his best to hold back from choking on.

"Have you lost your mind, woman? What do you mean, you might not come back?"

Lost in the humour of her dad's discomfort, Gabi hadn't fully registered what Nana had said. Nana had a dry sense of humour she said she'd picked up from the British. She was joking though, right? Gabi stared at her. She was smiling and didn't look in the least bit like she was teasing with them. What the fuck?

"Hugo, all my senses are in good order and always have been. No estoy loca. My mind is clear."

"Well, it sounds like madness to me. You can't just go off to Spain on a whim. What on earth are you thinking? What if something happens to you?"

Gabi's head twisted with the same thoughts, and the only thing stopping her agreeing with him, apart from the fact that it would stick in her throat, was that Nana must have good reason to want to go back to Spain after fifty-six years. She looked to the floor, bit her lip, and swallowed past the lump in her throat. A holiday was one thing, but the idea that Nana would stay in Spain made her stomach tighten. *Fuck.*

"And what if it does? The health care system is as good as here, maybe better. And I'm not planning to die yet." She crossed her chest. "God willing." She crossed her chest again and looked up. She picked up her drink and took a sip. "I want to visit my parents' graves and remember the fond memories I have of the life I left behind."

"What life? You don't know anyone there." Hugo cleared his plate and slammed it on the table. He paced around the room and rubbed his belly. "Jesus Christ, Mother."

"I made a New Year's resolution, and nothing you say is going to change my mind."

"You made a resolution four months ago and didn't think to tell me."

How dare he have a go at Nana? She didn't have to justify herself to him. "You're never here. What do you care?" Gabi said.

Hugo huffed, and his jaw tensed beneath his heavy jowls.

Nana turned to Gabi and smiled. "And Gabriela is coming with me."

Gabi stared at Nana, open mouthed. "I—"

"I need a chaperone, and I'd rather pay you than a stranger," Nana said.

The movie of Gabi's life rolled out in her mind's eye. It wasn't even close to award winning; it wouldn't even make a Z listing if there was such a thing. Working at the bar, the women she didn't know, and the hangovers that left her feeling shitty, there was nothing she'd particularly miss. Perhaps a break from it all would be good, and what harm would come from being paid to look after Nana for a few weeks or however long she wanted to stay? It would be an adventure, and she'd be doing Nana a service. A change of scene in her sex life would be good too.

"Mother, you need someone with you who can actually be of help to you," Dad said.

Arsehole.

"Gabriela is perfectly capable. She can work on her Spanish and explore her creative side."

Hugo shook his head and huffed through his nose. "You're losing your marbles."

"No, Hugo. I've never felt better."

Gabi looked from one to the other. He might be right, but Nana did look as if this decision had given her a new lease of life. She held up her glass in a toast. "Cheers, Nana."

Hugo plucked food from a dish on the table and ate it as if his life depended on it and mumbled something unintelligible.

"Will you come with me?" Nana asked.

Gabi had never visited Spain, and while she'd spoken Spanish with Nana as a kid, she'd had no reason to keep it up while working in a bar in a sleepy village in Devon. If she'd worked in London, things might have been different, but the idea of commuting had never appealed because she hated public transport. Spain conjured images of World Cup football, bullfighting, and the golfer, Seve Ballesteros. She wasn't a fan of any of them particularly, but she'd easily enjoy the sun, the hot Spanish women, and a chilled beer or wine at one of the many tavernas. "Yes," she said and took great pleasure in watching her dad look like he was about to explode. One nil to Spain.

2.

THE END OF MAY came around quickly. Gabi wished she hadn't bought a suitcase from the local charity shop when it suddenly developed a dodgy wheel halfway home. Dragging it up the hill to Nana's with a rucksack on her back was like a full-on workout, and it was too early in the morning to put her body through that kind of torture. Maybe she should have travelled lighter, but Nana had made it clear as they'd planned for the trip that she had no desire to think about their return. She was going to play it by ear, she'd said. The open-endedness felt a little daunting until Gabi started telling those around her that she was leaving. Her manager didn't beg for her to stay, and he found someone to take her job within two days. The new tenant taking over her flat was moving in later in the day. If it wasn't for her best mate, Issa, who cried when Gabi told her about the trip, it was as though she'd never meant anything to anyone. Issa tended to be overdramatic, but she'd promised to take good care of Gabi's stereo and espresso machine while she was away.

"We're going on a voyage of discovery. The future is our destiny," Nana had said.

Gabi had found the lack of certainty disconcerting at first, not knowing what lay ahead or what she might do when they returned. On reflection, she'd realised the sorry state of her life. She'd become comfortable with a lack of drive, though admittedly unhappy and unenthused by anything. She'd talked herself around the fear of leaving what she knew behind, because she had to be strong for Nana and settled with the idea that she could always move back into the farmhouse when they returned until she decided what to do next.

She stopped for a moment and leaned against the post box to take a few deep breaths. The farmhouse was shrouded in darkness, and she squinted to confirm what she was seeing. Nana stood outside her front door with two suitcases at her feet.

"You're late," Nana said as Gabi approached.

Nana leaned on her walking stick, looking typically Nana in her fuchsia pink rain mac with matching hat and handbag. It might be four-thirty in the morning, but with an untypical heat wave for late May, it was eighteen degrees. Gabi would have perspired just looking at her if she hadn't already sweated her backside off dragging her bloody case with its dodgy wheel. The two suitcases at Nana's side screamed out that they would need to pass through oversized baggage, which would mean another queue to contend with at the airport, but Gabi's first concern was how the hell they were going to get them that far when they had three train stations and the London Underground to navigate before they reached the airport.

"The taxi isn't due for another fifteen minutes, Nana."

"It might have been early, and then what?"

"The driver would have waited." It wasn't a long walk to Nana's, but it would have been easier for the driver to pass by Gabi's place, but Nana had insisted that they meet at the farmhouse and save the driver the bother of stopping twice.

"You know I don't like to be late, Gabriela."

Gabi put down her bags and stretched her back. She kissed her nana on the cheeks. The smell of soap and the foundation cream that she'd used for as long as Gabi could remember was comforting. Nana pressed her lips tightly together and stared down the road like a skittish cat. Perhaps she was more nervous than she let on. *Bless her.* At seventy-five and having not travelled abroad since she arrived in the UK, it was no surprise she might be a bit anxious about the journey. "We've got an itinerary. We'll be fine."

"Not if we miss the taxi to Exeter, we won't," Nana said.

"He's coming straight to your door."

"And if we're late, we'll miss the train to London."

"We're here, aren't we?"

"That's not the point. You could've been late."

Gabi rolled her eyes. "We have plenty of time between all our changes, so we don't need to rush, and a taxi will be waiting for us in Granada. You can relax. I've sorted it."

Nana patted Gabi's hand. "I know, Gabriela. I'm a little nervous."

Gabi took Nana's hand. "That's why I'm with you. And look, here it comes." The driver was early. Gabi was glad she hadn't been any later.

Nana used the cane to make her way down the steps and along the path, and greeted the driver with a jolly, "Good morning."

He opened the door for her, and she took a seat in the back, leaving Gabi staring at the bags and wondering whether it would have been easier to just buy what they needed in Spain. The driver opened the boot of the car and stood next to it, apparently not eager to help. She dropped their bags at the back of the car and smiled at him. "Nice morning," she said.

He grunted, giving the impression he was about as enthused at working at this hour as Gabi was being awake, and groaned as he lifted Gabi's case into his boot. *Wimp.* Gabi strained under the weight of Nana's first case, lugged it down the path, and smiled at the driver as he struggled to lift it. The second case was a fraction lighter, but it was still going to need to go through oversized baggage. Gabi had never had any inclination to work out before five a.m. The adverts for those early morning gym classes were a crock. No, it didn't feel great straining muscles before they'd fully woken up, and no, shifting overweight suitcases didn't set her up for the day. If she was at the flat now, she'd be turning over in bed and enjoying the restorative effects of a long lie-in before a strong sweet coffee. That would be the perfect set-up for the day.

She sat next to Nana and fastened her seatbelt. Her shirt clung to her back and beads of sweat formed on her brow. Nana was still wrapped in her coat and wearing her hat. "Aren't you warm?" she asked.

"It's better to be prepared than caught short, cariño."

"Hm."

"And I ran out of space in the cases," Nana said.

No shit. "An outfit for every season, eh?"

Nana took Gabi's hand and squeezed it. "I couldn't decide what to leave behind."

Gabi frowned. "How did you manage to lift the cases to the door?"

"I didn't, Gabriela. I packed them on the doorstep."

God help us getting through London. Her thumping head told her it was mid-morning already and quizzed her as to what had happened to the coffee. She stared longingly at the blue neon light of Caffé Nero as they drove past. A jittery feeling in her stomach prompted her to ask the driver to stop, but that wasn't on the itinerary, and Nana wouldn't like it if they strayed from their detailed travel plan.

Thirty minutes later and they were right on schedule, parked up outside St David's station with their bags sat in a line on the path. "Wait here and I'll go and find a trolley." Gabi said.

"Yes, cariño."

The distinctive coffee aroma called Gabi to the counter, and she ordered two double espressos. If Nana didn't want hers, Gabi would happily have both. Drinks in hand, she headed towards the trolley park. It wasn't easy juggling the two cardboard cups with a trolley that had a persistent lean to the left. What was it with bloody trolleys and wheels? With the determination of her craving-inspired body, she made it to the place she'd left Nana and their luggage, next to the lamp post just outside the station's main entrance where the taxi had dropped them off. Exactly where Nana should have been waiting for her. So where the hell was she? Where was their luggage? The absence of caffeine enhanced her worst fears and with a racing heart, she searched among the increasing number of travellers that occupied the path in front of the building. There wasn't a pink fuchsia hat in sight and the more she looked, the stronger the anxiety bit. "Fucking hell, Nana. Where are you?"

"Language, Gabriela."

Gabi turned to see Nana approach pushing their bags on a trolley. Gabi took a deep breath and her heartbeat started to slow, and then the fire rose inside her again. "Where did you go? You can't just wander off like that."

"A nice young man gave me his trolley. He was very helpful and polite. And those are rare qualities these days. So I took him

16

to the notice board, the one with the local attractions advertised on it. He was very grateful."

Gabi ran her fingers through her hair, pulled at the roots and took a couple more deep breaths. She forced a smile, and the trembling in her stomach eventually abated.

Nana patted her hand. "Come on, Gabriela, we haven't got time to stand around. I don't want to miss the train."

She turned the trolley like a pro and headed towards the station. If she hadn't wanted to get her pound back on principle, she would have dumped it right there. "I got you a coffee," Gabi said, balancing the two cups as she did battle with the trolley to get it back into the station building.

"You drink it, cariño. You look like you need it, and my hands are full."

"Stay close to me," Gabi said and wondered if she was taking her chaperone role too seriously. Nana's arms were at full stretch, and she was puffing like she had a forty-a-day habit. This level of exercise was likely to cause a heart attack and land them in A&E at the Exeter hospital rather than sunny Spain. "Slow down."

They reached the trolley park, and Gabi claimed her pound with satisfaction. She downed both coffees swiftly and inhaled deeply as the caffeine lit her up. They made their way to the platform.

"Stay here until I've loaded the luggage," Gabi said. The last thing she needed was for Nana to wander off again. This trip already felt like a labour of love, and she was beginning to wonder if she shouldn't have given her participation more considered thought. When the whistle blew and the train eased out of the station, she breathed a deep sigh of relief. She'd grab a nap in the three and a half hours it would take to get to London.

"What are we going to have for breakfast?" Nana asked.

Gabi would swear that Nana had waited until her eyes had shut before asking. She sat up and yawned from the weight of the tiredness that descended upon her. Nana hugged her coat and hat in her lap. Gabi's heart warmed. She was wearing the butterfly brooch Gabi had made for her birthday. "What do you fancy?" she asked.

"I don't know what there is."

"I don't have a clue either. Something plastic, probably."

"Can you go to the buffet car, please, Gabriela, and find out?"

Gabi would rather not have to run back and forth, but it seemed that was what she'd signed up for. Nana stared out of the window as they sped through the countryside, her hand trembling in her lap, and it occurred to Gabi what might be going through her mind. Was this the last time Nana would see this place? "Would you like me to put your coat and hat on the rack?" she asked as she stood.

Nana didn't take her attention from the scenery as she handed up the clothing. "Thank you."

Gabi made her way slowly through the four carriages to the buffet car to give herself time to process the sadness that had taken her by surprise. Nana hadn't given her any other reasons for the trip than when she'd announced it. Gabi supposed she wanted to see how Granada had changed since she was there and make peace with her parents' place of rest. Old people liked to reminisce and get closure on stuff, she guessed. Did Nana want to be buried with them? Gabi had never asked because it had never occurred to her that Nana would ever die.

It didn't matter how many times she studied the food options at the counter, it all looked unappetising. The woman behind the counter was called Sally, according to the badge sitting on a slant across the top of her right breast. Sally was a bright, cheery name, but that didn't translate to the woman's sullen appearance, which was a shame. She would be pretty if she smiled. On her second walk through the carriages to collect the food, Gabi noticed the other travellers, most in grey suits. Some read newspapers while others had their eyes shut. But for the thunderous rattle of the train, there was a dull kind of silence inside, an absence of joy, reaffirming Gabi's hatred of public transport. That was one of the positives of working in a bar. Everyone seemed happy, if not before a few drinks, then definitely afterwards. She was glad she'd never commuted for work. People looked so miserable. Why would she want to waste so many hours travelling for a job when she could be doing better things with her time, like chilling out?

Nana nibbled her bacon sandwich. She didn't comment on its taste, probably because there wasn't any. Gabi downed her third double espresso of the day and set to work on the ham, cheese, and pickle sandwich. It felt like lunchtime, and not only did she need to take the edge off the caffeine, but she was also ravenous.

"Promise me one thing," Nana said.

"What?"

"That you will make something of this trip?" She closed her hand around Gabi's and squeezed.

"Like what?"

"You have an opportunity, Gabriela. You are creative, and your talent was wasted at that bar."

Nana's hand was warm and soft and Gabi's clammy. Gabi frowned. She hadn't thought about anything beyond taking care of Nana. "I'll do my best."

"I worry for you," Nana said softly.

"There's nothing to worry about." Gabi stared out the window. This wasn't a conversation she was expecting, or willing, to have. Not now, nor at any time. She didn't need nagging about something she was acutely aware of.

"You are young. You should be happy."

"I'm fine," Gabi said and pulled her hand from Nana's. She hadn't realised Nana had noticed. Gabi's rebuff had been weak, and Nana's sigh telling. She had the urge to lash out, though at what or who she didn't know, and for what, she didn't understand. She couldn't remember when she'd last felt truly happy, but if she were to guess it would have been when she had been living with Nana at the farmhouse and before she'd fallen in love for the first time.

3.

"AISHA, COME QUICKLY, THERE is good news."

Mama was smiling and dancing at Aisha's bedroom door, delight gushing from her. She gesticulated to Aisha with a level of urgency that was impossible to argue against. It didn't matter what Aisha was doing, she must drop everything and go running. She must join in with the laughter and cheer in the living room. She must receive the good news that Conchita had already shared with her with enthusiasm.

Conchita had begged her to keep her secret weeks ago, and that had been easy to do because her sister's enthusiasm was not Aisha's. Who could know what love even was at seventeen? Who around here was still single aged twenty-four? Aisha would be reminded of her failing many times over the coming weeks, as always happened when a wedding had been announced. It would be more embarrassing for her family on this occasion, because her younger sister's wedding would come before her own.

"I'm getting dressed for work, Mama. What can be so important that it needs me to be there right now?" Her words would fail to reach her mama's ears; they were too busy prematurely ringing with the sounds of wedding bells and clinking glasses. Everyone would dance in the street tonight. Thankfully, work would provide her with a haven from the earlier celebrations and the questions and comments that would inevitably arise about her own intentions to marry. Hopefully, they'd all be too drunk later to force the point.

"Aisha, ven ahora," Mama said.

"I'm coming." The buttonholes on the front of her blouse were small, making it difficult to fasten the buttons quickly enough. She started towards the living room, still grappling with them.

"Aisha." Nicolás stared at her breasts and smiled. "Do you need a hand?"

She swerved to avoid him and slapped his outstretched hand. "No, I can do it."

He trailed behind her to the living room. It appeared the whole village had already arrived. Conchita stood at the centre of a crowd, her cheeks flushed and nodding her head and shifting her feet as each person took her into their arms and congratulated her. Aisha had not thought of her little sister as radiant, but she was tonight, and she looked even younger. Too young to marry. García, her now-betrothed, was stood at her side, fresh-faced and grinning like the boy that he was.

Aisha took a glass of wine, caught her sister's eye, and raised her glass in a toast to her good fortune. Conchita mouthed, "Thank you," then turned back to receiving the good wishes of those who surrounded her. Aisha hated this kind of attention, but that didn't stop the ache of unreciprocated longing reinforcing her sinful desires.

Nicolás raised a toast to the happy couple then turned to Aisha. He held up his glass to her. His thoughts weren't hard to read. He had beautiful eyes, as dark as the ocean, a rugged, handsome appeal, and the voice of an angel when he sang. There wasn't a woman in the village who wouldn't snatch up his hand in marriage if he were to offer it to them. Except Aisha.

His touch on her arm was gentle, though she still flinched inside. She tried to hide her response by moving towards the door. "We need to go."

"Yes, the others will not want to wait."

Her mama was making her way towards them. Someone had started chanting and another strummed a guitar. There was nothing quite like the announcement of a forthcoming wedding as a good reason for celebration, and no one did that better than them. Aisha had the urge to run.

"Isn't this the most wonderful news, Aisha? Your sister is to be married."

"Yes, Mama, it's great news." She wanted to add, *for her*, but stopped herself. "They look happy together," she said.

"And look at you two," Mama said.

She took their hands, and he smiled. Aisha fought the impulse to scream.

"You make a very handsome couple." Her mama drew their hands together.

Nicolás tried to hold Aisha's hand, but she pulled away. "Yes, Mama. Now, we need to go to work. I will join the celebrations later." She wouldn't be drawn into a conversation about *them* that would end in a fiery argument with her mama.

"We will join you later," Nicolás said and kissed Mama on the cheeks. "It is a special evening, and we can dance together until dawn."

Mama cupped his face and stared at him as if he was the son she'd always wished for. She heaved a deep sigh and looked at Aisha as she spoke. "You take good care of my Aisha."

Aisha wanted the earth to swallow her up and push her out into some other time and place. It wasn't that she didn't love her family. She did, very much. She loved them all and would give her life for them if she had to. She just didn't need—or want—a man to look after her. She wanted what she couldn't have, though her heart still tried to convince her it was a possibility every time she went to the city and performed.

She would sing of love in the street tonight. She would dance with wild desire. The music would feed her soul with hope, and her heart would open like a flower. The stars would appear brighter, and her steps home lighter. She wanted to know that joy for a short time, even if she couldn't grasp it and hold onto it. And the yearning would keep her awake until the sun started to rise. She would float away inside her dreams and wake as she always did with an ache so deep that she could lose herself inside its emptiness. When she rose in the morning and gathered the crops from the field, she would pretend that everything was fine.

Aisha had known that love once and thoughts of Esme still caused her heart to flutter, but Esme could never have been hers. It wasn't to be. Time had passed, and things had changed. As a strong, healthy woman, Aisha was supposed to make an excellent wife and bear many children, and for a gitana in the hills of Sacromonte, they were the only things that mattered.

Nicolás picked up his guitar and strapped it across his back as they left the house. They made their way through the gathering that spilled out along the narrow street. Their neighbours were dancing with her papa. He'd started a fire, so it would soon be ready to cook the food they would all share. Nicolás was right. When they returned, they would all dance together late into the night. It was expected of her.

"Are you not well, Aisha?" he asked as they walked.

Aisha stopped where the road was at its widest, where a tourist scenic spot had been constructed. The view of Granada, sprawled across the foot of the Sierra Nevada, made it a popular location for tourists to stop and take photographs, although she preferred the view late at night. Fewer lights would spill from the houses, so she could see the constellations. The Great Bear would often appear from the houses left of the Genil River, and Taurus the bull rose towards the Alhambra. And there was a stillness about the night in which she could find some solace. Behind her sat the white painted houses and beyond those lay their village and the narrow route further up the mountain. Their homes were carved into the rockface, each frontage as unique as the Roma families that had dwelled there for generations. No matter how many years that passed since their ancestors first made their homes there, that piece of their history was timeless.

"Do you ever dream of another world?" she asked.

Nicolás laughed. "Why would I do that? Our life is here." He danced a pirouette. "Besides, we have the prettiest girls in our village."

An attractive woman didn't escape Aisha's eyes either. But the women here were looking for a husband. And if they weren't looking for a man, then they weren't looking at all, and she didn't know anyone like that. Women like Aisha had to keep their secrets inside their dreams and deny their desires because the risk of bringing shame to their family and their community was too great. So, it was better not to look, not to see and be tempted, and not to draw attention. "You are free, Nicolás. Maybe it's different for you."

"You are free too, Aisha." He turned and took a pace away from her, lowered his head, and poked the ground with the toe of his shoe. "You can have any man you want."

He didn't need to ask her directly to go out with him. His longing was as easy to read as the signposts on the road. He was passionate and showed his heart to her unashamedly in the way he looked at her and spent time with her. She was grateful he hadn't asked her to marry him. Perhaps he knew deep down she would refuse. "I just wonder what it might be like to travel and see the world."

He turned swiftly and frowned. "Where would you go that is more beautiful than this?"

"I don't know. It's impossible to imagine what's out there, beyond Granada and Spain. Berlin, Paris, Los Angeles, London. They're places we've heard about, where the tourists come from, places I think might be like ours but different." She didn't know what she was trying to say.

His frown deepened. "You think I lack ambition because I am happy here?" he asked.

"No, I don't. I didn't mean that."

He was blinded by his desire and the fire that he wanted to give to her. His want would never be fulfilled. She didn't share his dream of them making a life together, though her life would be a lot easier if she did.

"If you wanted to go to America or Mexico, you could dance there. But you would leave behind your family and friends to make your way in that world that you don't know? And what will you do if you find you are still not happy?"

"I don't know." Though she might dream of a different life, she couldn't imagine leaving her family. The longing that drove her insane wasn't about her working in another part of the world. It was about her being able to love who she wanted to love and to express that love with her family's blessings. Was she wrong to want that? Husbands and wives had it.

"Can you not see how good life is? We are lucky to have each other, all of us. Ours is a strong and healthy community. Maybe one day you'll see. I just hope it won't be too late for you."

"To find a husband?" She was sick of the prospect of having to be a wife to a man one day and the feeling that that day was going to be forced upon her before she was ready. She would never belong to a man. Never.

"Of course. You are twenty-four already. It's odd that you're not married. People say it is because you're passionate about your work, but with every year that passes, you are giving them cause to ask new questions. I worry for you."

Aisha worried for herself too. She worried that she would have to settle down with a man and have a family. She worried for her sanity when she would eventually be forced to marry. It wasn't fair because there were no options. She couldn't entertain that thought right now. She would rather die than live a lie. But Nicolás was right. She didn't want to be considered an outcast or a freak. She wasn't. She was just not like the other women in their village.

She was done with the conversation. It could never go anywhere, and she wouldn't dance well if she wasn't feeling passionate. She lifted her skirt at the front and started to stride down the road, feeling her pulse rise with the promise of the music. They had to get to the pick-up point where Julio, Francisco, and Manuel would be waiting for them, and she needed to feel good. "No more talk of dreams. We will make the city dance tonight."

4.

Nana asked the taxi driver in fluent Spanish to take a particular route to the hotel, and they stopped outside the gates of a three-storey house. An external staircase, wide enough for three people, started at the street and rose in a sweeping arc to the left and up to a double-sized front door. A brick patterned arch defined an elegant entrance. The cream exterior looked clean and fresh, and everything about it said filthy rich. Gabi counted the windows and imagined eight ensuite bedrooms, probably more, and one of those high-tech kitchens with a central island and a fuck-off huge espresso coffee machine. It stood out against the terraced whitewashed houses with terracotta slatted roofs that they'd passed on the way here. Judging by the height of the well-trimmed hedges that spanned either side of the stately looking property, an equally well-manicured and extensive garden lay beyond them. Gabi bet the owners paid a gardener and probably employed maids too.

Nana pulled out the handkerchief she'd given her for her birthday and wiped her eyes. This had been her parents' house, the place she'd spent the first nineteen years of her life, and Gabi's heart ached as it dawned on her what Nana had left behind.

Now at their hotel, Gabi continued to watch Nana, studying the map she'd picked up from the table in her hotel room. "Would you like to visit the cemetery tomorrow?" Gabi asked.

How much had Granada altered in nearly sixty years? Gabi couldn't think of anything that had changed close to her home except for the Exeter city centre bypass that had recently been extended. But a lot would have changed after the Second World War, including the fact that they could easily travel across Europe now. Their trip to southern Spain would have taken days or even weeks back then. Thank God for progress.

"I'm in no hurry," Nana said.

Gabi was fascinated by the idea of being related to people she'd never had the chance to meet, although she didn't feel anything towards them. Given how Nana had reacted seeing her old house again, she was more concerned about how Nana was going to respond to seeing her parents' graves for the first time. "Is it far?"

"No. It's close by."

Nana pointed to a place on the map, but the tremor in her hand caught Gabi's eye. Nana looked up as she patted the map as if consoling a close friend and smiled. There was still a hint of sadness in her expression that hadn't lifted since seeing her old home earlier, and she'd been quieter than her normal self.

"We must visit Alhambra at some time. It's quite spectacular," Nana said.

"It's a fortress, isn't it?" Gabi had flicked through some of the tourist leaflets briefly while they'd waited in the hotel reception for their keys. There were a lot of historical sites and attractions that would keep them busy for a while.

"There are several palaces. They're Moorish."

Gabi's stomach rumbled. It had been a long time since the plastic sandwich on the train and the limp pastry she'd picked up at the airport because they'd been running late after a delay on the London Underground that had caused Nana to panic. "I'd like to see the markets too."

Nana touched the butterfly brooch attached to her blouse and sighed. She stood and straightened her skirt. "Vamos. Let's go and get dinner."

Gabi looked at her watch. "The hotel restaurant is open."

"No, Gabriela, no. I would like to walk into the city." She picked up her handbag and walking cane.

Gabi dashed though the door that joined their two rooms and grabbed some cash. By the time she'd returned, Nana was already heading down the corridor with a spring in her step, and Gabi had to run to catch her up. She had no idea where they were going, and Nana negotiated the cobbled streets with her cane like she was skiing a black run. The siesta had clearly given her a new burst of energy, and Gabi wished she had taken a late nap instead of wandering the streets.

The air was comfortably warm in a way that it rarely was back home, and the smell of dry earth quickly faded as they passed by gardens with roses and orange blossom trees. Spicy aromas spilled from a bar as they walked past, and clouds of tobacco lingered in the air. The occasional bad smell wafted from the drains. There was loud music, guitars, and clapping, and a crowd huddled around a group of flamenco dancers in the street. The audience's tapping feet sounded like castanets, and the strumming was fast, and furious, and electric. Gabi couldn't see what exactly was going on, but her heart raced, and an elated feeling stayed with her as they moved on.

Nana stopped outside a taverna within earshot of the music. A yellow and green striped awning shielded tables dressed in matching cotton cloth with red paper serviettes. It resembled the colours of the city's flag, intentionally no doubt.

"This one?" Nana asked.

The place looked nice enough, but then so had the other six they'd ignored, and it wasn't as if Gabi knew them like she did the bars back home. She couldn't tell what was a good one and what to avoid. Frankly, she was on the edge of a sugar-low induced rage, and she was about to pass out with hunger or murder some unsuspecting tourist. "Great."

Nana spoke to the waiter who, even though most of the tables had a reserved sign on them, seated them in a prime position overlooking the bustling street. Gabi didn't know whether it was Nana charming the men in their native tongue that seemed to have them eating out of her hand, or maybe they were just more attentive to a woman of Nana's age. She didn't back herself to get the same results if she'd done the asking.

"Some tapas are free," Nana said, "like olives and bread, and sometimes pan con tomate. If it has a pincho in it, then it costs. The longer the pincho, the more expensive. Hot tapas cost. You need to know this."

"Okay." The best they'd offered at her old bar was free crisps and peanuts, but with more attention being given to people with allergies now, the nuts had gone a couple of years back. The crisps went shortly after.

Gabi picked up the menu and squinted at it. The waiter placed two dishes of tapas on their table. Neither dish had cocktail sticks in the morsels of food. Gabi started on the tapas and felt the tension release as the food registered in her stomach. It wasn't only the sunshine that encouraged her to breathe more easily. There was something intoxicating about the place. Grubby, sometimes tatty, buildings leaned against majestic structures, and yet neither looked out of place. They appeared part of a grander, richer scene. The place had a unique feel and so different from England. Waiters with an unhurried, easy-going manner stood outside their restaurants smoking, encouraging passers-by with their effortless charm and bright smiles. Even when their offer was rejected, they laughed and chatted as if talking to a good friend. They appeared to have all the time in the world and all the world in their time. It was captivating. She was drawn to just sitting, and observing, and revelling in the aromas and the relaxed ambience. Besides, she hadn't spotted a women's bar yet; she hadn't been looking. That might be of interest later, but it wasn't like they were on a short holiday. She was in no rush. "I'm enjoying your company," she said.

Nana peered over the top of her menu. It was one of her gently quizzical looks that would normally have Gabi flushing with guilt. Only it didn't this time because what she'd said was true. Having dinner with Nana and watching the world go by, with the clicking and chanting from the street performers seducing her mind was calming.

Nana had talked about bullfighting when Gabi was younger. The dance between bull and matador, the art Nana had said—not the killing—was what drew people into the arena to watch. Gabi hadn't had a clue what she'd meant and no matter what, she didn't like the idea of an animal being treated that way. They'd watched the opera *Carmen* together on the television, the passionate plea of lovers forced apart by circumstances. Both were a cliché of course, but both summed up the feeling in the air, and the passion in the music coming from the streets. Granada was electric by Devon's standards, which didn't take much to be fair, and now they'd arrived, she was excited to explore.

She'd never seen Nana eat as much, let alone drink two glasses of wine. All right, they were small glasses, but she wondered how Nana was going to negotiate the cobbled streets safely back to the hotel. Nana had been quiet as they'd eaten. "Has it changed much?" Gabi asked.

"Has what changed, cariño?"

"Granada."

Nana looked around. "It's busier. More people and a lot of cars. Too loud. The shops and restaurants have changed. It was a long time ago, Gabriela, and for most of my teenage years, I didn't come into the city. It was unsafe."

"Did they sing and dance in the streets like this? I love it."

"Yes." She looked towards the group of people clapping and cheering and turned up her nose. "That's for tourists. We should visit Sacromonte for real flamenco by the Roma Gypsy descendants."

"I'd like that."

Looking out over the square, Nana stifled a yawn and rubbed her eyes just as Gabi was about to order another drink. Even though Nana had benefitted from that late afternoon nap, she must be shattered after their early start and long journey.

"Are you ready to go back?" Gabi almost said home, but they were a long way from the farmhouse.

Nana blinked. "Yes. I think I will. You stay."

"No, I'll go with you."

"No. I know the way. We just walked from there. And that neon hotel sign is bigger than the moon. It can't be missed."

Nana was exaggerating a little, but she made a good point. The evening had barely begun. She gave Gabi her look again that told her not to argue.

34

"Okay, fine. But promise me you'll be careful and go straight back." Gabi sounded like the parent she'd sworn she would never become, for the second time since they'd set off. She had agreed reluctantly, and it came with a twinge of discomfort. But Nana didn't seem at all concerned, and she had to respect that, or she would end up trailing her everywhere and that wouldn't work for either of them.

Nana shook her head. "I know this city like the back of my hand."

"Hm." Gabi doubted that Nana was as familiar with Granada as she once might have been, but there was little point in arguing. Gabi paid the bill and watched Nana as she started to retrace her steps. She looked remarkably spritely, wielding her cane, on the back of two glasses of wine. As she mingled with the others and Gabi lost sight of Nana's white hair, her pulse raced. *She'll be fine.*

Gabi gravitated back towards the music in time to see a dancer lift her skirt and reveal her knees and block-heeled shoes. The crowd cheered as she started to tap. She stood on a piece of wood with her back to a man. He perched on the stone wall of the water feature behind them, a guitar in his lap. Another man sat next to him, his palms resting on the top of what looked like a metal block he had clamped between his legs. He started tapping his fingers in a fast beat on the front of the instrument. The woman clicked her heels. Two other men who appeared to be a part of the group started clapping and moved to stand on either side of the woman.

The speed that she moved her feet and the sound that she made were mesmerising. Gabi couldn't stop staring, and she became immersed trying to work out the pattern in the beat.

Some of the other spectators around her were clapping, and she had no idea where to begin. The man with the guitar started to strum. There was nothing lazy or relaxing about this music. He had a dark intensity to his appearance. It was as if he was the music, all passion, fast and fiery.

Gabi had no idea how long she'd been standing with her hands clasped together in front of her, but when the woman leading the dance caught her eye and smiled, she became acutely aware of how odd the prayer position felt given she held no faith. It was astounding that anyone could move a body part that quickly, let alone several parts in coordinated, precise movements. She thought about Michael Flatley's tap dancing during the interval at Eurovision the previous year. That had been brilliant, but this flamenco was another level of genius. It was raw, fresh, and every beat seemed to ignite a fire inside her. She wanted to dance with them, to feel as uninhibited and as connected to the spirit of the music as they appeared. Nana said this was for tourists, and if Nana was right, Gabi couldn't wait to see the real thing. It was insane, in a brilliant way.

All these people were beautiful, like the stars in a Hollywood movie. They were olive-skinned, athletic, and alluring. Now that she'd quit her obsessive need to watch the woman's feet and had registered that she'd smiled at her, Gabi felt as hot as hell and in desperate need of a chilled beer. She tried to wet her lips, tried to breathe deeper. She failed at both. Her heart raced and her hands tingled, and she felt very self-conscious.

The woman glanced in her direction again as she danced a circle with her arm raised, clicking her castanets, and tapping her heels. Gabi was sure they'd locked eyes. It wasn't the kind of stare she used in England for the explicit purpose of getting laid. This was nothing like that. Not even remotely close. It was as if every cell inside her had stopped functioning and held her suspended inside the passion of the music, and then those cells had simultaneously come to life in a wave of electric vibration that had no end. And each glance the woman stole in Gabi's direction intensified the feeling. It was hard to breathe and impossible to not stare.

As the music came to an end, the crowd cheered, and people threw coins into the upturned hats that defined the boundary of the group's makeshift stage. Gabi stepped forward and dropped a note. She had no idea how much she'd given, but she knew what she'd experienced was worth more than she'd brought out with her. She was ushered from the hat by a man wanting to show his appreciation. Coins chinked, and she wandered away in a trance.

She was still thinking about the flamenco group when she got to the hotel and wanted to tell Nana about them. She poked her head through the door that separated their rooms to see if she was awake. Nana's bed was empty, and the sheets hadn't been touched.

She should have made sure she got back safely. She should have taken better care of her. *Oh shit. Where the fuck is Nana?*

5.

"You were on fire tonight, Aisha." Nicolás grinned, and his eyes sparkled with fire.

He was as passionate now as he had been at the start of the evening. Sweat darkened his white shirt under his armpits and across his chest, and his black hair shone. He had been pretty good tonight too. He always worked hard, and she always gave heart and soul to every performance, and tonight had been no exception. Music was the lifeblood that pumped through their veins. It was one thing they had in common. The only other good thing they had shared was their love for Esme. He didn't know about that and would never understand.

He handed Aisha a glass of wine. She watched flames lick the sides of the logs on the fire and the small red sparks that rose and then disappeared into the night. The smell of food created an aura around the street, though it didn't stir her appetite. A neighbour sang while others danced. She thought about Esme. They would have danced side by side here, never together, and Esme would have enjoyed the celebrations for Aisha's sister's engagement into the early hours.

"Someone dropped us five thousand pesetas, Aisha."

She knew who that someone was—the woman stood out from the crowd, a beacon in a storm. Aisha had spotted her staring as she'd danced. She could tell the woman was moved. She'd been transfixed, and she'd walked away slowly, looking dazed. Tourists came and went, of course. They watched many dancers around the city and listened to their music, and they enjoyed those moments as one of many on their long list of things to do here. But their hearts weren't open as this woman's had been, and so they would never feel the music touch their souls as she was sure this woman had. Aisha knew that feeling well, and she could see and feel it in others. There was more that had captured Aisha's attention. She had razor-short hair at the back, and it was spikey on top. Her jeans were baggy around her legs and tight at her waist, and her leather brogues completed the outfit. There was something in the way she stood, the way she looked at Aisha, and the way she walked. Small things that, when taken together, defined her as being like Aisha, a woman attracted to other women. Aisha could be wrong but was convinced she wasn't.

"Five thousand." He started to dance in front of her and held out his hand for her to take.

Aisha didn't get to enjoy the money because she had a duty to her family, and it was passed to her mama. Her family would be pleased. She hadn't been able to shake the feeling she'd returned home with since she'd watched the woman leave the square. She couldn't explain how or why one person could affect her without a word being spoken between them any more than she could explain why or how music inspired the soul. Such reasoning was known only by the gods and spoken of by the poets. Her sense of restlessness was like a wedge trying to prise open her heart. She couldn't let it do that, not again.

She took his hand and he lifted her to her feet, though she kept a physical distance from him.

"Aisha. Nicolás."

Conchita approached with García at her side and smiled at them. "It is good to see you two dancing together." She turned her face from the men and winked at Aisha.

Aisha had no desire to conspire with her over any fantasies that she might follow in her sister's footsteps. The men started talking, and Nicolás put his arm over García's shoulder as they wandered towards the hub of the celebrations.

"You are happy for me, Aisha?" Conchita's eyes were bright and alive with the love that oozed from her, and yet she was still a child.

"Of course I am."

Conchita adopted a dreamy expression, undoubtedly aided by wine. She was going to marry the man she loved. The joy Aisha felt for her sister couldn't quash the ache in her heart.

Conchita took her hand and squeezed it. "Being engaged is more exciting than anything you could imagine." She twirled around and laughed. "I feel like I'm floating up high where nothing bad can reach me. It's soft and cosy and warm. And I have the comfort of knowing he will be there for me and always protect me."

That wasn't Aisha's appreciation of the most important qualities that defined what it was like to be in love. Love was being at one with her, whether she was at your side or not. It was about cherishing her ideas even when they weren't the same as yours. It was touching her, and being touched by her without any physical contact, and knowing the essence of her in every cell in your body and in every breath that you took. It was your laughter in tune with hers. It was exploring, sharing, giving, and receiving, and feeling that you were the luckiest person alive to have known something so precious. She hadn't needed to read poetry to know what love was. "They become the fire in your veins and your reason for being, and when they're not with you, you're reduced to nothing more than the dust beneath your feet. Love is everything and without it, we are mere shadows of what we might otherwise become."

Conchita stared at Aisha, her mouth open and her eyes wide. "Are you happy, Aisha?"

Conchita's response clawed at her throat, but she held back. What would be the point? Surely Conchita knew the answer. Everyone in her family knew she wasn't happy. How could they not see that? But they would never ask her why because they wouldn't be able to entertain a conversation about what *would* make her heart sing like Conchita's did now. It was better that problems such as hers remained unspoken. They would continue to make excuses as to why she remained single until that situation was no longer tenable. Conchita's marriage would be that turning point. She'd always known her time would come and had been lucky her parents hadn't forced her to marry sooner. Denial never changed the truth, but what other choice did she have? She couldn't leave her family and the group, because she had nothing and would be nothing without them.

"Nicolás loves you."

She pulled away from Conchita and turned her back to her. "He's like an older brother to me."

"He's kind, and he cares about you. I've watched you perform. You are good together."

Aisha's heart hollowed at the thought of him in that way, and her sister's claims of his affection towards her widened the void. "We're good friends, and that's all we can ever be."

Conchita linked her arm through Aisha's and leaned into her. The sunset was a great distraction for the eye, but it wasn't enough to calm the building rage inside Aisha. "I don't want to talk about it tonight," she said.

"Is it because he was married before?"

Aisha closed her eyes and inhaled deeply. Esme's face appeared, hauntingly, and the emptiness in her chest expanded.

Esme was laughing with the young children they were teaching over something so insignificant she couldn't remember what. The browns and reds that tinted her hair were always more vibrant in the midday sun, but the children had run coloured beads through the narrow braids that shaped her face in a perfect oval, and she looked amazing. Her older cousin had given her the black skirt she wore, and it was two sizes too big, but she'd tied it with a red scarf around the waist, and it looked as if it had been designed that way. Her white laced blouse hung open at the neck, baring the top of her breasts and the rose quartz charm on a chain that Aisha had bought for her sixteenth birthday. No, her reasons for not wishing to marry Nicolás had nothing to do with the fact that he had married her first love. Esme, her best friend, who had died from embolism almost two years ago, the baby too. It had left them both bereft.

Nicolás had the community to console him in his grief while she had wept silently in the privacy of her room at night and come up with excuses to justify why she needed to dry her pillows every day in the sun.

"It's not easy to find a good match, Aisha."

"At my age, you mean?"

She lowered her head. "I didn't mean..."

Aisha didn't want to be harsh with her sister. Conchita meant well, but she couldn't let her lie about something they both know was true. Deception was divisive and destructive, and it would only weaken the already fragile bond between them. "Yes, you did mean at my age. Everyone talks about it. I'm used to the comments. What you must understand, Conchita, is that I'm not like you."

Conchita stared up at her, her eyes watering.

Aisha smiled. "It's good. You found your true love. I haven't. Maybe someday I will. Maybe I won't. But I can't marry someone I don't love with all my heart. Now that you have found García, you understand what that feels like." Aisha took her hand, and Conchita nodded. "Please don't think about me. You'll have a family of your own soon. I am happy."

Conchita sniffed. "I hate to think that you are not happy."

Conchita was blinded by the laws within which their culture thrived. Happiness was not a priority when it was derived from something so unspeakable as the love of another person of the same gender. Conform to the customs of generations or be condemned to live life outside of the community. Aisha would be banished for such a crime. She would disgrace her family, and she couldn't do that. "I'm lucky. I love to dance. That makes me happy."

"Then dance with me. Let us join the others and be happy together."

Aisha drew her sister to her and kissed the top of her head. She was still a child, and yet she was soon to be married. She would be considered an adult who would fashion her own life with her husband and have children. Aisha could think of nothing worse.

"Have you set a date for the wedding?" Aisha asked as they ambled towards the others.

"September 27th to the 30th. I love the autumn colours."

"It will be perfect."

Conchita continued to talk about the plans for her first dress fitting and her ideas for the flower arrangements. Aisha would hear it all again and again until she was tired of hearing about it. Did anyone care about her happiness? She doubted it very much. She would excuse herself after this dance and go to her bedroom, and she would settle for a while, alone with her dreams. And, for a short time, she would find some pleasure.

6.

No one at the hotel reception had seen Nana.

Granada might be reputed to be one of the safest cities in the country, but that didn't mean anything. It was getting dark, it had been a long day, and Nana was old and not the most stable on her feet. Gabi had a vision of her lying in the gutter down a dark and narrow, cobbled side street because she'd fallen over and passed out from the pain of a broken hip. Gabi shook off the image and another one replaced it. This time, Nana stared at the name plate of a road attached to the wall of a house, frowning, and trembling, and trying to steady her cane. Gabi felt her confusion and anxiety, and more disturbing visions of Nana's fate haunted her. Nana might think she knew the place like the back of her hand, but that was now an arthritic one that had probably changed as much as the city had in the last sixty years.

"Can you call the hospital and check to see if she's there?" Gabi said to the man behind the desk. He smiled but made no move to pick up the phone, despite her pointing repeatedly at it.

"Please try not to worry, Miss Sánchez. I'm sure she will be safe."

You don't know that. Arsehole. Her blood was close to boiling point, and she wanted to throttle the fucker. "Can you tell me the number? Please." Nana wouldn't forgive her if she forgot her manners. She couldn't wait. "I'll call the hospital." There was no way her Spanish was going to hold up to trying to explain the situation but right now, that was the least of her problems.

45

"Please, Miss Sánchez, we can help you. Please, take a seat."

I don't want a fucking seat. I want Nana. The ticking bomb inside her was about to explode, and this little fucker was going to get the full blast of it if he didn't pull his finger out. "I have to find Nana, now." She squeezed the words out before she choked on them. The air was being sucked from her chest faster than a burst balloon, and the pressure inside her head was increasing at the same speed. Where would she start looking? She could be searching all night and their paths still might not cross. The man smiled at her again, and she wanted to slap the charm from his face. She rammed her clenched hands into her pockets and bit her tongue. She hadn't realised how much she hated this feeling. *Calm down. Calm down.* Trying to breathe and calm her thoughts was impossible, like swimming against a tsunami.

"Maybe she took a stroll somewhere," he said.

"She's a seventy-five-year-old woman who walks with a cane."

"I understand, Miss Sánchez."

No, you clearly fucking don't do you, or you'd have phoned the hospital already. He started to do something on the computer, probably checking Gabi wasn't lying about Nana's age, or maybe checking that Nana existed and Gabi wasn't some fruit loop. Gabi launched herself towards the counter. She stopped short of thumping her fists on the surface and screaming at him or worse still, reaching across the counter and shaking him into action. "Please." Her voice sounded weak.

He picked up the phone and made several calls.

Nana hadn't been taken to hospital, although this fact didn't lessen the tension in Gabi's head or reduce her irritation with the man relaying the information. He broadened his smile, and her tension rose another level.

"I'm sure Mrs Sánchez will be back very soon."

Not if she's lying in a dark alley and no one has seen her, she wouldn't. *Fucker.* "Can you call the police, please?"

He raised his eyebrows and cleared his throat. "You said it has been two hours since you last saw her?"

"That's not the point."

He wiggled the red tie at his neck. "She will not be considered missing."

The great emphasis he had placed on the word missing didn't escape Gabi. That he was technically accurate grated even more. "I'm going to see if I can find her," Gabi said through gritted teeth. She forced a tight-lipped smile and turned her back to him. She took a deep breath to alleviate her heart palpitations, and another, and stood still until the dizziness had abated. She didn't need this stress. She needed a quiet night and a long sleep. She needed the comfort of...comfort of what?

"May I suggest you start at the river," the man said.

Fuck. She hadn't thought that Nana might have drowned. She turned back and glared at him, and the smile slowly slipped from his lips.

"It is the place many of our guests go for an evening stroll."

As she walked, she had to admit he was trying to be helpful, but she wasn't overreacting. She knew how vulnerable Nana was even if Nana didn't show it. Gabi shouldn't have left her to walk back to the hotel on her own. If something happened to Nana, she would have to face her dad, and she would feel eternally guilty. And pissed off that he'd been right about her being incapable of helping anyone but herself.

47

She started jogging, searching among what looked like the whole population of Granada for Nana's silver-white head of hair. After two hundred yards, her lungs were burning. She stopped, took a couple of deep breaths, and reverted to walking, scanning in every direction until she reached the river. The water looked deep, and the current was strong. Everything blurred in front of her eyes. Which way should she go?

She walked for ten minutes before she sat on the wall of a small plaza that overlooked the river, held her head in her hands, and allowed the tears to fall silently. She didn't want anyone to stop and ask if she was okay, because she'd break down completely. She needed to be strong for Nana. She rubbed her eyes and lifted her head.

"Are you all right, Gabriela? What happened?"

"Nana." She jumped up and wrapped her arms around Nana and held her tightly. The tears flowed, but they were out of joy and relief. "I was so scared."

"Cariño, about what?"

Gabi let her go and stared at her. "About you. Where did you go to? You were supposed to be at the hotel and when I got back, I thought something horrible had happened."

"Cariño, why would you think that? I feel safe here. I wasn't tired, so I took a walk." She perched on the wall and rested both hands over the pommel of her cane in front of her. "Sit down, cariño. Enjoy this wonderful place."

Gabi sat, not because she wanted to, but because she felt as though she'd had the wind knocked out of her. "I was frickin' terrified."

Nana patted her on the knee. They sat in silence. The elation seeped from Gabi as her insides unwound, and she felt sick. A flash of irritation gave way to exhaustion. She closed her eyes and willed herself to stay calm. Nana was safe, and that was all that mattered.

"I used to sneak out from my house and walk here with a boy." She sighed. "It was romantic and exciting," Nana said.

Gabi opened her eyes. Nana was smiling, and her cheeks had coloured. It was hard to imagine Nana being that young. This wasn't Grandpa she was talking about because she would have called him by his name. Intrigue got the better of Gabi as she watched Nana reliving the fond memories of that time. "Were you in love with him?"

"Juan was his name. Yes."

Her eyes watered, though she was still smiling as she gazed out at the river. She had been in love with someone other than Grandpa. All Gabi knew of Nana's history was that she and Grandpa had fled to England at the beginning of the Second World War on a shipping boat via Gibraltar. Grandpa had been a civil guard, and Great Grandpa, Nana's father, a senior guard commander. After Nana and Grandpa moved to England, he worked for the British government as a civil servant of some kind. He'd died before Gabi was born, and she'd never heard Nana talking about him. She'd had no reason to ask questions before, but now her head was filled with them. "If you loved Juan, why didn't you marry him?"

Her smile broadened. "It wasn't possible. He was a gitano."

"A what?"

"They are Romani Gypsies who originated from southern Asia. Some settled here hundreds of years ago, and many still live in the caves in the Sacromonte hills."

"So, why couldn't you marry him?"

"Franco killed gitanos without reason, and I was the daughter of a guard commander. I wasn't even allowed to speak to him, let alone walk with him."

Gabi's heart ached at the sadness she saw in Nana's eyes. The cruelty was hard to stomach. "If I loved someone that much, I couldn't leave them."

Nana sighed. "I hope not. I'm pleased the world has changed for you."

Nana must have been broken-hearted leaving behind the man she loved, but that made something else more confusing. "Why did you marry Grandpa if you didn't love him?"

Nana took a deep breath, and there was a long silence before she responded. "Circumstances, Gabriela. It wasn't safe for a young woman to travel alone, so being married gave me some protection." She pinched her lips together and took a deep breath. "And I did learn to love your grandfather."

How could you learn to love someone? That didn't make any sense at all. Love came from the heart, not the head. "Do you think he's still alive?"

Nana pressed down on her cane and stood. "I doubt that. Many gitanos were slaughtered during the war." She set off towards the hotel, and Gabi strode to catch her up.

"I'm weary, Gabriela. How was your evening?"

Gabi had the impression she didn't want to talk about Juan anymore. Gabi's evening was a blur. "I wandered for a bit then watched flamenco in the square." She recalled the dancer's block heels and the man fiercely strumming his guitar, their passion, and the fast beat that she hadn't been able to keep up with. "It was brilliant."

"My Juan was a flamenco dancer," Nana said.

My Juan. Gabi played the words of affection through her head. She linked her arm through Nana's. It was going to take a bit of adjusting to the fact that Nana had been in love with a man who wasn't Grandpa, but she was fascinated. "Will you tell me more about him?" she asked. "Maybe we can visit where he used to live? Maybe he's still there?"

"Oh, cariño, we will go to Sacromonte. I would like to see it one more time, and the dancing there will be the best in the city."

Gabi wondered whether Nana had a bucket list for this trip that she hadn't shared with her, and whether she'd been secretly plotting that this would be her final resting place. "Are we going to the cemetery tomorrow?" she asked.

Nana stopped walking and took a few quick breaths. "Maybe another day."

Gabi frowned. Nana had lost a little of the sparkle she'd had earlier, and she did look tired. She'd pushed herself too much when she should have been tucked up in bed.

Nana stroked Gabi's cheek. "I don't need you to look after me, Gabriela. I want you to explore for yourself. My legs are tired. I will go to the spa tomorrow. It's been a long day. A very exciting day, don't you think?" She smiled, concealing a yawn.

No, Gabi didn't, and she hated spas. She was knackered and utterly drained from the stress of travelling and the subsequent distress of thinking something awful had happened to Nana, and now she had to face the guy in reception again whose smile would say, "I told you so."

Gabi tilted her head from side to side to release the tension in her neck as they entered the hotel, scanned the faces behind the desk, and released the breath she'd been holding. She couldn't see him, thank God. She made her way quickly to the lift and kept it on hold while Nana bid everyone a good night. Gabi felt even worse for her behaviour and vowed silently to make amends with the man when she next saw him. She lowered her head and rubbed the back of her neck.

"You don't seem yourself, cariño. You're not coming down with something, are you? They say flights are the worst for germs."

"I'm fine. I made a bit of a fuss at reception when I was worried about you, that's all. They called all the hospitals."

Nana smiled. "Well, I'm sure the staff were delighted to help. They're so welcoming, aren't they?"

In her room, she found a small bottle of wine, a box of chocolates, and a card that said the staff were at their service no matter what they needed. It hadn't felt like that earlier, but then maybe she hadn't been seeing things all that clearly.

By the time Gabi's head hit the pillow, she was beyond exhausted. There was a rumble coming from Nana's room, like water gurgling down a narrow drainpipe. It took her a while to work out that it was Nana snoring. She sunk into the soft mattress pondering Nana and her old love, Juan. It had been a lifetime ago. The last thing she remembered was the flamenco woman's block heels tapping out the beat of the music.

7.

GABI HAD TAKEN FULL advantage of the swimming pool on the roof of the hotel in the week since their arrival, enjoying the hospitality at the bar and soaking up the rays, while Nana had relaxed with daily spa treatments and siestas. Nana looked younger and more refreshed for it, and Gabi questioned whether she should have opted for a facial and full body massage rather than Cava cocktails and vitamin Ds. She sipped her drink and cast her gaze across the rooftops below.

The array of vibrant colours marked the textile stalls at the market, and the rocky hills beyond that climbed from the city's perimeter into the sky in a series of dark jagged lines and peaks. The contrast with the rather flat and green landscape and generally damp and cold climate in Devon couldn't be starker. The vibe in Granada, like the promise of a deliciously smooth cocktail on a lazy Sunday afternoon, had piqued Gabi's interest. She'd wandered into the city each evening and sat quietly in the same bar, watching people come and go. She'd enjoyed the music and a free tapa with every drink and hadn't felt the habitual loneliness that had set in after Shay left her.

"The view is spectacular," Gabi said.

"What do you think of this?" Nana asked and held up a newspaper to Gabi.

"A two-bed apartment?"

"It has a large terrace and a small garden. It's a ten-minute walk into the city, so it's far enough out to be quite peaceful. I think I could manage it."

Gabi's heart skipped a beat, and a sinking feeling made its way slowly to her stomach. "Are you serious about buying here? Staying here?" Even though Nana had said she didn't know when she planned to return to England, Gabi had assumed they would at some point. Nana hadn't mentioned anything about buying a place. They'd booked their first three weeks at the hotel so they could unwind and then rented a self-catering property through to the end of September. If they planned to stay beyond that, Gabi had thought they would find somewhere else or extend the rental.

Nana looked up over the top of her glasses and smiled. "It would make a decent holiday home and if I, or we, decide to stay, it would be perfectly manageable. I'm going to do some investigating. I have a good feeling about this one."

The idea of not returning to the place she'd known as home jostled uneasily alongside the thought of returning to England alone. No, she couldn't go back without Nana. Nana looked so excited about the apartment, it warmed the chill feeling that had come over Gabi.

"It's been recently renovated, and it's owned by a Dutch couple. I'm going to arrange to view it," Nana said.

Gabi rubbed the back of her neck and inhaled deeply. Nana was moving ahead faster than Gabi could process, and as much as she wanted to object just to slow things down, she couldn't spoil Nana's excitement. A holiday home would be a great idea, and they would be able to visit at any time. "Shall I come with you?"

"Of course, cariño. Let me speak to the agent first and see what I can arrange." Nana closed the paper and stood. "I'm going to call them now and then head to the garden and read for a bit. I found a classic in the hotel library that looks interesting. *One Hundred Years of Solitude* by Gabriel García Márquez."

The title sounded depressing as hell. Gabi couldn't imagine anything worse than solitude, let alone a hundred years of it, probably because it pretty much summed up how she'd been living in her flat, and why she preferred the company of women at night to sleeping alone. All those years in isolation, though. No, she couldn't see how that would bring happiness. She craved company but not the transient kind that had become her norm. "I'm going into town to see if I can see the group I saw last week."

"Excelente. You should let your hair down a little."

Gabi ran her hand over the back of her head and laughed. "I'll do my best."

"Oh, and I think it's time to go to the cemetery tomorrow."

That would be one of the attractions ticked off Nana's bucket list. Gabi hoped Nana had a very long list. "Okay."

"I'll arrange a packed lunch from the hotel," Nana said.

Gabi curled her lip.

"I'd like to spend the day there."

"At the cemetery?"

"It's a serene place."

Yeah, dead quiet. Gabi was interested in her grandparents, but the idea of spending the day in the company of tatty tombstones and ugly stone sculptures made her shiver. "I'll grab lunch at the market."

"Will you look out for something for Maggie's birthday for me?"

"Sure."

55

"I had in mind an ashtray or a small vase."

"Will do."

"She likes reds and oranges and hates black. Reminds her too much of funerals and the war."

"She'd hate it here then." Most of the women wore black most of the time from what Gabi had seen. Black skirts, black blouses, black veils. Probably black knickers, not that anyone was likely to find out. Black was expected to be worn for a year after the death of a husband, but many widows never changed back.

"Autumn colours would be perfecto," Nana said.

An hour later, Gabi walked into the city, pondering the apartment that Nana had arranged to view. It had two spacious bedrooms each with ensuite bathrooms containing a bath and shower, a living room that was bigger than the whole of Gabi's old flat, and views overlooking the square and a local small supermarket. It also had a modern kitchen with a breakfast bar, and a terrace with a view of the Genil River that would pick up the evening sun. Nana was right, it would be perfectly manageable. Maybe Gabi should be a bit more open to staying, and even look for a job. She could explore the bars for opportunities. It was the holiday season after all, and her Spanish could just about stand up to tourist conversations, taking drinks orders, and listing the best places to visit.

The music in this street wasn't as good as the first night. A waiter coaxed her into his bar with a smile and a free first drink. She ordered a beer and glanced around as she waited for it to arrive. Women's perfume, men's aftershave, and a hefty dose of cigarette smoke formed a heady mix that reminded her of working her old job. The voices and laughter drowned out the street music. Though she would be better off in the balmy air, she relaxed easily with the familiarity inside the bar. She smiled at a woman smiling at her. Her white blouse hung off one shoulder and was tucked into a skirt that barely covered her ass. She had long wavy brown hair and a mock-coy smile that Gabi read as an invitation to introduce herself. Gabi thanked the waiter for her drink and raised her glass as the woman approached her.

"Have you been in here before?" the woman said in a distinctively Cockney accent.

Gabi shook her head. "You're from London?"

"Is it that obvious?"

"What can I say? I'm an EastEnders addict."

The woman laughed. "Where are you from?"

Gabi sipped her drink. "Devon. A village close to Lydford."

The woman nodded. "You look Spanish, apart from the hair."

"It's in my genes." Gabi tugged at her baggy jeans.

The woman laughed. "Holiday?"

"Kind of. You?"

"Just a week."

Gabi sipped her drink. "I'm Gabi."

"Lynn."

Gabi held up her glass, and Lynn clinked it with hers.

"Have you been to Spain before?" Gabi asked.

"No, you?"

"First time." Gabi raised her eyebrows and sipped her drink.

Lynn smiled as she eyed Gabi up and down. "Nice."

The beer headed down the wrong way, making Gabi cough. "Seems nice enough," she said and looked around the bar, heat burning her cheeks. She was used to being chatted up while on the other side of the bar. It was different being on this side, and she felt more vulnerable without her job to hide behind.

Lynn brushed Gabi's arm with her fingertip and held Gabi's gaze.

Gabi finished her beer and called the bartender over. "Can I get you another drink?"

Lynn shook her head. "Want to try a different bar?"

Gabi couldn't see anything wrong with this one. Admittedly, it wasn't a gay bar, but the atmosphere was easy going, and it was close to the square where the flamenco dancers were. What the hell? It would be nice to have some company. "Okay."

"Follow me," Lynn said.

"Where are you staying?" Gabi asked as they walked.

"A bed and breakfast on Jorge Carmen." She shook her head, tousling her hair, and ran her fingers through it then settled it behind her ears. "There's three of us. We work together."

"Where are they, your friends?"

"I left them in bed together." Lynn rolled her eyes.

Gabi laughed. "Nice, for them."

"They decided to hit it off the night we arrived and haven't gotten out of bed since. Going away with friends sucks."

"Unless it's you that's getting laid," Gabi said.

"True." Lynn made her way through a crowd of women and into a bar.

The voices were a higher pitch and the aroma sweeter. There were more women inside. "Is this a gay bar?"

"I think it's gay friendly to cater for us immoral tourists. You know there aren't any Spanish lesbians, don't you?"

"What?" Gabi frowned then realised Lynn was joking. Gabi shook her head. Why was it so difficult for some people to let others live? She didn't shout about being a lesbian, but she didn't hide the fact either. Yes, there were a few people who looked down their noses or had something derogatory to say about her short hair, but there would always be fuckwits in this world. "Sucks. You'd think it was 1905, not 1995."

"It's pathetic. What do you want to drink?" Lynn asked.

"Vodka Coke, please." Gabi looked around. She picked out the languages she recognised, German, French, and Portuguese, and something that sounded Scandinavian or Dutch.

Lynn handed Gabi her a drink and lifted her glass. "Happy holiday."

Gabi made her way outside and away from the crowd. "So, what do you do when you're not here?" she asked.

Lynn sipped her drink. "I'm a social worker."

"Tough job."

"Sometimes. Mostly it's rewarding, helping disadvantaged kids so they get a shot at life. The successes make it worth the hideous hours and shit pay."

"It's a proper job."

"What about you?"

"Bar work. And I make jewellery." She'd almost left off talking about the jewellery because she mostly felt embarrassed about it. She hadn't made many things and although what she'd done had been well received, she'd surmised it was because she'd given the stuff away either to her friend or to Nana.

"Are you any good?" She tugged at Gabi's jeans and held her gaze.

Gabi wondered if the topic of the question had changed. "I guess beauty is in the eye of the beholder, eh?"

"True." Lynn smiled. "You have pretty eyes."

Gabi blushed. She wasn't into Lynn, but it was still nice talking to her, familiar, like being back home. She was drawn to the music a distance away. Lynn leaned into her. The warmth against Gabi's ear sent a tingle down her spine. She put her hand on Lynn's waist.

"You have a gentle energy," Lynn whispered.

Gabi should say something positive in response but didn't want to encourage her. She wanted to get back to the square and to the music. She opened her eyes and froze as she clocked the woman walking past the bar, right in front of them. She was sure it was *her*, the flamenco dancer she'd seen on that first night.

Lynn backed away. "What is it? What's wrong?"

Gabi blinked several times and started to doubt herself. She craned her neck but couldn't see the dancer anywhere. "Nothing," she said. "I'm good."

Lynn looked in the direction Gabi had stared. She glanced around. "Did I miss something?" she asked.

Gabi turned to her and smiled. "No, it's nothing. Hey, look, can we take a rain check tonight? Maybe do this another night. My nana's waiting for me at the hotel." That sounded lame. She cringed.

Lynn sighed. "I'm leaving tomorrow."

Gabi pursed her lips. Lynn was sweet, but she didn't set Gabi's heart racing or cause the electric feeling in her stomach to intensify. Lynn was nothing like the dancer. "Shame," Gabi said and hoped she'd sounded more genuine than she felt.

"Maybe we could hook up when you're back," Lynn said.

Lynn looked sad and lonely. Gabi felt the echo of it touch her heart, but she couldn't make a promise she knew she wouldn't keep. "It's a nice offer, but I'm not sure if we're going back to England."

Lynn pecked a kiss on Gabi's cheek. "Well, it was good to meet you. I'll let you get back to your nana," she said.

Gabi smiled. "Have a fun last night."

Lynn lifted her glass. "Oh, I intend to," she said and headed back into the bar.

Gabi followed the music back to the fountain where she'd watched the group on that first night. The crisp sound of castanets came fast and furious, and the guitar was wild and intoxicating. She worked her way through the crowd, joined in the clapping and cheering, and the hairs on her neck prickled. And then she saw the dancer and stopped, breathless.

She held her long skirt by the hem up above her knees and swayed it back and forth, while her other hand above her head moved with the music. Gabi didn't feel drunk enough to be imagining the desire this woman stirred in her. It was very real. It was pure. Fresh. She was the most beautiful woman Gabi had ever seen, and Gabi's body wasn't going to let her forget it easily. The dancer's almost black hair floated freely around her tanned face as she danced, and her dark eyes took on the fierce stare of a hunter, shrouding her in mystery. Her full lips parted to reveal beautifully white teeth and when she chanted, Gabi felt the vibration in every note.

Whatever it was that this woman did, and however she did it, Gabi was affected in the strangest way. It wasn't just that she was stunning and alluring. It was the passion, the fire in her eyes, and as the beat quickened, Gabi became hypnotised by her, as she had been on that first night.

The dance came to an end too soon, and Gabi made her way back to the hotel in a trance. The dancer had awakened something inside her. This wasn't the predictable thrill she'd get from a night with the Lynns of the world. She could live without that and not miss it. This feeling, this sense, like the puzzle seeking a solution or the warm breeze gently commanding a response from her that she couldn't deny was captivating. It wasn't about missing something or living without, it was about discovering something powerful within her that she'd ignored for too long. It came with a large dose of excitement and a hint of alarm, and she had no option but to hold on tight and go with it.

Gabi considered what she would say to her, and her stomach tightened. Why was she freaked out about having a simple conversation that had come effortlessly with Lynn just an hour earlier? And yet, she couldn't look at this woman, couldn't think about her without her mouth parching and her heart racing. She would come back next week to see the group, and in the meantime, Gabi would summon the courage to speak to the dancer.

8.

"AISHA QUÉ TE PASA? You are not paying attention. Your sister needs our help for this most important time in her life, and your head is in the clouds."

Mama clapped her hands in front of Aisha's face, tugging her from her daydream. the one where the woman was stood outside the bar with another woman, holding her hip and whispering into her ear. She'd stolen a glance at the two of them, nothing more because Nicolás had been with her, but that glimpse had been enough to stir the fire that filled her with want. It was the same woman who had been at the square on Saturday, and she was intrigued by her.

The last thing she wanted was to be here, tending to her sister's wedding dress plans. She looked at Conchita and smiled.

"Which one do you think, Aisha?" Conchita grinned.

She held the length of white satin material at one side of her body and the white lacy cotton material at the other side. The satin would be soft against her skin and show the curves of her breasts and hips. The heavy lace had more of a traditional feel and reminded Aisha of the veils worn by the women in mourning. It wasn't a look that enhanced Conchita's youthful and joyful demeanour.

"Definitely the lace, Conchita," Mama said.

The woman selling the material nodded and expressed her agreement with a high-pitched squeal and fervent clapping of hands. Aisha's aunt, and abuela, and the other two elders of their village, who had to be involved in important decisions like wedding dress design, joined in the exultation. Aisha shook her head as they continued to fuss over Conchita.

One of the elders picked up a finely knitted veil from the shelf and ran it through her fingers. "Perhaps with this?" she said.

When an elder spoke, what they said might be presented as a question, but it wasn't, and any challenge would be perceived as a demonstration of insolence. Aisha would hate this kind of attention for her wedding and being told what to wear, and as she caught her sister's eye and received a thin-lipped smile in response, it was clear Conchita wasn't overly enamoured either. It was much easier for men, much less of a commotion for them to choose a suit. If Aisha married, she would wear trousers. She danced in skirts every day. She would choose a white tuxedo with a blood-red bowtie to represent the heart. She would pick a freshly cut rose to match, one with a delicious perfume, for a buttonhole. She would never allow herself to be subjected to this display.

The dress making would take weeks and involve several fittings. Aisha would be expected to attend them all to give her sister support. She didn't agree with the elders or her mama. Aisha widened her eyes and stared as her mama took the lace material, unfolded it, and wrapped it around her sister. Conchita looked like a fractured meringue. She also wore a deep frown as she looked down at herself and touched the material as if it was going to bite her.

"Are you sure, Mama?" Conchita asked.

"No," Aisha said and immediately felt the heat of the women's glares. They all edged taller and pinched their lips in one synchronised expression of disgust and shock.

"Ah, it speaks," Mama said and threw her arm in the air. "You wait until we have decided what is best for Conchita before you join us."

"The lace is old-fashioned." She paused. "Conchita, García will appreciate you in the satin far more. You are young, and the material is soft and inviting. The lace is stuffy and too heavy." She ignored the open mouths and the gasps and took the satin from the shop woman. She put the lace to one side and held up the material to her sister's bosom. "I think a low cut, to show him what will soon be his mozuela. Tight to the waist." She lifted the material at Conchita's side. "And open up the side of your leg."

Conchita blushed and giggled. She looked at where the material was being held high up her thigh and gasped softly. "Do you really think—"

"My daughter is not going to dress like a puta, especially not on her wedding day," Mama said, throwing her arms in the air. She ripped the material from Conchita and handed it to the shop woman. "What are you thinking, Aisha? Cállate. Ya has dicho suficiente. I really do not know what to make of you these days, but this attitude must stop."

Aisha watched one of the elders fanning herself. Her abuela and aunt stood with an arm around each other, each covering their mouths with their hands. Cloaked in their home-sewn black widow's uniform, they were as depressing as their regressive attitude. There was a weight to Aisha's sigh as she stepped back from her sister, shaking her head. She wanted for Conchita what she wanted for herself: the freedom to break from the traditions that would have them reliving the lives of

65

their ancestors. The feeling in her chest became leaden as she saw her sister's eyes glaze over.

Mama apologised to the shop owner and the other women present and expressed her deep concern for Aisha. Aisha allowed the words to brush over her. She'd heard them all before. She had no reason to feel embarrassed, or guilty, or sorry for speaking up. The shop sold the satin material because it would make a fine wedding dress. She wasn't wrong in her judgement. But her thoughts and ideas had come from her interactions with too many tourists and "others," her mama explained to the women. They stared at Aisha, shaking their heads, offering words of condolence to Mama, and making the sign of the cross as they muttered, "Dios mío" and "por Dios." Conchita looked down, and the shop woman picked up the heavy lace and held it against her.

Aisha huffed. She took a seat in the wicker chair in the corner of the room and crossed her arms. She watched the women fussing around her sister with the lace material. By the time they finished, they would have her dressed like the virgin she was, tightly bound and unreachable. It was a metaphor for the strangled life she would live with her husband. He would struggle for hours to get near her on their wedding night but when he did, the prize would be his, for he was the winner in their relationship. He always would be.

Dancing flamenco was more romantic than anything a man could ever offer. Flamenco *was* a woman. The first note, the instant awakening to a shared passion of such intensity. The peaks, and falls, and the rapture of the crescendo, and there were always many, and they were explosive, and she wanted more. She could slip the clothes from her body with ease and snuggle against her soft, warm skin. She could lose herself in the tenderness of her touch and die for a moment as the warmth of her breath brushed her skin, and she could discover unparalleled ecstasy in their final ascent together. That was what love felt like, in her dreams.

She closed her eyes and thought about the time she and Esme had gone to the field to collect oranges. She placed her hand on her chest above her heart and took a deep breath. It was a fond memory, but it had also changed everything for Aisha. She'd closed off her heart...

It had been a mild autumn that year, and the fruit were juicy and sweet. Esme had thrown her cardigan on the ground before she'd started to climb the ladder Aisha held against the trunk for her to get to the higher branches. Aisha had been so tempted to look up as Esme climbed above her, but she had looked away. She'd kept her head down until an orange had landed on it. Esme had laughed, but all she could see was Esme's legs and the skirt opening as she descended, and the point between her legs at which it became dark, though she knew what she would find there. That had been the moment just before Esme had screamed, and Aisha hit the ground with a thud. She'd breathed through the sharp pain in her back and the winding, and then opened her eyes and laughed at Esme sitting on top of her. Esme had helped her to her feet. When she'd groaned in agony, Esme had frantically but gently touched Aisha's arms and shoulders and ribs. She'd cupped her face and stared into her eyes, saying she was just checking her pupils. Aisha's pain had transformed into a sensation of deep longing.

She hadn't intended to brush her lips against Esme's but after it happened, Esme froze and stared at her for a very long time. "That must never happen again," she'd said. "It is wrong, and you will die for it." Esme hadn't changed towards Aisha after that, but Aisha had buried her feelings and hadn't let them surface since. They never spoke about the incident again. When Esme got engaged to Nicolás she changed, and Aisha became more distant with everyone.

"What do you think of this, Aisha?"

Aisha blinked until her focus sharpened. Still a meringue, only now with a hideous mask covering her beautiful face. "The satin would be better," she said. "And no veil. They're old-fashioned."

Mama raised her arm. "Why do you have to be so obstructive? Nos quemaremos en el infierno."

You will burn in hell for insisting on dressing my baby sister as if she's already in mourning? She took a deep breath and tuned out their fretting. She thought about the woman who had come and watched them dancing. With the colour of her skin, she couldn't place her in the world, but her appearance made it most likely that she was a tourist. What did it matter? Tourists came and went. Aisha could only dream.

9.

GABI COULDN'T SEE WHERE the cemetery started or finished. It appeared to stretch in all directions for miles. There must have been thousands of graves, perhaps a hundred thousand. Nana put down the bunch of flowers she'd bought. She removed a piece of paper from her handbag and studied it, then looked around.

"This way," she said. She picked up the flowers and set off.

Gabi followed her past row after row of raised black and grey marble graves laid out in a symmetrical pattern. Each tomb had sharply cut edges, and their surfaces shone in the sunlight. The grassed areas in between were lush, unlike the dusty areas she'd seen around the city. The tall white statues added height, giving perspective, and the oldest she'd spotted was dated 1824. Life was surreal. The statue had stood for over a hundred years, and the people buried around it had probably lived less than fifty, reduced to a name that no one remembered and a date or two engraved on a plaque that faded over time, whilst something constructed might stand for thousands of years. It was bizarre, but it reinforced how important it was to savour every moment and grab every opportunity.

A wall covered with small square plaques on small square doors provided tiny homes for people's ashes. It was spotlessly clean and dressed in fresh flowers that gave off a sweet smell. The colours brightened up the greys and whites, and it wasn't as morbid as Gabi had expected. She hated the cemetery attached to the church near home. It was dull and not well looked after like this one. Nana was right; it was serene and pretty, and she could see why Nana had opted for a packed lunch. The cemetery was like an open-air art gallery and history museum all wrapped up in one.

Nana stopped at a raised tomb. She pulled out a delicate black veil from her handbag, put it on, and made the sign of the cross at her chest. Gabi stood quietly pondering the significance of the mark of respect. She didn't have a veil, but she made the sign of the cross and felt the ache beneath it.

The name Flores, printed in white lettering, stood out from the centre of the black marble. This was Nana's family plot. Angel Flores was Gabi's great grandfather. He had died aged forty-two, and her great grandmother, Serena, had been just forty. "They were so young," Gabi said.

"My parents didn't support Franco. They'd planned to come to England after me, but with the war, Father thought he could do more good if they stayed and fought the regime from within. By the end, he had helped thousands of people escape through Gibraltar, including me and Miguel."

A shiver slid down the back of Gabi's neck, and she couldn't stop staring at their names and the dates that marked their short lives. She couldn't begin to imagine who he had saved, or what their children might be doing now, or where in the world they lived. Nana had lost her dad. Did his life mean anything to the people he had saved? "Sounds like he was a hero."

"He was considered a traitor and executed, my mother with him. The government took our house and everything we owned."

"Fuck." Gabi's stomach turned. He had tried to help people survive, and he had been killed for it.

"Yes, Gabriela."

She'd known nothing about his incredible feats of bravery. "You've never talked about this."

Nana took off the veil and put it back in her bag. "I think, after a time, we forget what was once important, cariño. Maybe I didn't want to open old wounds again. We all had busy lives and a future. I'm sorry, maybe I should have said something, but when is there a right time? And then time moves on and the past gets lost."

At one point, Nana had probably known Gabi better than Gabi had known herself, but after Gabi had moved out of the farmhouse and claimed her independence, she hadn't talked to Nana about her personal life. The past had been left in the past, but for the occasional flick through a photo album at Christmas time, faces and names she didn't know. It hadn't been a conscious choice on Gabi's part, it had simply happened that when they were together, that they talked about other things, like the garden or cooking or Gabi's jewellery. Something had been lost between them, and Gabi hadn't realised exactly how much Nana meant to her until now. She put her arm around her because she needed the comfort of that closeness again.

"We were in a privileged position, Gabriela. My father was trusted and well connected with the Spanish Intelligence Services. Miguel and I were able to settle in the UK. Father got Miguel a job working with the British Secret Intelligence. Together, they provided information about Hitler's collaboration with Franco."

Gabi's great grandparents had been executed, and her grandpa was a spy. It was too much to take in.

"Many other families died trying to escape. They were dangerous times."

"What about Juan? Is he buried here?"

Nana smiled softly. "Oh, no, Gabriela. He wouldn't be allowed to be buried here." Her wistful look gave way to a half-smile. She sighed. "When the war started, Juan and I talked about what we would like to happen to us if we died."

Gabi stared at Nana, willing her to elaborate.

"He wanted his ashes thrown into the wind from the Sacromonte hill at a spot close to where he lived. 'Verde que te quiero verde. Verde viento. Verdes ramas.'"

Gabi choked up. She didn't understand why Nana was quoting what sounded like poetry. "Green, how I want you green. Green wind. Green branches." But it meant something to Nana because she wiped a tear from her cheek, and Gabi's eyes welled up. "Do you want to be buried here?" she asked.

Nana took a deep breath and held Gabi's gaze. "I thought I would rest next to Miguel in the churchyard in Devon, but now I'm here, I've changed my mind. I think I want to be with my parents. This is my true home, Gabriela, and I'm glad we came."

Gabi's mum's ashes were in the same churchyard in Devon, and Gabi had assumed she would follow suit, not for any emotional connection, just because that's what normally happened. She hadn't really given it any deep thought, because she'd never known her mum, and she was too young to think about an event that was so far off. But knowing that Nana would be buried here made her feel suddenly very alone. She didn't want to imagine Nana being here behind some block of stone, because that would mean she wasn't here talking to her. And that was inconceivable. She rammed the thought to the back of her mind and looked skyward. Beautiful blue skies. Air. Life. "I'm glad we came too," she said and bit back the tears.

Nana laid the small bunch of flowers inside the plot. "I'd like to be alone for a while, Gabriela."

Gabi walked back to the entrance with a heavy ache in her heart. Nana seemed okay seeing the graves, but this history and saying goodbye wasn't new to her. Gabi's legs were like jelly, and there was an uncomfortable edginess in her chest. She was shocked by her great grandfather's story, and she felt small and insignificant by comparison. But she was also sad and nauseous. Nana had lost so many people that she loved, and one day, Gabi would have to say goodbye to Nana.

If Gabi died tomorrow, who would care? She looked back to where Nana was sitting on a bench with her hands in her lap. Nana was stoic, and kind, and the most amazing person in the world. She'd always loved her and been there for her, and never judged her. Gabi couldn't find the words to describe what life would be like without Nana. She ambled towards the market, her heart feeling as though she'd just put it through a shredder.

She took a seat in a square she didn't know the name of. The fountain in the centre was surrounded by a grassed area that had retained its colour, though it wasn't lush like the grass at the cemetery. It was like the battered grass the kids played on back home when the drier weather came. Water spurted from a tall spire at the fountain's centre and from several other lower points that formed a circle around it. The splashing noise, like a quiet waterfall, was pleasantly distracting. She threw a coin into it and made a promise to make something of her life, because she couldn't have the one thing she would have wished for: her mum.

She made her way to the market and struck up conversation with a stall holder. His smile belied the age that his

73

deeply creviced skin revealed. Gabi admired a series of framed sketches on fine cotton cloth that had yellowed with time.

"This is my brother's family in Kashmir. My great uncle drew them," the stall holder said.

There was a woman, always in a brown dress, and children in dirty white cloth robes, gathering crops, playing and laughing, cooking and eating, and around them in one picture were partly destroyed buildings and men carrying machine guns. They evoked both sadness and hope. "They're beautiful. Are they for sale?"

"No. They are just memories."

They were exquisite, and they gave Gabi a sense of what his family had endured, and maybe of what her great grandpa had gone through too. She had nothing like it to remember her family by, and that absence ripped through her like a bolt of lightning. She held her hand over her heart and closed her eyes and wondered what her life would have been like if her mum had survived. Gabi had always felt different, at school and growing up, and not having a mum was just something that had made that difference more noticeable. She'd had Nana though. And if her mum had lived, Nana wouldn't have been the Nana she knew, that same Nana who had brought her up and was still here now. She had no memories of her mum, nothing to hold onto, nothing to miss except perhaps the absence of something that should have been there, the illusion of what might have been. She didn't think it mattered but right now, she couldn't be sure because she felt turned upside down and inside out by the events of the day and needed things to settle inside her so she could know what she really felt.

"Would you like tea?" he asked.

She smiled weakly. "Thank you."

The herbal tea that tasted like sweet tepid water, seemed precious in that moment, and she chatted a while with him and discovered that he lived with his wife and three daughters in the hills in Sacromonte. Gabi thought about her mum. No, she had no memories of her to treasure, either.

The hand-woven rugs sold here were bright, and the patterns reminded her of the rug that Nana had in her dining room. One was particularly eye-catching. It had an elephant at its centre which seemed odd for Spain but presumably reflected his Indian roots. The reds were vibrant, the blues were pale and soft, and the gold regalia that hung around the elephant's neck and across its back jumped out at her. It wasn't Gabi's thing, but its detail was striking, and she admired the skill. There was a slight chemical smell to the wool, and its texture was coarse. The length of the pile was short and tight. It must have taken hours to weave, and yet it cost peanuts in comparison with a commercially produced rug of the same size in the UK. She hoped the people making the rugs here had enough food to eat. Gabi bought a silk fuchsia scarf from him that would match Nana's coat and handbag. She paid him double the asking price, and it still didn't feel like she'd given him enough.

She felt lifted by more vibrant colours as she walked past the clothing and textiles stands. Rugs seemed popular, but that wasn't what she was looking for. She moved beyond the fabrics and past the souvenirs without a second glance. She stood in front of the type of stall that always tugged at her heartstrings. Jewellery. Her initial excitement faded as she cast her eyes across the display. The pieces were for tourists. There were multiples of the same design, and it lacked the authenticity she'd hoped for. She wanted to be inspired by something that had been hand-crafted, something delicate, intricate, and unique.

"A wedding ring for a pretty lady, perhaps," the man behind the stall said.

Gabi looked up and saw him gazing beyond her. He had a broad smile and a cheery manner and judging by his flushed cheeks, a fondness for the person he was talking to. Gabi turned and held her breath.

"I will send Conchita to you, Matías. Right away."

The woman started laughing. It was *her*. Gabi's heart couldn't escape her chest quickly enough. She thought she was going to pass out.

"Promise me, Aisha, when your time comes you will bless me with the honour of designing your ring. I will create perfection for you."

Aisha.

"Matías, you will be waiting an eternity."

"I will wait. Your time will come," he said.

Gabi got the impression he was having a different conversation to Aisha. Hers was a pretty name. Gabi enjoyed the sensualness of it on her tongue. She swallowed hard and became acutely aware that she was feeling more flushed than Matías looked, and more embarrassingly, she was powerless to look away from Aisha.

Aisha smiled at her, and Gabi's heart raced. She wasn't wrong. It was the flamenco dancer. It became harder to speak, and her last thought before her mind went completely blank was that Aisha's hazel eyes were beautiful. Gabi couldn't stop staring into them.

"Hello," Aisha said.

Gabi forced herself to look away, to look around, to look anywhere except at her. She scrabbled for something intelligent or witty to say but was too bewildered by the vacant space between her ears and the desert that her mouth had become to be able to speak.

Aisha smiled at Gabi again and narrowed her eyes.

"Hi," Gabi said, or rather, she squeaked. She cleared her throat and tried again. "You're the flamenco dancer."

"Yes."

"You were incredible. I mean, are. I mean..." She didn't know what the hell she meant and was sure she looked like a babbling idiot. But there was nowhere to hide unless she ran off to never be seen again. What would be the point in that? An uncomfortable silence filled the space.

Aisha dipped her head a little. "Thank you. I'm pleased you enjoyed the dance."

"I did. It was awesome. I've never seen anything like it. How do you move your feet that quickly?" Seriously, she just said that. She closed her eyes so Aisha couldn't see her rolling them at herself, and when she opened them, Aisha's smile was wider.

"With a lot of practice."

Aisha swept her hair back. Where the dark brown caught the light, it unravelled golden and reddish strands. She was more beautiful up close. Gabi cleared her throat. "How old were you when you started?"

"As soon as we walk, we dance," Aisha said.

Gabi imagined her as a toddler. She would have easily drawn people to watch her. She had gorgeous round eyes and a look that would melt the hardest of hearts. "I couldn't keep up with the beat," she said.

Aisha smiled. "It is very fast."

Gabi closed her mouth and hoped that she hadn't been gawping for too long. "Do you play somewhere other than the square?"

"We play other places sometimes. Always at the square on Saturdays. How long are you on holiday for?"

"We're not. Well, it's a kind of holiday. I'm with my nana." She needed to explain. "She's seventy-five, and she's from here originally. She's lived in England since she was nineteen and wanted to come back to see her parents' graves and make her peace with her homeland I think." She left out the obvious bit.

"She sounds interesting."

The family history that Nana was a big part of was epic. "Yes, she is."

"What about you?"

"Am I interesting?" A tingling wave weaved through Gabi when Aisha laughed.

"I'm sure you are. I meant what are your plans while you're here?" Aisha asked.

Gabi would swear she wasn't thinking about sex, but it was suddenly very hot, and there was nothing she could do to keep the burning from her cheeks. "Everything. The culture, the food, the dancing."

Aisha picked up a silver bracelet with blue gems embedded in it and turned it in her hand. Gabi couldn't tell by the way she looked at it whether she liked it or not.

"I'd best let you get on," Gabi said and felt empty at the thought of walking away. It wasn't a line best suited to lead into continued conversation, but she was struggling to know what else to say and didn't want to come across as some crazy Englishwoman.

"You live in England." Aisha put the bracelet down.

"Yes."

Aisha's lips curled upwards, and her eyes narrowed. "What's it like, where you live?"

"Green and mostly wet. Flatter than here." Gabi looked towards the blue sky and hills the size of mountains.

"Green is my favourite colour," she said.

"Hazel is mine," Gabi said, looking into Aisha's eyes. Aisha appeared distant. The strain of the laboured conversation was vice-like around Gabi's chest. The handle of the instrument, the silence that with every second that passed, squeezed her tighter. Still, Gabi didn't want their time together to come to an end. "Could you tell me where to get a good coffee?" she asked.

Aisha smiled. "I can show you, if you like?" she said.

The vice released a fraction, and Gabi breathed more easily. "If you have time."

"Sure."

Gabi felt taller by Aisha's side. "Do you live close by?" she asked.

"In Sacromonte. Do you know it?"

"In the hills. The caves cut into the rock?"

"Yes. About fifteen minutes by bus."

Bus. She would prefer to hire a taxi for when she and Nana visited.

Aisha stopped outside the door of what looked like a house. With closer inspection, Gabi saw the name of the café engraved in the wood of the largest window frame. The upstairs windows were small, and a black chalk board that advertised a limited menu leaned against the whitewashed wall next to the front door. It was quaint and judging by the tanned skin and dark hair of the two women drinking coffee outside, it appealed more to locals than tourists. Gabi loved it.

"Here is the best coffee."

Gabi hesitated to turn away from Aisha, and Aisha didn't look like she was going to make a move either. It was now or maybe never. "Would you like to join me?"

Aisha smiled and nodded, and Gabi followed her into the café.

It was small and dark, and there was a strong aroma of tobacco. Aisha said something to the man behind the bar who dragged on the cigarette that seemed stuck to his lower lip. He led Gabi to the back of the room where they took a seat below the air conditioning vent.

The man from behind the bar brought over their order in a silver pot with a long spout. It was decorated with an Arabic pattern and complemented by two espresso-sized silver cups.

"Does everyone in your family dance?" Gabi asked.

"Yes, though some quite badly."

Gabi blew out a puff of air. "It's good to know there are others out there who can't dance."

Aisha sipped her coffee. "I didn't say they can't dance."

Aisha's smile told Gabi she was teasing her, but Gabi liked her directness too.

"What do you do?"

"I used to work behind a bar, and I like to make jewellery."

"Ah, did you like the market stall?"

Gabi knew her face had given away her thoughts before she had been able to censor herself.

Aisha grinned. "Matías is a good craftsman and a better businessman. He makes what sells easily. If you want to see something original, I can take you to his workshop."

"That would be amazing."

Aisha touched Gabi's hand, and she froze.

"You don't wear anything you make?" Aisha let Gabi go.

"No." Gabi sat on her hands. The thought of Aisha seeing anything she'd made caused her to want to flee. It was irrational, but it was for the same reason she'd never moved to selling her jewellery. Any criticism affected her deeply.

Aisha tilted her head to one side and stared at Gabi to the point that everything inside Gabi tingled.

"I imagine you are very talented." Aisha sipped her drink.

Gabi's throat tightened. Aisha was kind, she was stunning, and Gabi felt as if she'd just dipped into her soul and somehow made it bigger and brighter. She wished she had the same belief in her abilities that Aisha had, although Aisha was probably just being polite, and she hadn't seen anything Gabi had made. "Does this mean we can meet again?" she asked.

"If you'd like."

Gabi swallowed back the squeal of delight. The back of her eyes burned as shamelessly as her throat. She didn't know why she felt sad and happy at the same time, something to do with the cemetery, maybe. And it was overwhelming, and she felt stupid. She sipped her coffee and as Aisha stared at her, she couldn't stop grinning.

Aisha looked at her watch and took a deep breath. "Time escapes me. I probably should get home."

Gabi didn't want her to leave. She finished her coffee slowly and stood. "Thanks for bringing me here."

"Thank you for buying me coffee."

The awkwardness of earlier returned, and Gabi made her way out of the café in silence. She stood in the street as if waiting for an instruction, hesitating to be the one to break the spell that bound her.

Aisha turned away and pointed. "I'm going this way."

Gabi tilted her head in the opposite direction. "I'm staying at the Palacio hotel."

Aisha raised her eyebrows. "It's one of the best."

"Nana chose it."

"She has good taste."

"Yes, she does." Gabi half turned. "Can you meet tomorrow?"

Aisha started walking away, and Gabi's stomach took a dive.

"At eleven. The fountain at Los Patos."

Gabi's heart raced. Aisha had a great ass in jeans. She had no idea where the fountain was—there were so many of them— but she wasn't going to go back to the hotel until she'd found it. This was one date she wasn't going to miss.

10.

"Look, these tomatoes are perfectly ripe, Aisha."

That wasn't news to Aisha. Nicolás was trying to make conversation and trailed her around the field like a puppy dog. It was annoying. All she had that was hers and that no one could take from her were her thoughts, and she would like to have them alone. She handed out the basket for him to drop the three buffalo tomatoes he'd picked. "They are a good size this year," she said, because her mama would have something to say to her if she wasn't polite.

"I will pick peppers?" he asked. "How many does Pilar want?"

Aisha didn't care about the peppers or what Mama wanted. She just wished he would go away and leave her in peace. "Four or five."

The cherry tomatoes were sweet and succulent. She plucked three vines of them and added them to their gathering. "And two lettuce."

Nicolás put the peppers in the basket and touched her hand. She turned towards the onions though they didn't need any, and his hand slid from hers.

"You seem more distant, Aisha. Is it Conchita's marriage that distracts you? It's a very busy time for the family I know, but you must trust that everything will go well. It's a happy time."

It was a happy time for her sister, and Aisha had no doubt that everything would be perfect for the wedding. That wasn't the issue. Thoughts of the English stranger occupied her mind.

She hadn't expected to see Gabi again after the dancing. Bumping into her yesterday had fuelled her fantasies and filled her mind with false possibilities. She should never have agreed to meet her again. It was too risky, but she'd been caught off guard, and the more they'd chatted, the more she wanted to get to know her. She ripped the onions from their place in the ground, shook off the soil that clung to them, and threw them in the basket.

"Aisha, I want you to take me seriously."

"Nicolás, I do. You are an honest man. You care about...you care about people, and we work well together."

He leaned towards her, his hands clasped together, and his eyes narrowed as his frown deepened. "Not just our work together, Aisha. I want you to think of me as Conchita thinks of García."

Her heart launched itself into her throat, choking her, making it hard to breathe. As the silence extended between them, his appearance shifted to defeated, and he took a step backward and lowered his head.

"I want us to be happy together, Aisha. I hoped you wanted that too."

"It's too soon, Nicolás."

He pressed his lips together and shook his head. "Not for me, it isn't."

Why was it always what he wanted that mattered? She took a deep breath to maintain her calm. "I need to be sure." She would need to be forced was what she really meant.

"And you are not?"

She turned away and started walking towards the house. "It's not that simple."

He trailed a pace behind her. "Why, Aisha? Why is everything so fucking complicated with you?"

She stopped and faced him, her head inches from his. "Why are you shouting at me?"

He stepped back, ran his fingers through his hair and tugged at the back of his neck. "You always make excuses. Even Esme couldn't work you out."

The mention of her name in that way drove a knife through her heart. He couldn't say that about the one woman who did know her well, who only changed towards Aisha after she married him. "How dare you bring your dead wife into this? If she were still here, you wouldn't be knocking at my door, would you?"

He squirmed then lifted his head and adopted the posture of superiority that was his birth right as a male in their community. "What will become of you?"

She tried to stare into his eyes, but he avoided contact. Was his reaction intended to threaten? He couldn't know about her desires, because she had nothing to hide except the images that were guarded closely by her mind. She couldn't give any concern to what might happen should she lose her mental faculties, like Old María, and start speaking the truth. She couldn't show him any concern for his verbal assault either. She mustn't show any sign of weakness because that would lead to an intervention of some kind by her parents. "I will be happy, that is what will become of me." She started walking back to the house, and he followed her.

Mama greeted them at the door. She held a basket covered with a cloth. Aisha put the basket of vegetables they'd just collected on the table and started towards her bedroom.

"Aisha, you need to take this food to Señor Pérez," Mama said.

"Mama, I can't. I've arranged to meet a friend at eleven." There was no escape from Nicolás's questioning stare.

"These are not plans that I know," Mama said and raised her hand dismissively. "Señor Pérez is very old, and we have to look after him. I made fresh bread. Now take it and go."

"This is Conchita's job. Why isn't she doing it?" If looks could kill, she would have fallen swifter than a bird shot from the sky. The joy and excitement she'd harboured for the meeting with Gabi seeped from the wound her mama had inflicted. She might as well be lying prone on the stone floor, bleeding, on a slow route to her death. "Mama, I need to talk to you." She had to try to explain to her that she couldn't marry Nicolás, or any man.

"Not now. I'm busy. Your sister is sorting out necessary wedding preparations. You have nothing as important as that to give your time to. Ojalá, que no fueras tan insolente. Vamos." Mama thrust the basket at Aisha. "Tómalo."

Aisha took it and let it hang at her side. She didn't mean to be rude to Mama. She wasn't being listened to and that was infuriating.

"Allow me to escort you, Aisha. It would be my pleasure," Nicolás said.

Aisha turned towards him and tightened her grip. "I'll be fine."

Mama beamed at him, the saviour of her delinquent daughter. She could scream.

"This is a very good idea. Perhaps, Nicolás, you can help her lose her disrespectful attitude."

She launched another dismissive wave at Aisha. There was no point in challenging her because she would become angrier. Even if Aisha ran all the way to the old man's house and back, she would miss the bus she needed to catch to get into the city on time. At best, she would be an hour and a half late. Gabi would think she didn't want to see her. Some would say it was nature's way of getting her to do the right thing by her family. She didn't believe that.

"So, who is this friend you've arranged to meet?" Nicolás asked as they walked.

"No one you know."

They continued in silence. Aisha lengthened her stride, and the anger and frustration burned inside her. Being late was annoying, but not being free ate away at her like a parasite that couldn't be destroyed. There was no one she could talk to. No one she could share her dreams with who would understand what it was to be her.

"Is this friend a man?" he asked.

She stopped walking, turned to him, and put her hands on her hips. "This isn't a conversation I want to have. Not everything revolves around men and marriage, Nicolás. I'm not interested in either." Her heart pounded. She'd said too much. She bit her tongue and watched his response, hoping he hadn't picked up on what she was really saying.

He shook his head. "You would tell me if there was another man?"

She choked on the breath that she'd been holding, and a little of the tension slipped from her.

His mouth twitched as he spoke. "I really care about you, and if there was another man for you, it would break my heart.

But I want you to be happy. This would explain your reaction to me."

She felt sorry for him, pinning his hopes on her, but she needed to keep him sweet, or her parents would encourage her towards another suitor in their village and another man might be less patient with her. "There isn't another man. If I wanted to get married, then I would choose you, Nicolás. I'm just not ready for that yet. I love to dance. I want to meet new people and learn about the world." *I want to be able to breathe as me, not as we.* Their culture and their history defined them both, but where it nurtured him, it destroyed her.

He gave her a half-smile. It was better than a scowl and suggested he had bought into her story.

"I can still hope," he said and carried on up the hill with a little more of a spring in his step.

Thinking about Gabi lifted her spirits and drowned out his presence. She would get a message to the hotel and hope that Gabi could forgive her. Maybe they could go to lunch or take a long walk together along the river and talk sometime soon. She wanted to know more about England and the incredible life Gabi must have there. Gabi wanted to explore Granada, and Aisha could show her around. There was so much to see. What harm could come from them spending time together? Her heart answered the question, and she couldn't quash the feeling, though she knew she should.

11.

GABI SAT ON THE low wall of the fountain and turned her face to the sun. Her pulse raced, and her insides vibrated like soda inside a cocktail shaker as she thought about Aisha. She couldn't remember feeling this nervous and excited when she'd first met Shay, so that was a positive. When Shay had walked out on her, she'd felt the pain that came with rejection and worse still, being taken for a fool, but she hadn't missed her. The one-night stands had masked the loneliness that had haunted her since childhood in a way that her relationships hadn't, but she'd also come to dislike herself, because she wanted the stability of being with one woman in a loving relationship.

She'd thought about Aisha a lot since that first night, and although seeing her at the market and spending time with her yesterday had felt awkward, she was sure they'd connected. The music, the dancing, the food, the wine, the place. It was all very dreamy, and Granada was a beautiful city, but there was something else. She felt more at ease now that she wasn't hunting Nana down every five seconds. It was as if her history here had laid down roots for her to connect with, as if she were a part of this place she hadn't known before. It didn't make sense. It was a feeling of belonging, and maybe it wasn't hers at all. Maybe it was Nana's, and she'd somehow tuned into it.

It was nuts feeling the way she did about a stranger, and maybe she was in danger of making the mistakes she'd made before, thinking she was in love when really it wasn't love at all, but she couldn't lie. She felt crazy, bonkers, and a little intimidated, so this had to be different from Shay, and the one-nighters didn't count for anything.

As time moved on, she became edgy and wandered around the tiny square. It wasn't difficult to be seen, so Aisha couldn't miss her. She studied the Los Patos sign on the wall of a house, even though she knew she was in the right place. She'd walked the route three times from the hotel yesterday, and she'd arrived at 10:45 a.m. even with picking up a coffee on the route. The Spanish had a more laidback attitude to time, so being late was probably just the norm.

That didn't stop Gabi questioning if she'd completely misread Aisha's intentions, blinded by her own confused feelings. Her stomach tightened at the thought of being stood up. Had she pushed Aisha to say yes? She didn't think so. Aisha must have got caught up somewhere. Gabi didn't know which voice inside her head was right, but she knew which one she wanted to believe. She'd give Aisha a bit longer.

She looked towards each entrance to the square in turn as the minutes ticked by. Every second reminded her of feeling invisible, just as she was as a child at Nana's, watching the pendulum of the grandfather clock tick, not knowing, tock, waiting. Her dad's voice raised in anger. She felt it now, the gut wrenching feeling of being ignored while being talked about, when all she'd wanted was for him to hold her and tell her she'd be okay.

Time moved slowly. Half an hour slipped into forty-five minutes. She'd been fooled, like she was with Shay. Stupid, stupid, stupid, Gabi. That voice in her head, that didn't like her too much, had taken hold and the thoughts tripped convincingly through her mind. She shouldn't have come on the damn trip, and she should never have fooled herself into thinking that she had anything to offer someone as beautiful as Aisha.

She folded her arms to protect her aching heart and strode back and forth, the weight of disappointment dragging at her feet and the emptiness inside expanding. It could consume her and still she couldn't bring herself to walk away, because she didn't want to admit the truth. Aisha wasn't coming.

She sat on the ground at the base of the fountain, closed her eyes, and gritted her teeth to stem the tears. The let-down was worse because the anticipation had been electrifying. Gabi tapped her watch face. It couldn't be 12:15 p.m. already. Should she give Aisha another half an hour? She couldn't leave yet.

She'd been naïve, again, thinking things were different this time, here, with a woman she didn't even know. Logic was screaming at her to wake up. Walk away and don't look back. But logic paled against her heart's will and left her sat next to a flowing fountain of tears. How many coins would she need to throw in for her wish to come true? She wasn't the first person in the world to have been stood up or dumped in such a romantic setting.

The ache in her chest deepened, and she thought again about her mum, the absence of her and what she must have missed, and the tears rolled down her cheeks. The child in her wanted to be held and comforted, but as had always been the case, her mum wasn't there to take away her pain. The voice that had tricked her thoughts about Aisha subsided and the intense sadness eased, leaving her feeling weak and raw.

The walk back to the hotel was long, and when Nana greeted her with a gust of enthusiasm, it didn't even take a chip off her despondency.

"I was just coming to find you. What's wrong, Gabriela?"

"Nothing."

"Ah. Are you sure, cariño? Come and have lunch with me by the pool. We can chat, or maybe a swim will help."

She wasn't hungry but the idea of soaking her head in water to cool the burning behind her eyes wasn't such a bad idea. "Sure."

Nana picked up her handbag. "Get your swimsuit on."

Gabi did as she was told, and they made their way to the roof via the hotel reception, where Nana insisted on informing every member of the staff of their lunch plans. She was always so chatty, and the staff seemed to love giving her their attention. The receptionist that Gabi had almost assaulted when she'd thought Nana was in trouble plucked a purple flower from the vase on the desk and handed it to Nana.

"If there is anything we can help you with, please ask," he said.

Gabi followed Nana into the lift and crossed her arms.

"Would you like to go to a flamenco show one evening? In Sacromonte? That will cheer you up," Nana said as the lift set off.

"If you want." Gabi watched the floor numbers light up. She didn't want to go to Sacromonte. She didn't want to run into Aisha just in case Aisha had changed her mind. She couldn't think clearly. Her chin trembled. It took all her effort not to cry again.

"I thought you enjoyed the dancing at the square," Nana said.

"I did, but there's loads of other stuff you want to do," Gabi said.

"How about a visit to the Alhambra?"

"Sure." Gabi's optimism had drowned at the fountain, and her lack of enthusiasm came through loud and clear. The sadness that thinking about her mum had elicited was confusing. The feeling was new and the intensity unexpected, and she didn't know what to do with it to make it go away. She took a deep breath and smiled, though Nana's deepening frown suggested she hadn't been fooled.

They reached the pool area, and Nana made her way to the bar to order a selection of tapas. Gabi stripped off her shorts and T-shirt and jumped into the water. She swam to the bottom and tried to sit there, doing her best to burst her lungs. It was impossible. Against her will, she floated to the surface and gasped for air. The ache in her chest was of her own making, and she felt stronger for taking back an element of control. She knocked out a few lengths to vent off some steam, then stepped out of the pool and joined Nana.

"I got you a beer," Nana said. She took a sip of her sherry and sighed. "Do you know this was the first and only alcoholic drink I ever had before we escaped to England. I was given a small glass that last Christmas to celebrate our journey and new life. Pedro Ximenez is without doubt the best sherry in the world."

"Do you still miss your parents?" Gabi asked and dried herself down. She sat in the seat next to Nana and flicked her fingers through her hair to style it.

"Sometimes."

"I miss Mum," Gabi said. She sipped her drink, and a tear slipped onto her cheek. The view over the city, with its mountainous backdrop was spectacular, and she should be appreciating it because this trip was for Nana's benefit. But it was hard when the loss was so raw.

Nana took Gabi's hand and squeezed it. "It was hard for you, and very sad that Pamela never got to see you grow up."

"Grow up a fuck-up."

Nana sat upright in the seat and turned to face Gabi. She lifted her sunglasses and stared at her. "Don't you dare say that. You are kind, and generous, and beautiful, and I will not hear those words from you again. She would have loved you with all her heart."

Gabi shook her head and wiped her cheeks. "I didn't realise I missed her until coming here. It's stupid."

"Cariño, no, it's not." She took Gabi's hand. "I didn't expect to feel the way I do, returning after all these years. Memories, feelings, sometimes they come when we don't expect them. Maybe when we're ready to face what we couldn't at the time. Seeing my parent's graves, being here and thinking about Juan, the loss is stronger than when I was in England, but there is so much joy and love too." She motioned at their surroundings. "If you stay lost in that tormented mind of yours, you'll miss all this beauty and its opportunities."

A second beer helped Gabi relax. Since they were talking, there was another thing that had been niggling her since they'd visited the graveyard. "Was Dad a spy?" she asked. Had he followed in his father's footsteps? It would explain his behaviour and attitude towards Gabi.

Nana sighed. "No, cariño. I think your father..." She swallowed and pressed her lips together before taking a sip of sherry. "Your father spent his early years with a nanny and at boarding school, then military school after that."

"I know, but why is he so distant and angry with me?"

"I don't think he was close to anyone except Miguel, cariño. I'm ashamed to say that the role model he should have had in a father wasn't there for him, though he idolised Miguel.

"Grandpa was away a lot when he was younger?"

"Yes, Miguel moved between London and Gibraltar gathering intelligence, helping the resistance with my father. He was a good man at heart. If I had my time again, I would have challenged his decision to have your dad schooled away from home. It was harder for a woman then. A husband's word was final. I owed my life to Miguel because he'd helped me get away. I couldn't embarrass him. His ideas about your dad's career were fixed, driven by his own. Discipline and structure were more important to him than anything."

"Not to you though?"

Nana shook her head. "Rigid rules that suffocate individuality and passion are not right. I should have been there for my son, and I wasn't. The war made my relationship with Hugo difficult, because while he was being taken care of by a nanny, I looked after other people's children evacuated from London. In my mothering of those poor children, I lost sight of my own."

Nana looked dispirited, and Gabi wanted to take away her pain. "You're the best Nana anyone could wish for."

Nana smiled and put her hand to her chest. "Cariño, Gabriela. I love you with all my heart." She stroked Gabi's face. "You are a beautiful soul, and you will make many mistakes over the years too. I know I should have done better by your dad, and maybe I will always regret that, but I can't change what I did."

"Hindsight is kind of a bit late, right?"

Nana laughed. "True. But I have relived the moment I should have made a different decision many times. I'm sorry that he wasn't the dad he should have been. It's my fault."

Gabi couldn't swallow past the lump in her throat. Nana had wanted to do things differently, and because of how life was back then, she hadn't been able to do diddly-squat about it. It was heartbreaking. She wondered how her dad might have turned out had he been bought up by his mum rather than a nanny and the schooling systems, and her heart warmed towards him. "How's your sherry?" she asked, to change the topic and lift the mood.

"Excelente." She took a sip. "I'm going to see that apartment this afternoon, if you'd like to come. If we like it, maybe the owners will let us rent it until the sale goes through, then we can cancel the holiday booking."

"Do you want to stay here permanently?"

"I don't know, cariño. I feel at home here, and I never expected that. It's as if a part of me never left and is happy to be reunited."

Gabi felt as though her emotions had been sucked up inside a tornado and spat out in tiny pieces. The positive on the horizon had been Aisha, and the disappointment from being let down earlier resurfaced. She sighed and sipped her beer. There must have been a good reason for Aisha not showing up, surely? "Maybe I could look for a job?" she said.

"You have one. You're looking after me." Nana said and sipped her drink.

"And if you have too many more sherries, I'll need to carry you back to your room." Gabi laughed. "Anyway, I'm not going to be your paid carer if we're going to live here. You'll drive me up the wall."

Nana laughed. "Well, don't go looking for a job in a bar. You're better than that."

Gabi shook her head. "I'm not qualified for anything else," she said.

"Rubbish, Gabriela." Nana looked over Gabi's shoulder and smiled. Gabi turned around, and her stomach kept turning. Her heart raced, and she couldn't stop herself from blushing.

"Excuse me for interrupting you."

Aisha's wavy hair fell past her shoulders, and the sunlight passing through it reflected a range of rich browns and auburn red. Her black skirt stopped just above her knees, and she wore thinner heels and a loose-fitting red blouse. Casual and comfortable. She was a mirage calling to all Gabi's senses. Gabi's skin tingled as Aisha gazed the length of her body. She felt naked and vulnerable, and she ached for Aisha's hands to trace the route her gaze had just taken.

Aisha cleared her throat. "Gabi, I'm sorry I couldn't meet earlier. I had to run an errand."

Nana patted Gabi on the back of the hand and rested back in her seat. "Best you go and get changed, cariño." She smiled. "Go on, go on."

Gabi should have objected. Nana had ordered tapas, and Gabi had said she'd go to see the apartment, but she knew her words would be wasted. And the last thing she wanted was to spend the afternoon with Nana when she could be with Aisha.

Aisha stepped forward and held out her hand. "You must be Gabi's Nana. I'm Aisha."

Nana clasped Aisha's hand between hers, and Gabi could almost see Nana's thoughts as she smiled.

"It's lovely to meet you," Nana said, then looked at Gabi and frowned. "What are you doing still sitting here when this beautiful young woman is waiting for you?"

"Una hermosa mariposa," Aisha said to Nana.

If Gabi blushed any harder, she would explode from the heat.

Nana patted the silver butterfly pinned to her dress. She'd worn it every day since they'd left England. "Me gusta mucho. Es mi favorito. I have a very talented granddaughter," she said.

Aisha smiled at Gabi. "I'll wait in reception for you," she said.

Gabi grabbed her shorts and T-shirt.

"It was lovely to meet you," Nana said.

"You too." Aisha headed towards the door.

One of the waiters arrived with a stack of dishes balanced on various parts of his arm, and Gabi stared from the food to Nana. There was a line of dishes on the bar, all presumably destined for their table. She cursed silently.

"Go," Nana said and waved Gabi away. She looked towards the door that Aisha had exited through. "Now is a good time for you to enjoy yourself." She studied the tapas, looked up at Gabi and smiled. "Go, go."

Gabi kissed Nana on the forehead. "I love you," she said.

Nana brushed her off and ate a shrimp off a pincho. "Delicious."

Gabi ran back to her room and dressed. Maybe buying an apartment here was a stroke of genius, because it would mean she could be friends with Aisha. She didn't know Aisha well, but she hadn't let Gabi down. Aisha had intended to be true to her word, unlike Shay had ever been, and it had just been circumstances that had stopped her coming to the square. Her heart had raced seeing Aisha at the poolside, and that feeling didn't come from nothing. If there was such a thing as love at first sight, Gabi had felt it when she'd watched Aisha dancing on that first night, and in the awkwardness when they'd drank coffee. She couldn't be sure because the line between love and lust merged, and she'd got it wrong before. Anyway, she was getting ahead of herself and needed to slow down. She trembled inside as she headed towards the reception.

12.

THE PUNGENT SMELL OF raw onions, the thick cigarette smoke, and the sickly fried fat odours started to clear thanks to the increased airflow through the narrow openings in the top of the bus's windows. Gabi swallowed the last bite of the tortilla she'd struggled to eat since they'd got onto the bus. She sat back, thankful for the window seat Aisha had insisted she take and gazed through the scratched glass. These seats were designed for children, though being this snug against Aisha was worth the unpleasant journey.

The bus passed through what Aisha said was the main street of Sacromonte, where most of the tourists came to experience traditional flamenco, though the best flamenco took place in their homes further up the hill on a night after work. The bus continued along an increasingly narrow and winding road further into the hills. They took a sharp bend with a severe drop, and the tortilla did a quick flamenco with the acid in Gabi's stomach. If she'd known what was involved in getting to Matías's workshop, she would have suggested waiting until after her lunch had digested.

"That's the Alhambra," Aisha said. "You have to visit it sometime."

She pointed across the centre of the bus towards the reddish stone fortress opposite them. Gabi got a whiff of vanilla perfume and closed her eyes to fully appreciate the gentleness and warmth it evoked.

"The poets named it 'a pearl set in emeralds,' because it stands out from the forest of English elms around it."

"We English get everywhere." Gabi smiled and focused on the dark green trees densely packed around the palace. The vista was set in a deep blue backdrop that rose from the hills. "It's pretty."

"Yes, it is. 'Verde que te quiero verde,'" she said.

"Nana said that earlier. Does it mean something?"

"It means everything. Lorca wrote many poems about passion and love. He was the Gypsy Poet. He is one of my favourites."

Gabi loved the way Aisha spoke, full of admiration and excitement, and with a certainty that Gabi wished she had. "I never read poetry," she said. "I flunked school, to be honest."

"Poetry is the language of love. I have a small collection of books. I learned English reading them. I could show you the best second-hand bookshop here."

Gabi nodded. She wasn't into reading, but she'd go anywhere if it meant she could spend time with Aisha. "I'd love to."

"Tomorrow. I'll meet you at the coffee shop at ten-thirty?"

Gabi smiled. "You're going to introduce me to poetry?"

Aisha smiled. "Yes. I wish I could have met Lorca. My abuela did. The elders sat with him on many nights and talked and listened." She glanced around the bus and leaned closer to Gabi. "He was murdered by Nationalist forces during the Spanish Civil War."

"My grandparents were murdered by them too." Gabi took a deep breath as Aisha leaned against her arm. War was cruel, and both their families had suffered at the hands of the authorities.

"The civil guards were evil," Aisha said.

101

Gabi had avoided them on the street. In their green uniforms and baseball caps, with guns at their side, she was sure they would eagerly use, given the smallest excuse. "They're still scary here," she said.

"Is it the same in England?"

"No. The police don't normally carry weapons, and they don't patrol the streets like they do here. At least, not where I live. It's a quiet village, and you get more of a feeling of safety and support than fear."

"That sounds nice."

"I guess." She smiled.

"Being arrested for doing nothing wrong still happens here."

That wiped the smile from Gabi's lips. The concept was sickening. She stared out at the whitewashed houses that marked the neighbourhood from others within the city and wondered whether Nana had met this poet or Aisha's abuela. The houses looked less well kept, dirtier, greyer up-close set against the tall dark English elm trees. There was a weight to this history that she was a product of, and as foolish as it might be, she couldn't shake off the feeling that she had been affected by it.

"We're nearly there," Aisha said.

The bus slowed, and the air inside quickly reverted to the heady mix of odours that reminded Gabi of all the reasons why she'd never eaten from her local fish and chip shop. She fought the urge to fill her lungs, though she desperately wanted to breathe deeply. The bus crawled to a stop, and she couldn't get off quickly enough.

"Welcome to Sacromonte," Aisha said.

Gabi bent double and took in a few deep breaths. She felt Aisha's hand on her shoulder and rose slowly. "Sorry, a bit travel sick," she said.

"You look pale."

"I'll be okay." She took more deep breaths. "Just needed some air. I'm not good on public transport."

A plume of grey smoke clouded around them as the bus chugged on its journey, and Gabi coughed after inhaling a mouthful of fumes.

Aisha walked onto what looked like a huge vegetable patch and an orchard in bloom on the other side of the road. She plucked something from the ground and returned. "Here."

"Mint."

"It will help." Aisha ate some.

Gabi inspected the leaves for dirt and insects then popped them in her mouth and chewed. It was moist and lightly flavoured, and it cleared her head surprisingly quickly.

"It will settle your stomach."

"Is that basil I can smell?"

"Yes. We grow everything we need. Herbs, vegetables, fruit. Chickens roam. We have sheep and goats on the hillside, and cattle in the fields. That's chamomile," Aisha said, pointing to the wildflower. "And pink violet, and sweet chestnut."

As they walked, the landscape divulged the secrets of these people's lives, a world created through the toil of the generations who had paved their way. They could easily thrive without the commercial trappings that Gabi had come to think of as normal, things she'd tried and failed to create meaning from. The air that filled her lungs was alive with new fragrances and the view was uplifting and inspiring. Her stomach had calmed from the experience in the bus but looking at Aisha changed all that. She felt like dancing.

"This way," Aisha said.

A small wooden shed in a field, opposite the red door that fronted one of the caves, caught her eye. Matías stepped outside the shed and stood with his hands on his hips. His cheeks darkened as they approached.

"Welcome," he said. "Aisha tells me you like to make jewellery." He put his hand over his heart. "It will be my pleasure to show you around."

He had a gentle way, and his passion seemed to reflect the natural beauty that surrounded him. Gabi felt it touch her. "Thank you, both, so much."

"I have some very pretty wedding rings for you to see, Aisha." He led them into the workshop.

Aisha laughed. "I'll be sure to tell Conchita."

Who's Conchita? Gabi had a faint recollection of the name from the market, but she couldn't be sure of the context, because as soon as she'd seen Aisha, she'd forgotten everything that had come before. *Wedding rings?* Matías laughed. He turned his back to open the door, and Gabi felt like a cobra under the spell of the snake charmer. Matiás turned around, and Aisha smiled at him, breaking the spell. They stepped inside, and a shot of excitement tingled across Gabi's skin.

"You'll love it," Aisha said.

Another wave of tingling confirmed Aisha was right. Gabi was going to enjoy seeing the workshop too. It was cramped and dark inside, and there was a dearth of what Gabi would have considered essential machinery, such as a casting machine or a flexible shaft. She'd been lucky to use a local facility back home, courtesy of her friend Issa whose boyfriend's father was a goldsmith. How on earth Matiás could craft anything under these conditions was a miracle. Her eyes adjusted slowly to the dim light, and she noted the work surface was spotlessly clean.

"It is small," he said. "But I have everything here. Look." He dipped below the surface, opened a drawer, and pulled out a slim tray. He turned on a spot lamp and positioned the light over the tray, then pulled back the silk cloth to reveal the jewellery. The gold clasps were light in tone, highly polished, and held in each was a small gem. When seen together, they could be the wildflowers, blossoms, and green leaves of the terrain, and they were more vibrant and more pure than the stained-glass Gabi had admired in the church windows she'd passed. Dark emerald and sapphire, deep purple amethyst, blood red ruby, and fiery citrine. They were beautiful and she would love to combine the colours and make something with them that captured the landscape here.

Gabi leaned closer to the tray. On the other side of it was a selection of gold bracelets and chains, each perfectly crafted and subtly different in shape, size, and the pattern of the links. She reached out then pulled back her hand, afraid to tarnish their beauty with her sweaty fingerprints.

"They won't bite. Please, inspect them closely."

"They're gorgeous," Gabi said.

"You think so?"

"Truly."

"They are," Aisha said.

Gabi picked up the helix-shaped bracelet and studied it. It would look wonderful against Aisha's tanned skin. She put it back carefully, her hands trembling. "They're so delicate."

"They're stronger than they look," Matías said. "Please, take something. A gift."

Gabi took a pace back. "I can't."

"It would be my pleasure," he said.

"Will you do something else for me?" Gabi asked.

"If I can."

"Will you show me how you make this?" She pointed to the helix chain.

Matías smiled. "Yes. Come again, a week on Wednesday after the market, after six p.m."

Gabi pocketed her clammy hands and grinned. "Awesome. Thanks."

Matías laughed. "Perhaps you can do me a favour in return," he said.

"Anything," Gabi said.

"Persuade Aisha to allow me to design her wedding rings."

Gabi glanced from Matías to Aisha. She had the sense of movement slowing down and spiralling, the room becoming darker, and the garbled echo of their laughter in the background. Matías's cheeks were a beacon that reflected his obvious affection for Aisha. Aisha's eyes sparkled as she laughed. Gabi stood still, speechless. *Please don't let that be true*.

"When that time comes, I promise I will come to you," Aisha said.

Matías picked up the cloth, set it down across the jewellery, and returned the tray. He invited them for apple tea and home-baked biscuits, and they went into his house. The cave was modest, with a living space that included a kitchen area with a small woodburning stove and a sink. The toilet was in a block outside and was shared with the other occupants of the houses in this row, he said. The stone walls inside were cream, warm to the senses, and a single lamp stood proudly in one corner behind a red leather armchair. A filigree gold frame on the wall to the side of the chair held the image of a woman in a green full-length dress and was the only decoration in the room. Gabi had never seen a home as small or as sparsely decorated. She wondered who the woman was and whether Aisha's house was similar. Matías's earnest hospitality and effortless kindness gave the place a warm homely feel that the decoration alone couldn't achieve, and she felt in no hurry to leave.

"Where do you live?" Gabi asked as they headed back to the bus stop.

"Further up the hill." Aisha pointed to another group of cave dwellings.

"Are you getting married soon?" Gabi asked.

Aisha laughed. "No."

They walked side by side, their footsteps accompanying the birds' evening chorus. Gabi didn't want to ask her next question in case she was getting too personal, but she couldn't not, could she? "Who's Conchita?"

"My sister. She's seventeen and engaged to García, who is also seventeen. They are getting married in a few weeks' time."

"That's young."

Aisha looked at Gabi and sighed. "We dance young, and we marry young," she said. "It's our way."

Gabi didn't like the shiver that scooted down her spine. She didn't feel old enough to marry going on twenty-six, let alone when she'd been seventeen. "At that age, you're still a kid."

"Exactly."

They walked in silence. The next obvious question chased around Gabi's head like a ball in a pinball machine. It bounced off the sign that said, "Don't ask," and past the one that said, "No, really, don't ask," and balanced precariously over the button that, depending which way the ball fell, would either open a door to Gabi or slam it firmly shut. "And you didn't marry young," she said. Okay, it was a statement. The softer option.

Aisha stared at Gabi, and the tingling brushed across her skin again.

"No."

Gabi wished she could shut up, but she couldn't hold back now. Gabi wanted to marry someone—the right woman—one day, and she needed to know Aisha's thoughts on the topic, just in case. "Do you want to marry? You know, later, maybe?"

Aisha looked up the hill from where they'd just walked. "I dream of marrying someone I love with all my heart."

Someone, not a man. The distinction was important, Gabi was sure of it. They stood in silence at the bus stop, and Gabi stuffed her hands in her pockets to stop herself from reaching out. God knows, she wanted to touch her. Aisha gazed in the direction the bus would arrive.

"Do you have a big family?" Aisha asked.

"No, just my nana and my dad. He's in England."

"No brothers, or sisters, or cousins?"

"None that I know of."

Nana may have more pearls from her history hidden away that she hadn't told Gabi about yet. But if she had any distant relatives in Spain, Gabi wouldn't have the first idea where to start looking for them. Plus, since she wouldn't know them from Adam or Eve, she had no urge to start looking either.

"And your mama?"

"I was three when she died."

Aisha took Gabi's hand. "I'm sorry."

Gabi stared at Aisha's hand around hers. The warmth nudged at the loss and loosened it a little. "They discovered she had breast cancer when she was pregnant with me. She refused treatment until after I was born. It was too late for her by then."

"She was very brave."

Gabi watched the tears well in Aisha's eyes. She was relieved the despair that had surprised her earlier didn't reappear, just a hollow emptiness and a little heartache. "Yes, she was. I don't remember her at all, but I still miss her. Does that make sense?"

"A mama is important. I can't imagine being without mine. I think you are brave too."

Gabi shook her head. "How can I miss something I didn't have?"

Aisha narrowed her gaze. "Love, of course."

"What do you mean?"

"We know what love is. It's in our heart. A mama's love should be there, and if it's not, we know it's missing." Aisha hugged Gabi. "I'm sorry for you."

Gabi inhaled vanilla and closed her eyes. She didn't want their time to come to an end, but it would have to. And it did, and it was all too soon, because she could have cried for longer and felt comforted, and it would have been better than going back to the hotel. She eased out of the hug and glanced up the hill to avoid Aisha's gaze that would set the tears rolling again. "What about your family?"

"There's Conchita, of course." Aisha rolled her eyes. "Mama, Papa, Abuela, nine cousins, and too many aunts and uncles to keep track of, though we do, of course. We live close to each other. Our neighbours are also like family."

"It must be nice having a big family."

Gabi considered herself sociable by nature, but she wasn't used to a crowd, especially when it came to family gatherings. It had been her dad and Nana for as long as she could remember, and even then, her dad's positive contribution to their family dynamic was questionable. She hadn't enjoyed the sense of loneliness that she'd experienced at the cemetery knowing it was really just her and Nana left. With a big family, there would always be someone to turn to, someone to feel close to, someone there to hug you when you needed it.

Aisha's lips twitched at the corners, and her smile faded on a deep sigh. "My family mean everything to me," she said.

"Let me guess. Everyone gets under each other's feet, they're into each other's business, there's big drunken parties, and lots of blazing arguments."

Aisha laughed. "Exactly like that."

"Sounds fun."

The birds chirped in on their silence.

"Would you like to see the Alhambra palaces at some time?" Aisha asked.

The offer had the effect of the music, lighting up every cell in Gabi's body. "I was going to see it with Nana," she said.

"Why don't you let me be your guide? Maybe on Monday morning. I have school in the afternoon."

"School?"

"Some of the younger children in our village. I help them. It's not a proper school. Maybe you could come and show them how to make jewellery sometime. They would like that."

Gabi frowned. She didn't have the skills to teach kids anything.

"Simple string and bead bracelets," Aisha said. "They are aged between five and eight."

Okay, she could do that. She held out her hand. "Deal," she said, and when Aisha took it, she didn't let go until the bus came into view.

She took a seat at the back so she could watch Aisha walking back up the hill. She couldn't wait until the morning when they would to go to the bookshop. When the bus took the next bend, her stomach churned, and she stared out of the window to steady it. God, how she hated public transport, but she would take the bus anytime if Aisha was sitting next to her.

13.

GABI SPOTTED AISHA WAITING for her outside the café, and her heart raced. When Aisha greeted her with a kiss on the cheek, heat flushed Gabi's face and she trembled. She shoved her hands in her pockets and stared at Aisha feeling like a teenager and a little lost for words. "Hi."

"Hi." Aisha rubbed her hands together and appeared as nervous as Gabi felt.

"You're early," Gabi said.

Aisha held out cotton cloth wrapped around something small. "I made this for you."

Gabi peeled the cloth back and revealed a cube-shaped biscuit. She lifted it to her nose and inhaled. "Smells good."

"Taste it."

Gabi bit into the crunchy exterior and found a soft centre. Lemon zest burst on her tongue. "Um, that's amazing."

Aisha looked at her watch and around the street, and the smile she'd greeted Gabi with became lost and was replaced by a frown. "Come on, it's this way." Aisha set off at a pace and Gabi strode out to catch her up. "I can't stay long as I have to get back," Aisha said.

The lemon turned bitter in Gabi's mouth. She'd hoped they could spend the morning at the bookshop and maybe grab lunch together. Perhaps she'd upset Aisha, but she couldn't think of anything she'd done that might have offended her, and people didn't bring gifts if they'd been upset. But something wasn't quite right. "Is everything okay?" she asked.

"Yes."

Aisha's fleeting glance as she spoke wasn't convincing. Aisha increased her pace and led Gabi down a series of cobbled streets. She entered a shop with a window display of pieces of antique furniture, old clocks, and glass bottles that looked as if they'd been dug out of someone's back garden, and a handful of hardback books whose covers were faded and marked.

The smell of wood and wax struck her as they stepped inside. The room was crowded with large ornaments and furniture, and unidentifiable items that Gabi would have had thrown out as junk rather than given them house room. She would tell Nana about the place though because Nana would browse for hours in here. She followed Aisha to the back of the shop where the wall supported three shelves of books. Books littered the floor below the stacked shelves in piles knee-height. She breathed in the scent of old paper, musty oak, and leather. It was a little reminiscent of Nana's office back home, only more disorganised.

"Hola, Aisha."

The man behind the counter who greeted them looked older than the antiques in the window. His long grey hair gave him a wizard-like appearance, which seemed fitting since it would take some feat of magic to know where everything was inside the shop.

"José, this is my friend, Gabi. We've come to look at books."

"You know where they are better than me," he said and laughed.

"You need to get organised."

"And spoil the joy of discovery? I am glad you came in. I found something for you." He started searching through the books on the floor.

Gabi glanced at the titles on a shelf. *Gardening For All Seasons* leaned against the *Diary of Anne Frank*, which rested against *A Brief History of Humankind*. There were cartoon books with French titles and an English Guide to Granada that was probably a few years out of date. That joy of discovery he talked about would take hours if she was looking for a specific title.

"Here," he said and brushed the cover of the hardback he'd found before handing it to Aisha.

Aisha gasped. "Gabriela Mistral is in here."

Gabi looked over her shoulder. "Who's she?"

"She was a Latin American author. She won a Nobel Prize for her poetry. This is incredible. Thank you."

José smiled. "I knew you would appreciate it. It's a compilation of some of the greatest poets."

The shop door opened, and José excused himself to deal with the new customer.

Gabi watched Aisha leaf slowly through the pages, her lips moving as if tasting the words. It was sensual and mesmerising. Aisha's eyes narrowed, and she swallowed, and sighed, and held her hand to her heart. Gabi wanted to kiss her. "You really love poetry," she said, her voice affected.

Aisha smiled. "It opens my eyes." Aisha looked towards José. "I used to come here as a child on a Saturday when Mama came into town, and I'd help with stacking and sorting the books. José helped me learn to read stories and then poetry. Words are everything. Love, loss, suffering, passion, hatred, and joy, and everything we know or can dream of can be captured in just a few lines. It's compelling. It gives me hope. It makes my heart ache and sing." She sighed. "It makes me realise I'm not alone in the way I feel," she said softly.

Gabi wanted to hold Aisha so badly the strain of holding back was excruciating. "How do you feel?" she asked.

Aisha held Gabi's gaze with a thoughtful expression. "Confused. Trapped."

Gabi put her hand on Aisha's arm. Aisha looked towards where José was talking to the customer. Gabi let go, confused because yesterday Aisha had comforted her when they'd waited for the bus. "If you want to talk about anything," she said.

Aisha ran her finger over the cover of the book. "Maybe I will learn to write properly one day and put my feelings into words."

Gabi shoved her hands in her pockets. "I think you should."

Aisha closed the book and sighed. "Do you ever dream of a different life?" she asked.

Gabi shook her head. "Winning the lottery would be good. I wish my mum hadn't died and that I'd paid attention better at school, but that's more about hindsight."

Aisha stared at Gabi. "You're lucky."

Gabi smiled. "Maybe I just lack imagination."

Aisha shook her head. "No. You have options."

"Don't you?" Gabi's stomach turned leaden as Aisha stared at her. She hadn't meant to be flippant, but Aisha was serious and intense. The differences between their lives were huge, and Gabi hadn't been respectful of the challenges Aisha had already faced.

"Not like you," Aisha said.

"But you enjoy living here?" Gabi asked.

"I love Granada, I love my family, and I love dancing. But our laws are strict, and we aren't free to choose how we live or who we love."

That explained the tension that slipped between them at times when other people were around. "My dad went mental when I kissed a girl," she said, hoping it would encourage Aisha to talk openly.

Aisha lowered her head and ran her finger across the cover of the book.

"I was eight."

Aisha smiled.

"We'd built a snowman together. That was my first kiss." Gabi shrugged.

It had ended up as one of those tick tock watching the grandfather clock moments. Dad had shouted at Nana about Gabi being out of control and needing to see someone, though Gabi hadn't quite worked out who she was meant to go and see or about what. "He went ballistic, and he's never accepted me for who I am."

Aisha sighed. "It's important to get a parent's blessing."

Gabi shook her head. "Not for me, it isn't. We're not close, and he's not going to change his attitude, so there's no point in me wasting my time fighting for something he's not willing to give."

Aisha clutched the book to her chest. "I would want my mama's blessing."

Gabi wondered what it would have been like trying to get her dad's approval. It would have driven her nuts, and anyway, she was too stubborn to plead for anything from him. Just because he was her dad didn't mean she had to have his

116

permission or agreement for the way she lived her life. "If progress depended on attitudes like my dad's, nothing would ever change." If that's how Aisha lived, no wonder she felt trapped.

"It's about respect," Aisha said. "And knowing you have their support makes things less frightening."

It dawned on Gabi how much Nana's support had helped her, especially defending Gabi to her dad, and she could relate a little to what Aisha was saying. "I guess. I have my nana's blessing."

Aisha turned and ran her finger across the spine of the books on a shelf. "Yes, you do."

Gabi had hoped that Aisha might have talked more but touching on the need for parental approval had brought a halt to their conversation and subdued the atmosphere. "Do you have to work later?" she asked.

"I have errands, yes. I must take food to some of the elders who can't leave their homes. I have to bake bread and pick vegetables."

"You make me feel very lazy. I have nothing to do, and you work all hours."

Aisha held Gabi's gaze and took a deep breath. Gabi thought she was going to say something, but she didn't. Gabi wanted to ask Aisha who she wanted to love, but Aisha turned back to the shelf, pulled out a book, and set it aside. The moment was lost.

"Will you come for a drink with me?" Gabi asked.

Aisha shook her head. "I can't. I have to get back."

"Some other time, I mean?"

Aisha smiled. "I'd like that."

"Tomorrow?"

Aisha shook her head. "I don't know when."

Gabi had a sinking feeling. If she had her way, she would see Aisha every day. It wasn't enough to know there would be a next time; she didn't want this time to end, and not with this sense of an unfinished conversation. She wanted time alone with Aisha, to have her close without Aisha looking over her shoulder all the time as if she was being watched.

"I can still show you and your nana around the Alhambra, if you'd like." Aisha smiled.

Gabi held Aisha's gaze, and the warmth returned to Aisha's expression. "I'd like that very much." Gabi carried a claustrophobic feeling back to the hotel with her, and it made her feel tight, and vulnerable, and confused. The sense of being watched and that she was doing something wrong worsened, and she glanced over her shoulder, shoved her hands deep into her pockets, and strode out. She couldn't imagine living day in and day out, wanting something that you couldn't have. Aisha, who danced with intense passion and felt the language of the poets, was creative, and intelligent, and kind, but she was locked inside a world that would strip all that from her, and more, by not allowing her to choose how she lived or who she loved. Aisha loved Granada, and her family, and dancing. Gabi wasn't sure what that all meant, but she wasn't surprised that Aisha felt confused and trapped either. Just hearing about it, Gabi felt that way too.

14.

AISHA IGNORED HER MAMA'S repeated call and sat in the shade of the apple tree and continued to sketch with the small piece of charcoal she'd rescued from the discarded ashes of the previous evening's fire. She'd kept the image obscure so that anyone looking on might see a scene or an impression of their own making. She'd captured the essence of her feelings for Gabi in long sweeping strokes and the lightest touch separated from the deep-rooted frustration she'd depicted through thick, dark, looming blotches in a cloudlike form. She held it up and studied it, turned it ninety degrees and then another ninety degrees. It needed more work but looking at the long sweeping strokes made her heart flutter.

"Aisha."

Her mama had puffed herself up with fury and almost filled the doorway. She gestured to Aisha with urgency, though Aisha could see no fire that needed putting out. "I'm coming," she said though she made no effort to hurry. She tucked the picture under her arm, put the charcoal in her dress pocket, and made her way to the house.

"What is wrong with you? I call you, and there you are lazing like there is no work to be done." Mama turned and went inside to where Conchita stirred melted wax at the stove. "We have candles to make for the wedding. Conchita needs your help. I have vegetables to pick."

Aisha sighed as her mother left the house. She watched her hobble across the street and into the field, taking slower and more deliberate steps than Aisha had remembered. At least she was able to walk on this Earth, which was more than Gabi's mama could. The emptiness that she'd sensed comforting Gabi as Gabi had talked about her mum was still there when she thought about what Gabi had missed out on. Even though her mama's controlling nature was irritating beyond words, she couldn't imagine what her life would have been like without her. And she still had faith that her mama might listen to her, under the right circumstances, should Aisha summon the courage to talk to her about the reason she didn't want to marry a man. But it wasn't just about her mama, was it? There was her papa too, and the other villagers who would all have something to add to the mix. As Gabi had talked about her dad's reaction to her kissing a girl, Aisha had known she would never get her papa's blessing.

She hadn't wanted to hurry back from the bookshop, but she'd lied to her mama about where she was going and had been worried about being seen and her mama finding out. She shouldn't have been distant with Gabi because she wanted to talk to her more. But being that close had been awkward, so she'd gone quiet. If only she was brave enough to go for a drink with Gabi without concern for the consequences. She wanted to go. She wanted to be free. She wanted to be like Gabi.

She went to her room, traced the image she'd drawn with tenderness, then tucked it under her bed along with the charcoal. She would finish the sketch in the privacy of the night. It was only a picture, a dream, and she would never let them stop her dreaming. She would try to think of a way to make them listen to her. She had to do something, or she would die.

Conchita stopped stirring the wax and smiled at Aisha as if she'd been waiting for her to return. She looked down at the chain around her own neck.

"What's that?" Aisha asked, knowing her sister wanted her to.

Conchita touched the chain and started to dance. "It's an early wedding gift from García. Isn't it the most beautiful thing you've ever seen?"

She had the dreamy joyful appearance that Aisha associated with being in love, airy and carefree. "Is it not enough that he's giving you a ring?" Aisha regretted snapping, and when Conchita backed away and tended to the wax, she couldn't look at her. Her throat became thick and tight, and she pressed her palm to her lips. She wasn't angry with her sister. She was jealous.

Conchita's shoulders rose and fell with her sobs as she stirred the wax.

Aisha went to her side and stared at the wall in front of them. "I'm sorry. I didn't mean to snap at you." She put her arm around Conchita's shoulder.

Conchita shrugged her off, turned to face her, and glared. Her eyes were wet with tears. "You can't be happy for me, can you?"

Aisha lowered her head and picked at the surface. "I am, Conchita, I promise. I'm sorry."

Conchita ladled the wax into twelve small round candle moulds. Her movements were sharp and her hand trembled, spilling the wax across the table. She cursed Aisha.

Aisha took the ladle from her and put it down. She held her in her arms and kissed the top of her head. "I'm sorry, Conchita. I didn't mean to hurt you."

Conchita pulled away. "You always hurt us, Aisha."

Aisha swallowed hard against the urge to retaliate. It wasn't her sister's fault that Aisha lived a hollow shell of an existence, that she wanted to be with a woman not a man, and because of that, she was imprisoned by rules that were slowly strangling the life out of her.

"Why are you always so indifferent? You barely talk to us anymore."

"I work hard for us all," Aisha said.

"You work hard, and you're not here. Your head is always somewhere else, somewhere better. You are one of us, but you are not with us."

Aisha's heart thundered, and her throat ached with anger and disappointment. If it wasn't for the money Aisha earned dancing, they would live in virtual poverty like many others. "You have no idea what goes on in my head or my life."

"Because you don't let anyone in, Aisha. How can we know? How can we help you to be happy?"

The thrust of Conchita's argument threw Aisha backwards a pace. Her little sister wasn't a child anymore. She was a young woman who could see Aisha's struggle for happiness and wanted to help. But how could Aisha trust her sister? Even if Conchita took her secret well, which she didn't think she would, it would put Conchita in a difficult situation within the community. She would have to lie to their mama and papa and to her future husband. She would become a silent part of the closeted life Aisha lived, and that would make Conchita unhappy in the end, as it had Aisha. "You can't help me. No one can. This is something I have to sort out on my own."

Conchita wiped her cheeks. Aisha picked up the ladle and continued to make the candles. Conchita left the room.

Mama entered the house and lifted the basket of vegetables onto the table. "Where is your sister?" she asked.

"Taking a rest." Aisha stared at the pot.

"Good. I need to speak with you."

Aisha's stomach dropped. She stirred slowly, deliberately, to control the tremor developing in her fingers and give the quaver in her voice that would be sure to show if she spoke too soon the time to still. "What about, Mama?"

"You were at Matías's workshop on Tuesday."

There was never any doubt that her mama would find out about the visit, and she was glad she hadn't lied about that. Nothing was sacred in the village. Aisha bent closer to the moulds and tried to give the wax her full concentration, but it was impossible with her stomach churning and knowing what was coming next. She went back to stirring the pot with her back to her mama. "Yes."

"Who was the woman you were with?"

"A friend."

"No one recognised her. She's not from the village."

"No." Aisha turned from the stove. She had to be strong and stand her ground without coming across as defensive or guilty. She had nothing to feel ashamed of, and no one was going to stop her seeing Gabi again. She was a friend, and Aisha wanted to get to know her. It had been a long time since she'd felt this happy, and she wasn't ready to give it up, even though she knew she probably should. She was drawn to Gabi in the way she'd been drawn to Esme, and that was a fact she absolutely needed to keep from Mama. She gulped down her breaths and stood taller, clasping the ladle tightly in her hand. Wax dripped onto the floor. Mama looked as if a bee had flown up her nose.

"Is she from Granada?"

"No."

Mama twitched her nose. "Spanish?"

"Yes."

Her expression softened as if she was about to smile. She didn't. "Where in Spain?"

The scenario would have been more amusing if Aisha didn't care, but because she did, it was daunting. The one person who had mattered to Aisha, her mama had never questioned her about, because Esme had been one of them, and the natural conclusion was always that a gitana only had eyes for a gitano.

Thinking about Gabi made her nervous in front of Mama, but if she was evasive, her mama's natural nosiness would flip to suspicion, and then she would watch Aisha more closely. "She's visiting from England with her nana. Her nana was born here and lived with her family until she escaped the war. Her Nana's parents were killed by Franco. She has come back to give her respects to them at the cemetery. She probably knows some of the elders here. Gabi is her escort, to make sure no harm comes to her." She reeled off the information Gabi had said in as laid back a tone as she could and added a little detail to help direct Mama's thinking. "Gabi—"

"Gabi?"

"The woman I took to see Matías's workshop. We met at the market at his stall. She makes jewellery, and she wanted to see some authentic work. His is the best, and he's going to teach her."

Mama lifted her eyebrows and said, "Really?" in a tone that captured either disbelief or intrigue, or some combination of both. Aisha couldn't decide. She'd intentionally left out important details like Gabi watching their performances, tipping them a large amount of money, taking coffee with her, and going to the bookshop, because those things were not for sharing with anyone. Those things were hers alone. If word got back to her mama, she would answer the questions as they arose, but until that time, saying less was the best approach.

"And her nana was born and raised here, you say?"

"Yes."

Mama scratched her head. "Hm. Perhaps we should invite them here. Maybe Abuela knows this Nana."

Aisha widened her eyes. Relief gave way to a whisper of elation, which then became obscured by something resembling abject fear. She wiped away the beads of sweat from her forehead. The ladle was coarse against her palm, and she put it down carefully. The smell of the wax became nauseous. "Yes." She poured a glass of water and sipped until it was empty, but still felt queasy. Her mama would notice Gabi's short hair and the way she dressed, and she wouldn't like it. "I can ask them," she said.

"Excellent. Ask if they would like to join us for the Fiesta de Santiago celebrations in July when everyone will be here. Now, how are the candles coming along? We will need three hundred to line the street for the celebrations."

Aisha was working as fast as she could. She released a long breath. The fiesta was weeks away. It would give her time for these feelings to abate. She stirred the wax and filled a second mould. The anxiety lifted as Mama chatted excitedly about Conchita's wedding arrangements, including a carriage and six horses for the bride.

Aisha only had thoughts of Gabi. What would she make of Aisha's home? She winced at the smallness of it that could either appear as cramped or cosy. The darkness was relaxing to tired eyes or depressing to the unsettled mind. The cool climate, a welcome relief from the summer's heat or a chill that revealed Aisha's concealed fears.

She watched her mama wash the vegetables. It must be easy being her, and Abuela, and the other elders. They lived without expectation of the world changing, and around them, it didn't. Their contentment was assured by maintaining the status quo. No yearning tainted their blood and drove them insane. Change wasn't just frightening to them. It was terrifying, and it wasn't welcomed, because life worked as it should the way things were. Except for Old María, who they'd all assumed had lost her mind because she hadn't had children. The inability of a woman to become a mother infected the soul, the elders said as they'd made a cross at their chest, as they always did. Everything that wasn't accounted for by Gypsy laws rested in the hands of God, and both were to be feared.

She eased another batch of candles from the moulds and set them aside to continue to harden and reset the mould with wicks and fresh wax. She threw another block of wax into the pot and stirred until it softened.

"It pleases me to see you enjoying yourself," Mama said. She folded a cloth and put it in the drawer. She came to Aisha and put her arm around her waist and kissed her temple. "How are things with Nicolás?"

Aisha stirred more vigorously. "Mama, I don't want to get married."

"Don't be so dismissive, Aisha. Of course you do. You must." She stroked a loose strand of hair from Aisha's face. "No quieres ser solterona, Aisha."

Aisha would rather be a spinster than married, given the choice. Mama's smile thinned her lips. Her insistence was about necessity, not passion, not love. It didn't matter that Aisha's heart would break. What was important was that the act of Aisha's marriage would bring great relief to the family. Surely, her mama could see that.

"He's a good man, and you could do a lot worse. Pedro has approached your papa to ask about your intentions. He is keen to date you."

Aisha shuddered. "Pedro hit his last wife."

Mama pursed her lips. "You are making this impossible, Aisha. When people imagine there is a problem, it attracts those with a history, and we only want the best for you and the best is running out. Pedro works hard and has a house of his own. There are worse men."

"He has two children, and he will want more."

"There is nothing more beautiful than children, Aisha."

Would she shame her family by not having children and not getting married? She knew the answer was yes. On every count, she was guilty. But love shouldn't come with guilt like this. She moved into the centre of the room to create space between them, defeated by her mama's insistence. She ran her fingers through her hair. In her mind, the screaming tugged at the bars of the cage that trapped her, but she needed to remain calm and give herself more time to adjust. She shook her head. There would never be enough time to adjust to marrying a man. "I will think more seriously about Nicolás," she said.

"I will tell your father to talk to Pedro and explain that you soon plan to get engaged." Mama grinned. "I am so excited for you, Aisha. You will be so happy."

Aisha went back to the stove and stirred the wax vigorously, rage increasing the pressure inside her head as the wax yielded to the heat.

She would make the candles until there was no more wax to cast. She would go to her room and sketch, and she'd think about Gabi and the green, wet landscape of her home and the English elms. The colour of life is green. "Don't you see the wound I have from my chest up to my throat?" One line alone summed up how she felt. One day, she would claim her life and find release from the pain she suffered. One day, she would be free.

15.

MONDAY MORNING HADN'T COME around quickly enough. Gabi had spent most of her time since visiting the bookshop worrying whether Aisha was okay, whether *they* were okay, and what Aisha was doing. She had worked hard trying to curb her irritation with not being able to see Aisha and failed miserably. She'd walked miles around the city and still couldn't shake off the uneasy feeling. It was ridiculous because they weren't *they*. Though Gabi felt there was something between them, and she'd sensed the shift in Aisha's mood like lead closing around her heart. She'd done a lot of rationalising with all that walking and decided she would let Aisha go if she had to. So the weekend had passed like when she was the kid watching the grandfather clock again. Tick, not knowing, and tock, waiting to find out. A sick feeling about her decision to let Aisha go had given way to secretly hoping that when they next met, Aisha would be back to how Gabi thought of her, and then perhaps Gabi could stop trying to protect her heart with false declarations of being able to walk away.

She'd read a few of Lorca's Gypsy poems, over and over again, about love and the moon. She didn't grasp it all, but she'd been captivated by the pictures he created with his words and learned how the gypsies had lived and died at the hands of the Guards. It hadn't been a fun or a light read, but she'd felt the power in poetry that Aisha had described. Lorca had been murdered by the Civil Guard for being a homosexual. It was hideous, and the uneasy feeling set deep in her gut as she'd wondered whether this kind of persecution was still being perpetuated within Aisha's culture, by her own people, against Aisha. It had been hard to sleep after that.

Excitement and anticipation weaved through her now, as she stood at the bus stop.

Nana had insisted that they use local transport to get to the Alhambra even though Gabi had voted that they take a taxi. Nana leaned on her cane with one hand and propped her sunglasses higher up her nose with the other. "We need crockery for the apartment," she said.

Gabi smiled.

Nana's offer on the two-bed had been accepted, and the owners had agreed they could rent the property until the sale was completed. They'd cancelled the holiday rental and were moving into the apartment on Friday. "Do we need anything else?"

"I will go to the market for herbs and spices later in the week. We need to think about feeding ourselves again."

"Home cooked food is going to be great." Gabi was grateful for the slight breeze that took the burn out of the sun. "It's going to be a hot one," she said.

Nana looked skyward. "Did you put sun lotion on?"

Gabi laughed. "Yes, did you?"

"Of course."

Gabi linked her arm through Nana's. "Did you ever meet Lorca?" she asked.

"What makes you ask?"

"I read some of his poems. Aisha's abuela met him, and I wondered if you had. Maybe you've met her too."

"I met him once. Such a clever man. We sat around the fire as he read." She sighed. "Juan had been so excited that he rode to my house and threw stones at my bedroom window to wake me. I sneaked out. Everyone was excited by Federico, except the Nationalists of course."

"Weren't you afraid to get caught?"

Nana clasped her hands in her lap. "I was young, and the thrill was worth it. When my parents found out, they stopped me from seeing Juan, of course." She scratched her chin. "He was smart and quick. We never got caught. That's why he was the best ratcatcher."

Gabi frowned. "Ratcatcher."

"All the boys and young men hunted rats. They needed to eat."

"That's disgusting."

"Not when you're starving, cariño. For some, it was their only protein. I once stole mutton from our fridge and gave it to Juan. One of our servants got blamed and lost his job. I didn't steal meat again, but I did give Juan eggs, and cheese, and rice when I could."

"Have you eaten rat?"

"Yes."

Gabi shuddered again, wondering if it tasted anything like chicken or beef.

"His mother asked me to eat with them. It was a goodwill gesture for the food I had given them. It would have been wrong to refuse their generosity and besides, I would have done anything to be with Juan."

"They were okay with you and him?"

Nana shook her head. "They insisted he marry a girl from the village, and I'm sure he would have after I left. We talked of being together, but if the war hadn't separated us, I have no doubt the Guardia would have. His parents wanted him to stop seeing me, but they didn't trust that I wouldn't have had him killed in revenge."

The omelette Gabi had eaten for breakfast turned in her stomach. The bus arrived, and she stepped onto it. A thick cloud of tobacco smoke, potent perfume, and the smell of old fish oil, and the omelette turned sour. She swallowed the acid back down and headed for a window seat. Nana gave a cheery good morning to everyone she passed before sitting next to Gabi.

"You like this girl?" Nana asked.

Gabi stared out the window. "Yes."

Nana straightened her blouse behind her back and settled with her cane between her legs and her hands in her lap. "She's gitana."

"Yes." Gabi didn't want to talk about the challenges they might face being together. It was too early to think about that, although she'd put herself through enough torment all weekend and hadn't found any answers. She willed the bus to gather speed so they could get some air before the curdled egg made an unwanted appearance.

"Does she like you?"

"I think so," she said.

"She came to the hotel to find you."

"She's kind. Doesn't mean anything."

"I saw how she looked at you. She likes you." Nana patted Gabi on the knee. "I know you've been hurt before, cariño. It can be hard to trust your heart to someone else's hands, but if you don't, then there will always be a shadow where there should be a brilliant light. To love and feel loved in return is to have lived."

Nana had blossomed since they'd arrived, like she'd been reborn in her natural home. "Juan was the one, wasn't he?" she said. "Not Grandpa."

Nana had intimated as much at the river, but Gabi hadn't appreciated the depth of Nana's feelings for Juan until she began to realise her own for Aisha. It must have broken Nana's heart parting from him.

"It was always Juan." She looked at Gabi and smiled. "It always will be. I kept his place in my heart a secret for so many years, but I never forgot how it felt to be loved by him. Now, I can set things right. I can talk about him. He was handsome and brave, gentle, and kind. I miss him terribly."

The bus pulled up next to the entrance to the Alhambra palace, and Gabi spotted Aisha in jeans and a long-sleeved white shirt with the sleeves rolled halfway up, baring her tanned forearms and revealing a multi-coloured string bracelet around her wrist. Pure joy radiated from Aisha's smile, and Gabi felt a huge dose of relief that the connection between them was still there, and the light in her heart that Nana talked about appeared brighter. Her stomach fizzed like sherbet, and she almost tripped as she struggled to coordinate her feet in the simple act of walking. It might be madness to think she was in love with Aisha because they barely knew each other, but the way her heart ached over her concern for Aisha and the warm fuzzy feeling going on inside her was too good to ignore. It was telling her something serious was happening.

Aisha smiled at Nana. "Hello," she said.

Nana hugged her and kissed her on each cheek. "Call me Estrella."

Gabi's heart hammered at the thought of kissing Aisha's cheeks and when Aisha turned to her and said, "Hello," she thought she might pass out from the furnace that had ignited inside her. Aisha stepped closer, held Gabi's shoulders, and kissed her cheeks. The moment was over in a flash, leaving Gabi weak and holding her breath. Gabi stared at Aisha unblinking, her cheeks tingling from the touch, and inhaled the vanilla perfume that lingered around her head. "Hi," she said.

Aisha narrowed her eyes and half-smiled, then she turned her attention to Nana. "How about we start with the Court of Lions?"

"I wonder if it's as formidable as I remember," Nana said and set off.

It will be beautiful, Gabi thought, because everything looked beautiful in that moment. Even the poorly executed renovation work looked bright and exciting.

"Have you been here many times before?" Aisha asked Nana.

"A few, with Juan. We panned for gold and silver in the river with a dream of making our fortune and running away together."

"That's so romantic." Aisha smiled.

"I thought so." She touched the locket around her neck. "Who knows, maybe he made his fortune at some point."

"That's a pretty locket," Aisha said.

Gabi had never seen this piece in Nana's extensive collection, and she'd been through her jewellery boxes many times as a kid.

"Juan gave it to me."

"He must have loved you," Aisha said and glanced at Gabi and smiled.

"We loved each other, a long time ago."

"You are lucky," Aisha said.

"I was."

"Here it is, Fountain of the Lions," Aisha said, leading them into the courtyard.

Gabi stared up at the domed light in the roof in front of them, at the golden honeycombed surrounds, the symmetrically patterned tiles, and filigree-patterned walls. The lions around the fountain were worn, and it was clear where repairs had worked and where they hadn't. To her eye, it wasn't anything special, but it was magnificent because of Aisha. Aisha was breathtakingly gorgeous, and Gabi wished she could be alone with her. She wanted to kiss her and hold her and talk.

"The lions are a symbol of power, strength, and sovereignty," Nana said.

"Yes," Aisha said.

Gabi loved Aisha's accent, loved everything about her.

"The hydraulic systems that produce the water from the lion's mouths were once thought a mystery. So much so, that a poem was written about it."

Not another poem.

"It's still here." Aisha pointed to the side of the fountain.

"Magnífico," Nana said.

While Nana bent to look at the inscription on the wall, Aisha stared at Gabi and tugged her sleeves higher up her arm. The material slid back. She fiddled with the collar of her shirt and wetted her lips. Why did Aisha's look of vulnerability feel exhilarating, and terrifying, and enticing? Gabi chuckled as Aisha tugged her sleeves up her arm again, and they slid back down.

"I'd like to rest here a while," Nana said, rising from the plaque. She sat by the fountain and closed her eyes.

Aisha turned to Gabi. "Would you like to walk along the river for a while?"

Nana opened one eyelid. "Excelente. Give me half an hour, and I'll be ready to go again."

Nana tilted her head towards the sun, both eyes now closed, her chest rising and falling with slow, shallow breaths. Her age showed more when she was resting, in the downturn of her mouth and the relaxing of her jaw. Gabi, reassured that Nana was fine, headed towards the river with Aisha at her side.

The essence of vanilla wafted around Gabi, and Aisha half-smiled, the meaning of which needed no words to be appreciated by Gabi's core. "Have you ever panned for gold?" Gabi asked.

"As a child, for fun. I don't think anyone has found anything for years."

Distanced from the palace, beside the gentle hush of the river, Gabi enjoyed the cooler air, the fusion of fragrances, wildflowers, pine, aniseed, and sweet honey. She walked closer to Aisha's side, matched her easy stride with the comfort of an assured lover, and with the natural sway of their rhythm, accidentally brushed against Aisha. A jolt from the charge tingled down her arm.

Aisha blushed but made no move to create space between them.

"Did you always want to be a dancer?" Gabi asked.

"Yes." Aisha stopped and picked a flower from the riverbank and handed it to Gabi.

The dark blue petals, perfectly symmetrical and as delicate as tissue paper, were beautiful. She brought the flower to her nose and inhaled the mild nutty aroma.

"It matches your eyes," Aisha said. She picked another flower and turned it between her fingers. "What would you do, if you could do anything?" she asked.

Gabi stared at the river and thought about the bar, her flat that was no longer hers, and waking up with women she didn't know in her bed. She had no plans. She'd drifted her way to this point, guided by the eddies of a life lived with only a fleeting consideration for the consequences and a deep fear of being alone. "I don't have a career. I worked in an office for a bit and hated it. I worked evening shifts at the bar, so the days were mine—"

Aisha's hand trembled as she held the flower, staring at it. She kept her head down. "Is there anyone special?" she whispered.

Gabi moved closer to Aisha her heart raced. "I'm not with anyone, if that's what you mean."

Aisha glanced up, and then swiftly fixed her gaze on the flower.

Blushing suited her, and Gabi wanted to kiss her even more. "There was someone, before," she said.

Aisha blinked and swallowed and took several deep breaths. She looked mildly uncomfortable, but not enough to end the conversation or return to the palace.

"I misjudged the situation," Gabi whispered. "I was naïve and got burned."

Aisha nodded. "Do broken hearts mend?"

Aisha seemed to have gone in on herself a bit and Gabi desperately wanted to hold her.

Aisha sighed and looked towards the river. "The day makes promises, the night leaves empty and cold. The heart swells on the tide of desire and cowers in the shadows of fear. Love, ever-present, and free. Not so for the heart unclean."

"Unrequited love," Gabi said.

"I could never have been with her. I think that's the worst kind of pain," Aisha said.

Gabi thought about Nana and Juan. "I think you're right."

They stared at the river, side by side. Gabi wanted to take Aisha's hand but stopped herself, because a couple were heading their way and that was the way things would be. She waited until they passed. "Are you still in love with her?" she asked.

The flow of the river and the birds chirping overhead as they returned to their nests in the trees filled the wordless space.

"She will always hold a place in my heart," Aisha whispered.

"That's how it should be," Gabi said.

Aisha looked weary from revisiting the memory. "I've never talked about her to anyone," she said.

Gabi took a step back. She struggled to find the right words, given the enormity of Aisha's confession. When she'd been dumped by Shay, Issa had been there for her with two bottles of Chardonnay and an extra hot curry. "I promise never to say anything," she said.

Aisha nodded. "Her name was Esme. We were best friends. I had loved her since we were very young. I never told her how I felt, but she guessed and made it clear she didn't feel the same way. Being a lesbian is not acceptable in our culture. She married Nicolás and died two years ago. Complications in childbirth." Aisha's eyes watered, and her chin trembled. She ran her fingers through her hair and blew out a long breath, and the tears slipped down her cheeks. She wiped them away. "My heart still hurts when I think of her." She turned to Gabi. "Is that normal?"

Gabi wrapped her arms around Aisha and held her close, because Aisha needed comforting more than she needed anything right now. "Yes, it is," she whispered and inhaled the spicy notes in Aisha's perfume and loss squeezed her heart.

Aisha eased away.

"Love fills the heart, and loss rips it to shreds. We can love many times and differently, I think," Gabi said. God, she'd been reading too much poetry. But she meant the words and hoped Aisha would feel comforted by them.

Aisha shook her head. "I don't think my heart can love that deeply again," she said.

Aisha's admission landed hard in Gabi's chest. Hopeless and deflated, she looked towards the ground. "It isn't easy letting go, but if we don't, then the future is just the past relived again and again."

Aisha smiled and nodded. "Perhaps."

Gabi held up the flower. "Let's make a wish," she said and tossed it into the river.

Aisha threw her flower in and laughed, and it was as if the last few minutes hadn't happened. Gabi watched the flowers bob downstream, feeling the pinch of Aisha's admission that she didn't think she could love again.

"What did you wish for?" Aisha asked.

Gabi shook her head. "Can't tell you." She smiled. "You?"

"What I've always wished for," Aisha said.

She had that expression again. The one that said she knew what she wanted and wanted what she couldn't have, and the intensity in her gaze caused Gabi to tingle inside. She moved closer until Aisha's blouse brushed her shirt. The warmth and the scent, and the sense of loss they both shared, were a potent drug that Gabi couldn't escape the effects of. She didn't want to run away. She wanted to touch and kiss, and this was the wrong time and place. Aisha was tantalisingly close. She closed her eyes and felt the warmth slip away. She opened them, took a deep breath, and smiled at Aisha's flushed cheeks.

Aisha dipped her head and fidgeted her hands at her side. "We'd better get back to your nana."

"Yes, I guess we should," Gabi said, and they ambled slowly back to the concrete lions in silence.

Nana stroked the tiles on every wall and dipped her hand into every fountain, as they wandered around the palaces, reclaiming what had once been old memories, dreams and wishes. Gabi admired Aisha from every angle with a gentle vibration low in her belly and decided without doubt, that she was more exciting, more interesting, in much better shape, and more formidable than anything the Alhambra could offer.

"I think I'd like to go back to the hotel now," Nana said.

Gabi would stay all day if it meant she could spend more time with Aisha. The words of the poem had haunted her. *A heart unclean.* Was that how Aisha thought of herself? Gabi walked to the bus with an ache in her heart and a wish that she had to work out how to fulfil—time alone with Aisha.

"We are having a celebration on the twenty-fifth of July," Aisha said as they waited at the bus stop.

"The Fiesta de Santiago," Nana said.

"Yes. We have our own celebration. There will be flamenco. Everyone in the village will be there. Would you like to come?" Aisha asked. "Mama would like to meet you both."

Nana leaned heavily on the cane. "What's your mama's name?"

"Pilar. Pilar Moreno."

Nana pinched her lips together, narrowed her eyes, and shook her head. "I don't think I know her. I said to Gabriela, the best flamenco is in Sacromonte. It would be a pleasure. Please thank your mama."

Aisha turned to Gabi and smiled. "It starts at eight p.m."

Gabi nodded. It was more than a month away. She had to see Aisha before then or the time in between would be like serving a life sentence. The thought of meeting Aisha's parents and family made her feel uneasy. Aisha's life was hard, and Aisha wasn't entirely happy. She was stuck, and Gabi was annoyed with Aisha's parents and frustrated that Aisha couldn't do anything about it. She didn't like the feeling of helplessness that irritated her chest and tugged at her heart either.

Gabi hugged Aisha quickly and brushed hot cheek to hot cheek as they said goodbye.

Aisha hugged Nana. "It was lovely to see you again," she said.

Nana smiled from Aisha to Gabi and back to Aisha. "Thank you for the tour. I'm looking forward to a long siesta when we get back."

Gabi smiled. She would rather spend the afternoon with Aisha.

"She's very sweet," Nana said as they sat on the bus back to the hotel. "And beautiful."

"She is." Gabi stared out the window and felt the physical distance separating them. "Why didn't you come back to Spain before?" she asked. Gabi would return, no matter what, if it meant she would get to see Aisha one last time.

Nana patted Gabi's leg. "I thought about it after Miguel died, but it was never the right time. I didn't want to see Juan with a family of his own. I wasn't ready to let go of my parents, and I was nervous about reopening these memories." She looked towards the palaces. "England was my home, and I thought I'd end my days there. It was easier that way."

"What changed?"

"I was approaching seventy-five. If I didn't do it soon, I never would. I found the idea of not seeing Granada again unsettling. And that feeling wouldn't go away. I had to come back, to rekindle my heart before my time ran out. I want to die with the happiness I had when I was here. Daft, I expect. But I feel closer to Juan, and more at peace. I think you know what I mean."

Gabi took Nana's hand and squeezed it. "I do." She felt for all that Nana, Aisha, Juan, and her grandparents had lost. "I don't think my heart can love that deeply again," Aisha had said, and the words stuck in Gabi's throat. But she wasn't ready to let go of Aisha either.

16.

MATÍAS'S HANDS WERE BUILT for farming, though he worked with the dexterity of an accomplished pianist. He cut, soldered, and moulded the precious silver metal with ease, and by the end, the rough cut of two birds of peace joined at the wing emerged.

Gabi turned them in her palm. "That's brilliant."

He cut another piece of metal and hammered it into a thin metal round sheet. He wound the sheet carefully around a wave-shaped wooden pole and stretched its edges, so they touched. He compressed the centre to create curves that formed right angles to each other moving in opposite directions, like petals. The fundamental shape of the spiral appeared.

He handed it to Gabi. "It's very basic."

"It's awesome."

He stood and motioned to the seat. "Now it's your turn."

Gabi's hands trembled as she started to work. She blew into her palms to reduce the clamminess. Moulding and soldering, she lost track of time. She frowned at the shape of the metal in her hand. It was crude, but it was a start.

He inspected the bird shape. "You're good," he said.

"I have a lot to learn."

"I have met others much older who know less."

She lowered her head. "Thanks."

"Would you like some herbal tea or water?"

"Either, thanks."

"Try the spiral while I'm gone."

"I don't want to waste the—"

"You won't," he said and smiled.

He left the workshop, and with the pressure of being watched gone, she relaxed and started to enjoy herself. She worked slowly, taking great care to deliver precision at every step, ensuring the metal sheet was a consistent depth across its surface, that she stretched it evenly at its edges, and pressed with equal firmness to create the two curves at right angles to each other. It looked like a butterfly with its wings tucked up, lacking in the contours Matías had effortlessly created.

She had a vague recollection of the door opening behind her and something being put down on a surface as she eased the silver into position. The bloody metal wasn't shaping as she wanted it to. She huffed as she worked. She sat back and stared at the piece on the stake. The light pressure on her shoulder made her jump from the seat. She held her heart as it thundered, and the familiar perfume registered. She turned to Aisha and laughed. "You nearly gave me a heart attack." She removed the piece she'd been working on and set it on the table among the other bits, embarrassed that Aisha would see it.

"What are you making?"

"It's nothing."

"It looks like something."

Aisha leaned over her shoulder and picked up the doves joined at the wing that Gabi had made. It was too crude for Gabi's liking, but the warmth sent Gabi's thoughts spiralling in a more perfect formation than the helix she'd just tried to hide.

Aisha stepped back and picked up two cups from a box next to the door. "I brought your tea." She held a cup out to Gabi and sipped from the other. "It's mint," she said.

Gabi nodded. "A nice surprise."

"Mint tea?"

"No. You."

"I wanted to see you."

The time that Gabi had lost, following her vague recollection of the door being opened, dawned, and the tips of her ears burned at having been watched. She rubbed the back of her neck. "How long were you stood there?"

Aisha smiled. "Long enough to enjoy seeing you at work."

Aisha moved closer. She picked up the butterfly-shaped piece. "This is clever."

"It's supposed to be a spiral. I've never worked with—"

"I love abstract. It allows for imagination to explore possibilities."

"What do you see?"

Aisha inspected it closely. "Freedom. Movement. Expression."

Gabi widened her eyes. She hadn't thought about jewellery that way before but now, she couldn't not see it, and it brought the piece to life even though it had a long way to go before it would be finished.

"If you turn it like this, it's almost two hearts overlapping," Aisha said. She put the piece back on the table and stared at Gabi.

Gabi's core throbbed. "We're moving into the apartment on Friday," she said. "Would you like to come and see it?"

Aisha released Gabi from her gaze and Gabi sipped the tea, grateful for the chill.

"I can't on Friday."

"Saturday?"

Aisha shook her head. "Monday evening?"

"Paella?"

"I love paella."

"Nana makes the best."

"You have her talent."

Gabi spluttered. "Ha. I don't know about that."

"I do."

Gabi's stomach fluttered. She wasn't as good a cook as Nana, but she had thrown together a few Spanish omelettes over the years. They were perfect for a hangover. "Monday it is." She ripped a scrap of paper from a packet, wrote down the address, and handed it to Aisha.

Aisha turned towards the door as it opened and slipped the note into her skirt pocket. She sipped her tea and smiled at Matías. "Thanks for the tea," she said.

"Freshly picked this morning and made this afternoon," he said and headed towards Gabi. "How did you get on with the spiral?"

Gabi held up her effort, her cheeks burning hotter than a welding iron. "It's a start," she said.

"This is very good. Very good. A little more pressure to the wood before you stretch will help keep the shape you are aiming for."

Gabi wiped the perspiration from her lip.

"She has a good eye," Aisha said.

Matías turned to her. "Yes."

"You were looking for someone to help you," Aisha said.

Gabi shook her head.

Matías rubbed his chin and frowned. "I was."

"Don't hesitate because she is a woman, Matías." Aisha slapped him on the back and laughed. "Women are equal to men, you know."

Matías nodded. "Yes, yes. I know. I know. Ana-María was more skilled than me."

Gabi frowned.

"Matías's sister," Aisha said.

"She was the inspiration in our business. I stopped making real art when she went to live in America."

Gabi wondered if that was the woman pictured on the wall in his house. "I would love to help, if you're happy to teach me to use these tools."

Matías looked from one woman to the other and grew in stature as his smile broadened. "Why not? If you have the time."

"I have plenty of time. One condition."

He nodded.

"Anything we sell, the money comes back to you and the business."

He shook his head. "We must work as a proper partnership."

"You teach me, and I'll help to make the jewellery. I gain new skills, and you grow the business. That's fair."

"And maybe later, when things are working well, you can review the plan," Aisha said.

There it was again, that "she knows what she wants look," that would easily slip through Gabi's defences if she had any left. Matías stared at Gabi, and she wondered if he'd noticed the effect Aisha had on her. She held out her hand. "Deal."

Matías shook hands and beamed. "This is something I never dreamed of," he said and hugged Aisha.

They stood for a while, looking at each other. Matías raised his finger in the air. "I have some drawings you might like to see." He left the workshop in a hurry.

Gabi smiled. "You just got me a job," she said.

Aisha walked across the workshop and leaned towards Gabi. The warmth kissed Gabi's ear, and she held her breath, her heart racing.

"You're welcome," Aisha whispered.

A shiver chased down Gabi's neck and spine, down her arms and to her toes. Aisha stepped back. Gabi moaned silently at the ripples of desire trembling through her. Had Aisha noticed?

"I have to get home," Aisha said.

Gabi sighed. "Do you have to?"

Aisha looked to the floor and then the door. "I have work to do."

"I'm going to come to the square on Saturday to watch you."

Aisha smiled. "I will dance for you."

"I'll only see you."

Aisha laughed and shook her head. Gabi didn't know what to make of that, because she'd meant it, and when Aisha left and Matías returned with his plans too soon, her head was still in a spin. Saturday couldn't come quickly enough.

17.

"WE WILL HAVE A spring wedding," Nicolás said. "Then it won't spoil your sister's special occasion."

Aisha pressed her hand to her chest where the tightness was more oppressive than the storm clouds that hung ominously overhead. The rain would pass quickly as it always did at this time of year, but the sorrow in her heart would deepen. "There's no hurry to set a date," she said. Her heart refused to think about the exact time her limited freedom would end.

He took her hand as they walked towards the pickup point. "I am the happiest man alive," he said.

Aisha let his hand go and repinned her hair, though it didn't need adjusting. She was angry with her mama for speaking to her papa, who had taken it upon himself to speak to Nicolás after he'd confirmed Aisha's intentions to Pedro. "Please, Nicolás, promise me, not a word to anyone until a date is set." She lengthened her stride to move further away from him. When they were around other people, she could easily keep her distance and pretend that this wasn't happening. She could forget that she was promised to him. She would lose herself in the music and dance to nourish the life that had been drained from her today.

"My lips are sealed for your love," he said and chased around her like a puppy dog as she walked.

She was going to be sick. He appeared less handsome though he had made a special effort. His hair was slicked back and shining black, and his cheeks dimpled around his smile. He smelled of a sweet perfume and cinnamon. His hand was warm, and he'd held hers softly. He had managed, through persistence and passion, to trap the frightened bird, and now he was free to caress it with tenderness. She could dream all she liked, but there was no means of escape from the cage that had been put in place to contain and control her. She tugged at her blouse to free it from her neck and inhaled deeply, in fear of fainting.

"We will have three children. Two boys and a girl," he said. "We can name the boys José and Jesús after our papa's. The girl will be called María del Pilar, after our two wonderful mamas. She will be as beautiful as you, and the boys will be as strong as me. They will dance, and sing, and play music together."

"You are greedy."

He laughed. "I want what any man wants, a family of my own. Is that greed, or is it not the will of God to bless the product of our love in this way? I want our blood to flow long into the future. Yours and mine together, through our children's children. They will be smart, courageous, and passionate, and our daughter will have your spirit. They will want for nothing, Aisha. We will give them the world."

What did he know about giving the world? That she should subject her daughter to a life fated by her gender and rules that favoured the past filled Aisha with horror. She could never do such a thing and live happily. Perhaps, if they were married for a few years and she bore no children, it would be grounds for him to divorce her. Then no one would want her, and she would be left in peace. Alone, yes. Pitied, perhaps. Happy, no. She had to give up any hope of joy, or she would end up crazier than Old María.

She thought about Gabi and being at the river. She'd opened her heart because she trusted Gabi, and although she didn't regret saying the things she'd said, maybe the advancing of her engagement to Nicolás would have been easier to accept if she hadn't opened Pandora's box. She'd left the Alhambra with a feeling that there was something between her and Gabi, and she couldn't let go of the desire that tugged at her heart and excited her mind as if it didn't exist. "We have to concentrate on dancing tonight," she said.

"I will dream of our future while you dance," Nicolás said and sang while they waited for their transport.

Aisha sat in the back of the van and closed her eyes. She couldn't bear to look at any of them. They were all honest men. Manuel had a wife and two children, Julio had three boys, and Francisco's wife was pregnant with their first child.

And they all represented the life she'd come to detest.

She imagined herself in another country that had no name, dancing in the street alone, the wind blowing her hair, and the cold filling her lungs. There'd be the uncertainty of whether people would throw coins for her to be able to eat at night. Where would she sleep? Where would she make her home? How could she leave with no means of supporting herself? Her mama and papa would sit at the table in their house, mourning their loss. Her sister and husband would christen their first child. Abuela would sew and tell stories to the children. Pictures would be taken down, and the tales used to explain her betrayal of them would eventually quiet. The elders would sing and dance around the fire as if nothing had changed because for them, nothing had.

"You are trembling, Aisha. You are sick," Julio said.

Aisha opened her eyes. The perspiration on her face chilled, and she shivered. She was shaking and nauseous. She couldn't bear to be disowned by her family. The cost for her to trust in love was too high, and the consequences too devastating. If she ever summoned the courage to leave Granada to be with a woman, she had to be prepared to never return. She would have to be certain that love would last a lifetime and be strong enough to withstand the ache in her heart left by her family's rejection of her.

Julio leaned through to the front of the van to where Nicolás was sat next to Manuel. "Aisha is sick," he said.

"I'm fine." She didn't have a temperature. She was unwell, but not for the reasons they would think.

"We're nearly there," Manuel said.

"I'm fine. Keep driving." She closed her eyes and shut out the sound and smell of the men around her. Sweet Gabi. When Gabi had stepped closer, Aisha had thought she was going to kiss her. She'd dreamed of the softness of her lips and the tenderness of her touch, and Gabi's body touching hers. Gabi appeared now in her imagination, on the outside of the cage, and although Aisha stretched her arms through to try to get to her, Gabi was unreachable. Why had she bothered to make a wish when those around her had the power to destroy it in a heartbeat?

The music might not bring life to her wishes, but it would soothe her soul. She would dance for Gabi, with Gabi in her heart, and she would dream, because dreaming was safe.

The van came to a halt, and the back doors opened. Nicolás looked her up and down and held out his hand.

"Let's make this town sing." She stepped out of the van and took a deep breath. She smiled, and his frown disappeared.

"I was worried about you," he said.

"There's nothing to worry about." She headed towards the fountain and her heart skipped a beat when she saw Gabi sitting on the wall with her legs outstretched and her feet crossed at the ankles.

"Hi," Gabi said.

She smiled and warmth filled her. "I didn't expect to see you this early."

Gabi raised her hands. "I didn't want to miss a dance."

Aisha looked back towards the van. Nicolás approached with his guitar, behind him the others with the board and drum. She wished she could run into the night with Gabi. "I will be busy until late," she said.

"You don't mind if I stay here all evening, do you?"

Aisha laughed. "It would be impossible to stop you. And, no, I don't."

Gabi leaned back, and Aisha felt assessed and admired as they set up their stage and started to dance. Every time she caught Gabi smiling, it was the most delicious feeling and soon, it numbed her troubled thoughts and allowed her dreams of love to set her free. And for those few hours, where her imagination ignited every movement, every sensation her body desired, she knew what it would be like to be touched by Gabi.

As they packed away, Gabi approached. "Will you come for a drink with me?" she asked.

Aisha turned towards Nicolás. He was watching her. Fuck him. She smiled. "We're going to Casa Torra."

Gabi looked towards the men and back at Aisha. "Okay, maybe another time."

Perhaps Aisha should be more cautious with Nicolás around, but she wasn't ready to say goodnight to Gabi. Surely, there was no harm in a conversation, and especially since Mama had invited Gabi to the Fiesta celebrations and was therefore familiar with who Gabi was should he decide to say something to Mama. "Meet us there."

Gabi shoved her hands in her pockets, shuffled her feet, and glanced around. "I don't know. I don't want to get in the way."

"Follow the road past the church." Aisha pointed. "Take the first left and it's the first bar you come to. It's easy to find. Casa Torra. We'll be there soon. Please say you'll come."

Gabi nodded. Aisha stole glances in Gabi's direction as they packed away.

"Who is that?" Nicolás asked.

Aisha had to quash any inquisition, and there was only one way to do that. "She's a friend. Mama has invited her and her nana to our house."

Nicolás raised his eyebrows. "Why?"

"Because they are good people, our people," she said. Aisha couldn't be sure of the truth, but Estrella had talked about spending time with a man called Juan, panning for gold in the river, and he was most likely to have been a gitano.

He nodded his head and slowly smiled.

"Gabi is going to come for a drink."

He laughed. "I have no wish to indulge in women's talk tonight. I feel like celebrating."

He was high on their future engagement. The line that had separated her from Nicolás before, as friends, had been clear. Being promised to him, the line had shifted, and she was more accountable to him. If she married him, which she had no intention of doing, there would be no line at all, and she would be bound by his word until death parted them. "You promised," she said.

"Our secret," he whispered. He pressed his finger to his lips.

Aisha shuddered at the thought of him. She walked through the street thinking about Gabi. She spied her as they entered the bar and went straight to her table. The men went to the bar, laughing and talking, and she was glad to be rid of them.

Gabi motioned to the glass of Rioja on the table. "I didn't know what to get you."

Aisha sat opposite her and took a sip of the wine. "Thanks." She felt alive with the dizziness of being close to Gabi, and every bubble that popped filled her with joy.

Gabi smiled. "It's nice in here." She looked around. "Busy, but—"

"Yes." Aisha checked to see the men were occupied.

Gabi followed her gaze. "Who is he? The man who plays guitar?"

"Nicolás."

"Is he related? He seems very protective of you."

Gabi's frown deepened and her eyes narrowed, and it was clear she hadn't warmed to him. Why should she? Aisha had a good idea what he would be thinking, and guilt pricked her conscience. "He is." She sipped her drink. "He married Esme. We've danced together forever. He's like a brother to me." She took another sip of wine to settle the discomfort from not being entirely open with Gabi about his intentions to marry her. Firstly, no matter what he thought, she wasn't going to marry him, and secondly, she didn't want to raise something that might scare Gabi away. And it wasn't a conversation for this time or place. Still, she found it hard to look Gabi in the eye without feeling as though she was deceiving her.

Gabi glanced towards him and back at Aisha and took a slug of her drink. Her tight-lipped smile revealed the discomfort that Aisha felt. Perhaps she shouldn't have invited Gabi to join them. "How was your day?" Aisha asked and smiled.

"Hectic. We moved into the apartment yesterday, so I've taken Nana shopping. The place came furnished, but she's a sucker for ornaments so I took her to the bookshop we went to. She picked up some cushions and drapes from the market. Makes it feel more like home, she said."

"Home?"

"Yes. I wouldn't be surprised if she decides to stay."

Aisha leaned back, her heart beating faster and a flutter of excitement in her stomach. Gabi had a job with Matías and somewhere to live. "And what about you?"

Gabi etched small circles with her fingertip on the tabletop. "That depends, I guess."

Aisha cleared her throat. "On what?"

"What happens here. With the job. I can't imagine leaving Nana on her own. I feel different here too. I met someone here."

Aisha widened her eyes.

Gabi laughed. "She's interesting, and sexy, and dances like I've never seen before."

Aisha blushed and sipped her drink. She looked towards Nicolas to check he wasn't watching her.

Gabi's expression caught Aisha's breath. Heat expanded from her chest in a flurry of sparkles. At first, it was like being bathed in softness and comfort. The vibrations in her stomach intensified, and the ache between her legs felt electric and exciting, and she wondered whether everyone could see her pleasure. She glanced around and, satisfied that she hadn't become a beacon of light attracting everyone's attention, took a deep breath. Gabi could read her mind, she was sure of it.

"I can't wait until you see the place. It overlooks the river and the hills. I think you'll like it."

"It sounds nice." She wanted to stare at Gabi. She wanted to hold her hand. She wanted to kiss her. She finished her drink, aware that Gabi was staring at her and that Nicolás was laughing, and talking, and keeping a close eye on her.

"Come for a walk with me," Gabi said.

The warmth of the drink merged with the fire in her belly. She felt choked by the business and noise that she wanted to escape from. She smiled at Gabi, whose expression soured as Nicolás approached.

He smiled. "Good evening."

Gabi nodded. "Hello."

He turned to Aisha. "We're heading home now," he said.

Aisha's stomach dropped.

"Can you get a taxi later?" Gabi asked.

Aisha watched Nicolás's frown deepen as he stared at Gabi. She could imagine what he thought about Gabi's appearance. She didn't dress like them, or look like them, or behave like them. Aisha's stomach tightened. If she didn't return with him, it would lead to questions from Mama that she didn't want to have to answer. Not yet. She wasn't ready.

"We have a van, thanks," he said.

Aisha shook her head and smiled at Gabi. "We'll take that walk another time," she said and stood.

Gabi nodded.

Nicolás looked from Aisha to Gabi and smiled. "Let's go," he said and squeezed Aisha's arm.

"I'll see you Monday," she said.

Gabi nodded.

Aisha left the bar and when she looked back, Gabi was heading in the other direction with her head lowered. She glanced at Nicolás and wanted to wipe the smile from his face. "Did you have to be so rude?"

"What's happening on Monday?" he asked.

She wanted to tell him it was none of his business. "I'm going to help make curtains for their new place," she said and strode ahead of him.

She stayed silent for the journey home and struck by more than tiredness, said goodnight to Nicolás before he could suggest anything else. In bed, she wrapped her arms around herself and imagined it was Gabi holding her tightly. Warm tears caressed her cheek, and she strengthened her grip. She thought about seeing Gabi again, and her mind calmed, her body became heavy, and she drifted to sleep.

18.

"MIO CARIÑO, THIS TASTES delicious. A little more paprika, then some lemon close to the end, and it will be excelente."

Nana wore a soft pink, cotton dress that she'd picked up from the market, her locket, and the butterfly brooch. She'd applied eye shadow and blusher, which she never normally did, and had set her hair. She looked elegant and had made a big effort for what Gabi classed as a casual dinner with Aisha. "I feel I missed something on the invite," she said, looking down at her beach shorts and vest.

"I forgot to say, I'm popping out this evening."

"Where to?"

"Señor Cortez invited me for a drink."

"Who?"

"Pablo, the man from the house at the end of the street, with the infinity pool and the pretty fruit and olive trees."

They'd noticed the grand house when they'd walked past, and they didn't need to get Nana's binoculars out to get a good view of its rear gardens from their terrace. The place was like the mansion where Nana had spent her childhood, that they'd driven past after they arrived, though it was smaller, a lot less pretentious, and the terrain less guarded. She'd imagined leaning over the edge of the pool with a cocktail in her other hand, the water trickling through her fingers into infinity, enjoying the view of the hills. The land around the property was terraced with rows of citrus, plums, and figs that would provide a good harvest. Grape vines trailed the trellises, giving shade to an extensive patio area. She could see Nana enjoying the gardens there and clearly, the company.

"I've seen Pablo a couple of times," Nana said. She cleared her throat. "He's going to show me his citrus sinensis arancio."

"I bet he is." Gabi laughed.

"It's a sweet orange tree. The best in Granada."

Gabi couldn't tell whether it was the blusher or an increase in body heat that flushed Nana's cheeks. It was nice to see her happy and making friends. "Sounds great."

"He has orchards of punica granatum he's going to show me."

"Are you testing my Greek?"

Nana smiled. "Latin, Gabriela. He owns the local grenadine factory. He's very interesting," Nana said and patted Gabi's arm.

"You'll be back for dinner, though, won't you?" Gabi said.

"Oh, no, cariño. Pablo's making us dinner, so I'll be back sometime after midnight."

Gabi closed her eyes as the heat swept through her. Her stomach fizzed, and her heart raced. Being alone with Aisha was everything she wanted, and it made her as nervous as hell. She'd thought Nana was dining with them, and the fact that she wasn't was fantastic.

"I'll be off then," Nana said. "Say hello to Aisha for me."

Gabi nodded because excitement had stolen her voice.

"Oh, and maybe wear that nice scent. Not too much, or it will upset the paella."

"Go." Gabi pointed to the door, laughing.

"Oh, the bunch of flowers on the table in the hallway is for Pilar."

160

Gabi hadn't thought about gifts. "Is there a custom here? Should I have got something for Aisha?"

"I picked up some jellied fruits from the market for her, along with the ashtray for Maggie that had slipped your mind."

Gabi winced.

"The jellies are next to the flowers."

Gabi went to Nana and kissed her forehead. "What would I do without you?" she asked.

Nana patted her arm. "Don't burn the paella," Nana said as she opened the door. "The crust should be brown and rich with flavour."

Gabi had no appetite for food. Her stomach was busy challenging the *Guinness Book of Records* for the number of somersaults thrown in a minute. Nana shut the door behind her, and Gabi punched the air repeatedly. She ran around the living room puffing up the cushions and setting them back down, grinning and laughing. She repositioned the ornaments on the window ledge, added more paprika to the paella and tasted it, and wiped down the kitchen surface. The wine and beer were perfectly chilled, and the Rioja had been left to breathe for an hour already. She removed Nana's place setting from the table on the terrace and found the candles. She put two tealights in cups and set one each side of the table's centre where the paella would rest. They could watch the sunset with the sound of the river. She went back to the living room and checked everything looked right before heading to her bedroom to change. She donned three-quarter length denim shorts and a clean, baggy T-shirt, and ran a little gel through her hair to set it. She still didn't feel ready.

A knock at the door sent her stomach into a spin and flooded her in tiny electrically charged vibrations. Telling herself to relax and calm down had the opposite effect. She clicked her fingers together and blew out a puff of air to release some of the tension. The knock came again. Her hand trembled as she opened the door, and her heart pounded behind her ribs as she caught sight of Aisha. "Hi," she said, glad for the relief that came from releasing her breath.

Aisha held out a bunch of yellow, orange, red, and violet flowers mixed with stems of green leaves, and grasses. "They're from our garden, for Estrella from Mama," she said.

"Nana has a date with the man at the end of the road," she said, and Aisha stared at her with that look in her eyes that turned Gabi inside out with a mix of desire and vulnerability. "She left those for your mum. The gift is for you." She was rambling. "Sorry, come in."

Aisha took a step and stood just inside the front door. Gabi brought the flowers to her nose and inhaled. Sweet rose, honeycomb, and candyfloss. She was taken back to the farmhouse when she and Nana used to bake cakes. Those summer days, with the sunshine, smiles, and delicious homemade lemonade had been few and far between, but they had been the best. "The smells remind me of summers in England. Come through."

Aisha's scent drifted into Gabi's consciousness, and she had to hold back from throwing Aisha against the wall and kissing her. "That door leads to a bathroom," she said, indicating to the door closest to the front entrance. She headed to the kitchen to find a vase and as the water ran, she took deep breaths.

Aisha followed her. "I'm really sorry that Nicolás was so rude to you on Saturday," Aisha said.

Gabi set the vase on the countertop. She wanted to say that he was a knob, but Aisha looked a bit tense, and Gabi wanted her to feel comfortable. She'd noticed the effect he had on Aisha, how he made her appear guarded and restless. He put Gabi on edge too. He was a bully, and she didn't want to talk about him tonight because it would bring the mood down. "I ignored him." She smiled. "Can we talk about something else tonight?"

Aisha half-smiled. "The paella smells good."

Gabi laughed. She glanced at the dish on the stove. "It's one of Nana's family recipes, tried and tested over time, so it should taste good. Paella is one of my favourites."

"Mine too."

The warmth in Gabi's chest reached her hands and they tingled from the urge to reach out and take Aisha into her arms. "Would you like red or white wine, or beer? I think there's vodka or sherry if—"

"Red wine, thanks."

"Here." Gabi handed her a drink.

Aisha gazed the length of Gabi and smiled. "I love your shorts."

"I made them from some too-short jeans years ago. I'll make you a pair," Gabi said, and Aisha laughed. Gabi loved the notes in her voice, loved Aisha's flowing white skirt that begged to be explored to discover the delights that lay beneath its folds. She loved the dark red blouse that screamed to be loosened to expose the top of her breasts before being slipped from her shoulders. She loved the low-heeled sandals that wouldn't

163

break a window should they be flung from Aisha's feet in the heat of passion. She cast the image to the back of her mind. "I like to sew," Gabi said and led them onto the terrace.

"We make most of our clothes," Aisha said.

Gabi studied the neat cut of the collar of Aisha's blouse and the tidy seam where the ruffled fabric joined the top of the arm with the shoulder. The stitching and alignment were impeccable. "Did you make that?"

"Yes."

Gabi's core throbbed, not because of the dress but because Aisha looked perfect. "It's beautiful."

Aisha lowered her eyes, and her cheeks flushed. She turned from Gabi's gaze and looked towards the hills. "Do you like Granada?" she asked.

"Yes," Gabi said. The day they'd arrived seemed light years ago. "It's hard to explain, and it sounds daft if I say it out loud, but I feel kind of settled here."

Aisha nodded. "Its beauty calls to you. You walk within it and quickly, you become a part of it. To leave it behind would be to sacrifice an aspect of your soul."

Gabi took a sip of wine, studied the hills, and stilled inside. "That's deep."

Aisha smiled. "Sorry, I didn't mean to be."

"I like deep. I read some poetry and didn't really understand it. But you do. You see things like an artist. They don't just paint a picture. They feel it and turn it into something that other people can appreciate. You change lives with your words."

Aisha lowered her head. "I'm not that good."

"You've changed mine already." Gabi noted the way Aisha's mouth twitched a little, the heart shape of her face, her neck where her pulse raced. Aisha took a deep breath, and an electric feeling coursed through Gabi. "You have talent. You could learn more."

Aisha put her hand on Gabi's. "You're very kind."

Gabi's heart thundered. "I mean it. And it's very sexy."

Aisha blushed and pulled back her hand.

"You're attractive, and clever, and…" *And I want to kiss you.* She sipped her drink before she let the words slip out. Heat flushed Gabi's cheeks, and she cleared her throat. Aisha stared at her as she sipped her drink, and the heat intensified. She wanted to kiss Aisha but couldn't think how to get them to that point without coming across as clumsy or desperate.

Aisha blushed, picked up her drink and sipped it, and stared at Gabi. "I would like to teach one day. Languages, literature maybe. I enjoy teaching the children."

"You could do that."

"I want to travel so much though."

"You could travel the world and teach."

"That would be amazing. Have you been to other countries?"

Gabi thought about her trips away from home: the one to Exeter, hardly a metropolis; the weekend she'd spent in London with Lillian, her first girlfriend, because Lillian had an idea that they might move there and work there; and that one night out in Bristol with Shay that had ended with an argument and Gabi heading home on the train alone. "Not until coming here."

Aisha frowned. "I thought you would have. We see so many tourists, I assumed travelling was normal."

Gabi shook her head. "I hate public transport."

Aisha's laughter weaved through Gabi.

"I never thought about it. To be honest, I haven't done anything interesting. But coming here has opened my eyes. I made a promise at one of the fountains that I would do something with my life."

"What are you going to do?"

"I don't know. I'll work on the jewellery and see where that takes me."

"You could do anything, if you wanted to."

I could kiss you. Gabi held her breath. She lowered her head and ran her finger along the edge of the table and breathed out softly. Aisha's hand trembled as she toyed with the stem of her glass, and Gabi wondered what she was thinking.

Aisha glanced at Gabi, sniffed the air, and frowned.

"Oh, fuck." Gabi darted from the table and whipped the pan from the stove to the sound of Aisha's tuneful laughter.

Aisha joined her in the kitchen. "I'm sure it will be delicious."

Gabi turned off the cooker and poked at the paella. "I think I caught it in time."

Aisha put her hand on Gabi's arm, and the back of Gabi's neck tingled.

Aisha lowered her head, wafted her hand over the food, and inhaled. "It smells good."

As Aisha stood, she was close enough to kiss. Her shallow, fast breaths, unblinking gaze, and the slight quiver in her lip as she smiled were undeniably allied with Gabi's racing heart and the thrill that swept through her and pulsed at her core. Gabi leaned forward.

Aisha held up the oven glove. "You'll need this."

Gabi groaned and clasped the pan handle with shaking hands, her heart thundering. The pan rolled like a wave as she lifted it onto the surface. It landed with a thud and a shrimp escaped and landed on the countertop.

Aisha popped it into her mouth. "Perfecto."

Aisha licked her fingers, and Gabi's mouth watered. She could almost taste the saffron on Aisha's wet lips, and feel the softness, and their perfect shape.

Aisha brushed against Gabi's arm as she picked up the serving spoon and, locking eyes with Gabi, held it out to her. "You'll need this too."

Gabi took the handle, her fingers touching Aisha's, and they held the spoon together, staring at each other. Gabi's focus narrowed to the want she saw in Aisha's expression. "Thanks."

Aisha let go of the spoon. "Where are the plates?"

"Plates." Gabi blinked and tried to recall where they were. She cast her eyes around the kitchen. "Ah, yes, plates. They're in the dresser in the living room."

Aisha cleared her throat as she brushed past Gabi. She froze, and her skin tingled. She closed her eyes and took a deep breath. How could she be so nervous about making the first move? She watched Aisha return with the plates and enjoyed the gentle sway of her hips, the quiet smile on her face, and the intensity in her eyes. It was impossible to think let alone control anything.

Aisha held out the plates. "These?"

Gabi took a pace towards her and kissed her.

Aisha dropped the plates on the floor. She gasped as the shattering of china interrupted the moment. Gabi laughed and Aisha kissed her.

Warmth, and tenderness, and a hint of wine stirred something deep inside her. She had a sense of arriving, and that this was where she'd always been heading, where she was meant to remain. With her hands on Aisha's waist, and Aisha's arms around Gabi's neck, Gabi guided her backwards. They kissed deeply as Gabi crunched through the broken china and pushed Aisha back against the wall.

Aisha caressed the back of Gabi's neck and ran her fingers through Gabi's hair. Gabi breathed softly as their tongues met, and the pulse in her core became more insistent. She drew Aisha closer. Warmth radiated through her body. Aisha held her face in both hands, bit her lip, and kissed her firmly. Gabi moaned in pleasure.

Aisha pulled out of the kiss and stared at Gabi with wide eyes and flushed cheeks. "I—"

Gabi ran her thumb across her wet lips. She smiled, though Aisha's vulnerability caught her off guard and caused her fingers to tremble. "You okay?" she whispered.

Aisha nodded. "I'm sorry about the plates," she said.

Gabi laughed. "You're so cute."

Aisha laughed and stroked Gabi's cheek. Gabi thought she had a look of wonder, like she'd discovered a new precious gem. She kissed Aisha's nose and the top of her cheeks under each eye. She kissed her tenderly on the lips and more deeply. She eased out of the kiss, created a space between them, and smiled. "I love kissing you."

Aisha's fingers trembled as she stroked Gabi's cheek again. "I thought this was wrong," Aisha whispered.

Gabi wrapped Aisha in her arms and Aisha leaned against her, her hands firm and warm on Gabi's back, her heart thundering in sync with the beat of Gabi's heart. She pressed her lips to Aisha's hair and took slow deep breaths to calm her desire. "This is right, and if anyone tells you differently, they're lying."

Aisha eased back from Gabi. She smiled and her eyes became glassy. "Thank you," she whispered and kissed Gabi again.

When she moved away her cheeks were wet with the silent tears she'd shed. Aisha's vulnerability and beauty stirred in Gabi a fierce desire to protect her. She stroked the strands of hair from Aisha's face, traced the shape of her ear down to her chin, and brushed her thumb lightly across her tear-stained cheeks. "I'm here for you," she said.

Aisha nodded.

Gabi kissed her slowly, unhurriedly.

Aisha moaned softly, and Gabi stepped back and smiled.

"The paella's getting cold," Aisha whispered.

Gabi smiled. "Are you hungry?"

Aisha shook her head. "You?"

"For you, yes."

Aisha traced a line from Gabi's shoulder down over her breast and slowly over her taut nipple.

Gabi tried hard not to gasp and let out a whimpering sound. "That's going to get you into a lot of trouble," she said.

Aisha traced the line back from Gabi's stomach and stopped with her hand on Gabi's breast. "I like how you feel," she said.

A shock wave zipped to Gabi's clit, and the throbbing sensation there left her breathless. "Seriously. You have no idea what you do to me." She took Aisha's hand and kissed her palm.

"I think I do now," Aisha said.

Gabi kissed her until the paella had gone cold and the night had drawn in, and then the last bus took Aisha away, and Gabi smiled as she cleared up the broken crockery with warmth in her heart.

19.

AISHA GENTLY UNEARTHED THE carrots and dusted the soil from them before carefully putting them in the basket. She cradled a tomato in her palm, determined its readiness for picking, and let it hang with the others for another day. She selected the ripest fruit from the vines, inhaled their rich fragrance, and smiled with the memory of kissing Gabi.

The sensation that had developed low in her belly had been so strong, it had alarmed her. She had wondered whether it was her penance for straying onto this immoral path, and that she might die for her transgression. She'd been relieved when her breath had returned. In Gabi's arms and hearing Gabi's honest words, she'd felt safe and vindicated in her lust.

She touched her lips. Gabi's mouth had been gentle and enquiring, and the softness of her lips and skin had been like touching warm silk. The blissful state had stayed with her on the journey home that she hadn't wanted to take. It had kept her awake until dawn, and she'd willed the sun to rise, fearful that if she slept, she might wake to find it had all been a dream. She'd got up earlier this morning, filled with kindness and joy, and welcomed her mama to the day with a pot of coffee and an omelette.

She broke three stems of mint and inhaled their aroma, reminded of the mint she'd given Gabi when she'd felt ill after the bus journey. How she'd wanted to kiss her then too. Warmth and softness filled her, and she suppressed the urge to laugh out loud or shout out her joy to the hills.

Hers wasn't a heart unclean. It was a heart complete with love and in perfect harmony with another. Its vibration was more tuneful than the notes of a song, more intense than the dance that would give character to those notes, and more lyrical than Lorca had captured in his Gypsy ballads. It made the fields greener, the crops sweeter, and the sun brighter. It carved a wider smile on her face that would be hard to shift. Her dream was no longer a dream, and reality gave her hope. But she had to be more careful. It was a dangerous time, wearing her heart so openly, and she could easily give herself away.

"Aisha. Aisha."

She jolted as if that fear of being found out had just happened. "Conchita." She released a breath and smiled. "Isn't it a beautiful morning?"

Conchita planted her hands on her hips and looked skyward. "It's going to be hot." She frowned at Aisha. "I need your help with the napkins for the wedding. There's so much to cut and stitch and it's going to take me forever, and—"

"Of course." Aisha hooked the basket in the crook of her arm and started towards the house. She turned when Conchita hadn't moved. "Are you coming?" Conchita ran to catch up and they walked side by side across the field.

"You seem happier," Conchita said.

"I am."

Conchita glanced at Aisha. "It's not like you."

Aisha laughed. "I had fun helping at Gabi's nana's and woke up refreshed." Aisha hadn't seen Estrella, because she'd had to leave to catch the last bus, and she hadn't exactly helped them with anything by breaking their plates, but a little white lie or two that served a purpose wouldn't do any harm.

"Aren't they the people coming in July?"

"Yes, Estrella was born here. She was in love with one of us, a man called Juan and had to leave because of Franco and the war. It's exactly as Lorca described. She will know some of the elders." She'd embellished the story with each rendition.

Conchita linked her arm through Aisha's and matched her stride as they headed back to the house in silence. They sat and started to sew a lace trim onto the cotton placemats that would be used on the main table at the wedding. Each was to be embroidered with the initials of the bride and groom for a lasting memento of their special occasion.

Conchita looked up at Aisha for the fourth time. She seemed poised to say something but sighed and sewed another stitch.

Aisha rested the place mat in her lap. "What is it?"

Conchita raised her head but avoided eye contact. "Can I ask you something?"

Aisha's heart thundered. She clasped her hands in her lap, stiffened her back, and swallowed. Her world collapsed in front of her eyes, and she blanked out the image. If her sister had guessed something, then she would deal with the question as best she could. She would lie to her face if she had to. "Yes," she said and hoped Conchita hadn't picked up her tension.

Conchita glanced at her and then stared at something over her shoulder. "What do you think it's like?" she asked.

Aisha sank into the chair and released a breath. "What?"

"You know." Conchita motioned to her lap. "When we do it."

Aisha smiled inside, though Conchita was frowning and looked in need of reassurance. "I imagine it's the most wonderful feeling in the world, like being kissed."

Conchita's lips parted, and her eyes widened. "Do you think it will hurt?"

Aisha reached across and took her hand. "I'm sure it will feel warm, and tender, and soft, and—"

"Soft. I thought—"

"I mean, soft inside." Aisha laughed. "Like his tongue when he kisses you."

Conchita frowned. "His kisses are firm and rough, and he grazes my cheek sometimes."

Aisha frowned. "Then tell him to be gentle."

"Should I?"

"Yes. He is with you to please you, not just to take for himself."

"I thought that was the way it was supposed to be."

Aisha shook her head. She knew too well what they'd been told to believe. Conchita might be marrying a man, but she should still look after her own needs. "Well, it's not. You can tell him what you want, and he has a duty to give to you as you give to him."

Conchita looked down. "Even that?" she asked.

"Especially that. If he hurts you, you tell him to stop."

"Have you done it before?"

Aisha shook her head. Gabi hadn't made any move to undress her or to touch her though she had wanted her to. "I might not agree with all our laws, but I honour them." She would burn in hell for all the lies, she was sure of it.

"Then how do you know so much?"

Aisha brought her hand to her chest. "Don't you know it in your heart, how it should feel when you come together through love?"

Conchita sat, wide-eyed, shaking her head. "I never thought about it."

"Well, maybe you should."

Conchita picked up the cloth and went back to sewing.

Aisha plotted to visit Gabi, and if Gabi didn't object, she would like to break the most sacred of all their Gitano laws.

20.

AISHA CLASPED A BAG of sweet treats she'd picked up as she'd walked through the market. She paced around and fanned her face with her other hand. She stopped to knock on Gabi's apartment door. She giggled with the giddiness, pressed her hand to her stomach, and took three deep breaths to calm her nerves. She tapped on the door and listened, praying that Gabi was in.

"Come in. Come in."

It was Estrella's voice, and Aisha felt the pressure release. She opened the door as Gabi's nana approached.

"Hello, Aisha. What a lovely surprise."

"Good morning, Estrella."

"Gabriela is just taking a shower."

The image of Gabi naked, wet hair, water trailing her body, over her breasts and down to the part of her that Aisha desperately wanted to explore did nothing to help her control her desire. She was sure she was blushing redder than the skyline in the painting on the hallway wall. She turned her attention to it and studied the sunflowers in a rich green meadow bowing towards the setting sun. She imagined lying in the grass, holding hands with Gabi and talking about love.

"It's a pretty picture, isn't it? My friend Señor Cortez, Pablo, knows the artist. Do you like art, Aisha?"

"It's of the fields to the north. Yes, I do like art." She held out the bag. "These are for you."

Nana smiled and took the gift. "Would you like a coffee?" she asked. She poked her head through the door leading to the bedrooms. "Gabriela, Aisha is here." She headed towards the kitchen.

Aisha stared at the door for a moment and imagined walking into Gabi's bedroom. Her stomach did a spin. Nana had unpacked the small meringues and set them on a plate by the time Aisha reached the kitchen.

"I'm sorry, but I'm going to have to leave you again. I'm on the hunt for a fruit dish, and Pablo has promised to take me to see a local potter."

Aisha smiled. "I need to replace the plates I broke," she said.

Nana waved her hand, swatting her away. She took a sweet and ate it. "Gabi said it was her fault. We have plenty of plates. Hm, these cakes are good."

"They're soplillos de la alpujarra."

"Yes, Juan's mother used to bake them. You can't get anything like this in England. They melt in your mouth. They're far too tempting, and I must resist having more." She patted her stomach.

Aisha smiled. "Mama bakes them too, but I got these from the market." Her mama hadn't known about her plans to visit Gabi, otherwise Aisha would have baked them herself. She hadn't wanted to raise suspicions. She still wasn't ready for questions.

A knock at the door grabbed Nana's attention, and she excused herself. She shouted down the corridor to Gabi to tell her that she was going out. "Have a lovely day, cariño," she said and closed the door behind her.

The quietness intensified the butterflies in Aisha's stomach, and the dizzy excitement of earlier returned with fierce determination. Her hands trembled, and her mouth turned drier than scorched earth in the heat of summer. She gazed out the window, over the river and towards the hills to distract from being consumed by her burning desire. She'd spent years yearning, dreaming, and denying the sole reason her heart pulsed with passion, and now she'd kissed Gabi, she had to know what it felt like to make love to her.

She turned at the sound of footsteps behind her. Gabi approached in a T-shirt and shorts, her hair spiked and wet, leaving Aisha breathless.

"This is a very nice surprise."

Aisha's heart raced, harder and faster, and she thought it might burst, and her insides vibrated. Her hands were clammy and trembling, and if she didn't do what she came here for, she might become too afraid. And that would be a wasted opportunity. She grabbed Gabi's T-shirt at the waist, tugged Gabi to her, and kissed her. Mint. So soft and warm. The throb between her legs was undeniable in its need for attention. She ran her fingers through Gabi's hair and kissed her harder, adoring the sensation of Gabi's tongue in her mouth.

Gabi eased out of the kiss. "Hm, and a very good morning to you too."

Aisha tugged at the waistband of Gabi's shorts and traced her fingertip across her belly. Gabi broke eye contact and released what sounded to Aisha like a strangled laugh. Aisha ran her hand higher.

Gabi jolted and groaned. "You're killing me here."

Aisha tugged Gabi to her and kissed her tenderly. Gabi's skin was hot and soft and prickled as Aisha ran her fingers across it, and Gabi moaned with desire and urged her to explore. She moved her hand higher, imprinting the shape of Gabi in every cell in her body. The heat in Aisha's core intensified as she touched Gabi's breast, and Gabi gasped when Aisha tweaked her nipple. She had never imagined being able to give so much pleasure from such a simple act. Slowly, she lifted Gabi's T-shirt over her head and took Gabi's nipple into her mouth.

"Oh, my God, you feel so good." Gabi closed her eyes, tilted her head back, and held Aisha to her chest.

The firmness of Gabi's nipple on her tongue and the soft flesh of her breast against her lips was exquisite and intoxicating. She felt delirious. She teased Gabi's nipple, fascinated by the effect that mirrored in her own body, the fizzing at her core, and the throbbing between her legs. It was incredible, and amazing, and exactly like the rise in a musical score. Only, she didn't want the fall to come. She wanted to keep climbing, higher and higher.

Gabi eased Aisha from her and blew out a puff of air. She caressed Aisha's face and kissed her softly. She picked up her T-shirt.

"I want to make love with you," Aisha said, and the way Gabi stared at her caused her heart to race. She was sure this was what Gabi wanted too.

Gabi scratched behind her ear and her forehead. She bit her lip, glanced out the window, and released a long breath. She turned back to Aisha and locked eyes with her. "Are you sure? I mean, really sure?"

Aisha took Gabi's T-shirt from her and threw it to the couch. She undid her own blouse and cast it aside, then unfastened her bra and let it drop to the floor, closely followed by her skirt. She drew Gabi to her, breast to breast, stomach to stomach. The warmth, and the softness, and Gabi's woody scent reaffirmed the rightness of the decision she'd taken when they'd kissed for the first time. "Yes, I am *really* sure," she said. "My parents don't—"

Gabi kissed her softly, tenderly, and unhurriedly, and it felt as if she was able to explore every part of Aisha with featherlike touches. When Gabi traced the line of Aisha's back, she felt the effect in her neck and down her arms. When Gabi touched her stomach, she felt a jolt low in her belly, and when Gabi cupped her breast, she felt sparks of energy everywhere. Her knees weakened, and she led Gabi to the couch before they gave way completely.

Gabi moved on top of her and kissed her neck. She enjoyed the spikiness of Gabi's hair at her fingertips and the sharpness at the base of her neck. The tingling sensations that came from Gabi's kisses intensified as she moved down Aisha's body. And when Gabi took Aisha's nipple into her mouth, Aisha gasped as the explosive sensation coursed through her. She cried out and opened her eyes. Gabi looked up and smiled.

"You like that?" Gabi said and went back to Aisha's nipple.

Aisha jerked and bucked beneath her. "It's too much, and it's not enough," Aisha gasped. "I want to feel you everywhere."

Gabi kissed her lips. "You are beautiful."

Gabi looked deep into her eyes as she put her hand between Aisha's legs. When Aisha gasped at the gentle pressure of her cotton pants against her sex, Gabi's expression didn't change. She put her hand on Gabi's shoulder, and the pressure between her legs increased. She became transfixed by the intensity in Gabi's gaze, and the surge of heat caused her to freeze. Gabi moved slowly towards her and kissed her with such tenderness, and yet she felt the effect of it where Gabi's hand rested against her. Gabi kissed her again. The sensation between Aisha's legs changed as Gabi touched her directly. She arched her back and felt Gabi's fingers sliding against her. She jolted as Gabi moved over her clit, and when Gabi did it again and again the heat became all-consuming, and she closed her eyes and squeezed Gabi's shoulder, desperate for her to stop and desperate for her to continue.

Gabi slipped inside her, and she cried out and opened her eyes. Gabi was staring at her intently. The tenderness and warmth became fiery and intense and then calmed, and she could breathe again. The sensations started inside her again, and the fire rose with Gabi's slow thrusts. She felt as though she was losing her mind, and she let it go willingly. She drowned in the sensations and craved more. In all her dreams, she hadn't imagined this. All the carnivals, all the dances, all the music, and all the thrills in the world couldn't compare to this feeling.

She cried out louder when she couldn't take anymore and trembled with the sense of falling stars lighting up every cell in her body. She became weak, and she slumped back into the couch. Her heart thundered, and she panted for breath. Gabi kissed her, and the memory of Gabi's nipple against her tongue sparked a fire deep in her belly. She groaned at her insatiable desire, opened her eyes, and started to laugh. Gabi smiled. Aisha felt the quiver in her lips and her heart thundering in her chest. "I love you," she whispered, and she started to laugh, though she didn't understand why.

"Te amo," Gabi whispered.

Gabi kissed her and Aisha touched Gabi's breast and the feeling deep in her belly ignited again. She would take great pleasure in doing for Gabi what Gabi had done for her.

21.

GABI GOT OFF THE bus close to Matías's house and nipped into the workshop and picked up some clasps and the tools she needed. She walked up the road to the place where she'd arranged to meet Aisha. She was early, so she put down the heavy rucksack and leaned against the wall with the sun on her face. She inhaled the clean air, wondering if she'd gone overboard buying so many things for the kids to make jewellery with. She hadn't been able to decide, and unsure of how a child's mind worked, she'd wanted to give them options so no one felt left out. Maybe she should have found some bigger needles in case the smaller ones were too tricky to work with. She rubbed her hands together. Her stomach knotted. It was hard to know which was more nerve-racking—seeing Aisha when their lovemaking was still at the forefront of her mind or meeting the kids Aisha taught. The sensation between her legs answered the question. She sat on the wall and leaned forward to try to stem the flow of blood to her clit. It didn't work, so she sat up and enjoyed the feeling instead.

Aisha walked towards her, swaying her hips, and Gabi squeezed her legs together. This was going to be a long day. The wraparound sandals accentuated Aisha's ankles, and Gabi wanted to kiss from them to where Aisha's skirt started, and just keep going. The skirt was shorter than the others Gabi had seen her wear, and it made Aisha's legs look longer. Gabi would rather be pressed against the firm muscle of her thigh than heading to a kids' school. Aisha's short-sleeved blouse was open at the neck and revealed more than Gabi thought appropriate for the kids to see. She looked radiant.

"Hello," Aisha said.

Gabi squinted up at her. "I was just thinking how fuckable you look."

Aisha laughed. She bit her lip as she gazed the length of Gabi. "And?"

Gabi cleared her throat and stood. "That's not helping." She picked up the rucksack.

"You look very fuckable yourself," Aisha said and set off.

Gabi enjoyed the way her hips moved, but she needed to focus on the morning's tasks, or she'd come across as if she'd lost the plot, which in all fairness, she felt close to. "Tell me a bit about the children, so I can prepare myself."

"There are two girls and three boys aged between five and eight. They can't go to school, because that would involve paying for transport, and uniforms, and books, and their families don't have that kind of money."

"That's shit."

"The children don't seem to mind too much. They come when they can. I teach them maths, and Spanish, and a little English. The boys prefer to play football, and the girls like to sew. Sometimes we bake cakes and eat them. They're all very excited that you are coming."

"I have to say, it's really intimidating."

Aisha laughed. "They won't bite you."

"Can you be sure?"

Aisha tilted her head. "Well, one of the boys might, but I'll keep an eye on him."

"Seriously?"

Aisha smiled at Gabi. "Thank you for doing this. It will mean the world to them."

"I want to kiss you." Gabi said and shoved her hands in her pockets and lengthened her stride.

Aisha laughed. "I'd be fine with that if we weren't in full view of the street."

There was no one around, but Gabi knew what she meant. Public displays of affection were always going to be off the agenda anywhere they might be noticed, which was looking like that meant anywhere in Granada. It sucked, but it was a price Gabi was willing to pay, for now. To be able to spend time with Aisha was a bonus she hadn't planned on when setting off on this trip. It didn't stop her wondering about how she might be able to get Aisha alone and far enough away from Sacromonte that they could relax together and enjoy the freedom that Gabi knew as normal. "Can you take a day off sometime?" she asked.

"What are you thinking?"

"I don't know exactly. But if you can take a day off, I'll come up with something. I'd like to take you somewhere you've never been before."

Aisha smiled. "I've never been outside the city."

Gabi frowned. "Really?"

Aisha shook her head. "We can't afford to travel, though I've dreamed of what it would be like."

"Not even with the dancing?"

"We live off the land. I don't get paid to teach. The money I earn dancing keeps us out of poverty, but there's nothing left for luxuries."

"I didn't realise." She avoided Aisha's eyes. She wished she'd known, wished she could do something to help.

"It's okay. We have what we need to survive, and we don't waste anything. Though I'd like to see other places, like history and art museums, and I'd like to go to the theatre. I'd like to study poetry, and music, and science, and talk to more people like me. There is so much to learn."

"I wasted my school years," Gabi said, and she felt shit about that. If she could have gifted her education and opportunities to Aisha she would, and Aisha would have done something incredible with them.

"It's difficult to appreciate what you have when you don't want for anything."

Gabi fell silent and felt even more of a shit for chucking away what Aisha would have treasured. Children's laughter broke through her pity party, and Aisha directed her to the back of a building and into a small, gated area.

"This way."

Gabi's stomach did a jig, and her heart raced. And then she saw their faces as each one of the children looked up at her in turn, a Mexican wave of big smiles, white teeth, tanned skin, and dark hair. They were beautiful, and she had to bite back the sudden rush of emotion.

"Children, this is Gabi. What do we have to say?"

"Hello, Miss Gabi," they said slowly in unison in English.

Aisha smiled. "We've been practising."

"Hola a todos," Gabi said.

The two girls giggled. The boys jumped to their feet and ran towards a dog-eaten, brown-skinned football.

One of the girls, no more than six years old, got to her feet and came to Gabi. She took Gabi's hand and led her back to the other girl and pointed at the ground.

Gabi put the rucksack down and sat with them. The girl touched the back of Gabi's neck, toyed with her short hair, and smiled.

"I'll get some drinks," Aisha said.

Gabi widened her eyes. "You're leaving me here alone?"

"I'm just going inside. I'll be back in a minute."

The second girl, sitting cross-legged, pointed at the rucksack. Gabi noticed a scar on her cheek that looked like a burn mark. There was something captivating about her that Gabi couldn't define.

"What's in there?" she asked.

"Do you like to sew?" Gabi opened the bag and started to unpack.

The girl nodded. "My name's Marta."

"Would you like to make some jewellery?"

Marta nodded. She dived into the pile of bags and started looking inside them.

Gabi's initial response was to create some sense of order, but she held back from controlling the girls and watched their eyes light up as they discovered the coloured leather laces, beads, carved wooden shapes, and the metal animals that Gabi had thought would be good for making a charm bracelet.

"My name's Verónica," the girl who had been playing with Gabi's hair said.

"What do you want to make, Verónica?"

She held up a metal figure. "What's this?"

"It's a dolphin."

"It's pretty."

"Would you like to make a chain for it?"

Verónica held the dolphin between her fingers and looked at it from every angle and frowned. "Can I keep it?"

Gabi smiled. "Yes. You can keep everything in here and what you don't use today, maybe you can use another day."

Verónica opened her mouth and didn't close it. She scrambled to her feet and went running in the direction Aisha had gone. She was just about to disappear out of sight when Aisha appeared with a tray of cups and a jug of juice.

"Hey, Verónica." Aisha lifted the tray as Verónica threw herself at Aisha's legs and hugged her tightly.

"Thank you, Aisha. Thank you." She ran back to where the bits lay across the dirt and sat down. "How do I make a chain?" she asked Gabi.

"Hm. Let's see. What kind of chain would you like? We can do something silver, or there's leather, or there's cord. We could make a braid with three colours. What do you think?"

"A braid," both girls said.

Aisha set the tray down next to the girls and poured drinks. The boys came running and formed a circle around the rucksack. They gulped down their juice and watched Gabi braid the chord and fix a clasp by squeezing the metal firmly around the braid.

"Can I try that?" the taller of the three boys said.

Gabi handed over the tool and clasps and watched as all three boys started to weave a braid with leather strands. The boy struggled to fit the clasp. He was all fingers and thumbs and not enough strength to get the pliers to work.

"It's a bit tough and fiddly. Have another go." Gabi fed the boys more materials and sat back and watched them work. This was easier than she'd imagined, and it was wonderful to watch their eyes light up and big smiles fill their faces at the smallest success.

The taller boy stood and went to Aisha. He held out a tri-coloured bracelet creation. "This is for you," he said.

Aisha ruffled his hair and tugged him to her. She kissed his cheek and he blushed. Gabi blushed too.

"Why don't you give it to your mama?" Aisha said.

He looked at Gabi. "Can I make another one for Mama?"

"These are all yours to play with. Make lots and give them to your friends. If you need help, just ask."

He sat and rummaged through the bits then set to work. All the children were deeply engrossed. Aisha indicated for Gabi to follow her. She picked up the cups and followed her to the side of the building.

Aisha led her through a door into an area that had a small sink and running water. Gabi had barely stepped inside when Aisha grabbed her and tugged her out of view.

Gabi knew what desire looked like, but she didn't get any time to savour it before Aisha's mouth closed over hers. She held Aisha's head, pulling her closer, kissing her harder, and feeling the effect of the kiss in the throbbing in her core.

Gabi jumped as the door moved, and she pushed Aisha away from her. She wiped her mouth and turned away from the door, her heart racing.

"Gabi, I made this for you."

She turned and smiled at Marta. Aisha was smiling at her too, looking like nothing in the world had just happened. Gabi bent down to Marta, who opened her tiny hand to reveal a wooden heart on a black leather thread. "That's beautiful."

"Raffa did the pressing thing. It's too hard for me." She indicated with her fingers and thumb and smiled.

Gabi lifted her chin and ruffled her hair. "You did an amazing job. Are you going to do some more?"

Marta shook her head. "I don't have anyone else to make them for."

Gabi looked down and cleared her throat. "Well, how about you make some things for me, and I'll take them to the market and sell them for you. The money you make you can keep."

Marta looked to Aisha with wide eyes. Aisha nodded, and Marta looked at Gabi. "Really?"

Gabi nodded. "Absolutely."

Marta threw her arms around Gabi's neck and squeezed her. "Thank you. Thank you," she said, then let go and ran out of the room.

She kissed Gabi tenderly on her cheek and whispered, "Thank you."

"Thank you for bringing me here."

Aisha smiled. "I've been thinking. I'd like to go to the beach."

"What, now?"

Aisha laughed. "I'll need to arrange things at home."

Gabi took Aisha's hands, the excitement bubbling inside her. "I'll hire a car. We can find somewhere secluded, have a picnic, and watch the sun go down."

Aisha kissed her on the lips quickly. "I'd like that. But I have to catch the last bus home."

Gabi frowned. "I can drop you back home."

Aisha shook her head. "No, it's okay. I'll get the bus."

"Is it to do with Nicolás?"

"It's him, it's Mama, it's the fact that people are always watching, and I don't need anyone asking questions about you."

"Fuck them."

"Yes, and I still have to live here."

Gabi pulled Aisha into her arms. "I know. I'm sorry," she whispered and kissed her tenderly.

The rucksack was almost as heavy on the return journey as it had been on the outbound one. Only now, her bag was filled with pieces of jewellery for sale. Whether they had no one to give them to or they preferred the idea of making money, Gabi didn't know and frankly, didn't care. She smiled all the way back on the bus and didn't register the distinctive aroma, though it must have been there. She smiled all the way back to the apartment too because she couldn't stop herself, and the only thing that would have made the day perfect would have been if Aisha had come back with her.

22.

AISHA TOOK OFF HER sandals and stood on warm sand for the first time. She squeezed her toes and watched the tiny grains close around her feet and wondered how far she might sink. "It's different from the soil. Warmer and softer," she said.

The gentle breeze brought more heat than it did in the hills, and the lapping of the waves created more noise than she imagined they should, given the idleness of the sea. "I never realised how blue it was," she said. "The sky and the sea together. It's hard to appreciate the scale of it without feeling so small." She felt vulnerable and a little scared, and she didn't know whether it was because she was here alone with Gabi, or it was just that she was somewhere she'd never been before and this immense blue space in front of her seemed to extend into infinity.

"The sea is fickle. Sometimes it's as grey as thunder clouds, and sometimes it's emerald, like it reflects emotion."

"It's happy today," Aisha said.

"Are you happy?" Gabi asked.

Aisha noted the mild concern in Gabi's expression and smiled. "Nervous about being here with you, but yes, very happy."

Gabi nodded. She hoped Aisha could stop looking over her shoulder and enjoy the experience. It was quiet, and they were highly unlikely to come across someone who knew either of them.

Aisha looked out to sea. "It's so big and looks like it never ends."

Gabi took her hand. "It takes you to North Africa at some point, I think."

"I'd like to visit Africa," Aisha said.

"It's not great for people like us," Gabi said.

Aisha sighed. Closer to the sea, a man and woman lay side-by-side on their fronts, a parasol shading their heads, their bodies basted and shiny. A woman in a wide-brimmed hat sat reading a book in the shadow of the rocks higher up the beach.

They set out their mats and offloaded the rucksack on a small patch of sand behind another rocky outcrop for privacy.

"How did you know about this place?" Aisha asked.

"Nana. Tourists don't come here because it's small, the route in is narrow and bumpy, and there aren't any facilities."

"I want to touch the sea," Aisha said and ran. She stood where the waves gave way to a ripple of foam that disappeared down into the sand. The tug as the sea drew back threw her off balance. Gabi stood at her side and held her hand. Her heart raced.

"We're invisible here," Gabi said.

"I like invisible," Aisha said. She inhaled deeply, and the warmth and vibration stirred inside her, and pleasure pulsed through her veins. They stepped into the water, and the sand became solid. At ankle depth, Aisha stopped and gazed around. "It's heavenly," she said. "It's so warm. It smells like the fish market, only less fishy."

Gabi laughed.

It was a wonderful sound, light, and just lovely, and it melted her heart. She squeezed Gabi's hand, and they stared out to sea together. A tear slipped onto her cheek. The tiny hairs on her arms prickled, and she could find no words to express how she felt. Gabi put her arm around her and held her close, and any debate about the rightness or wrongness of what they were doing had been taken away by the sea to somewhere deep down or beyond the horizon.

"I love the sea," Gabi said. "The coastline near where we live is very pretty. You'd like it, but the water is always cold, and the beaches are mostly pebbles."

"Have you missed it while you've been here?"

"No." She smiled. "I didn't realise exactly how important Nana was to me until we made this trip. She's always been there for me, after my mum died and with my dad working away from home, but I didn't see her as I do now. Wherever she is, I don't want to be too far away."

Aisha stared at Gabi. "She's lucky to have you."

She didn't dare ask about them and what their future might hold. She didn't know the answer herself. She was hardly able to ask anything of Gabi, though she was sure she wanted to be with her. But to be together, they would have to leave Granada. Aisha wouldn't be able to face her family after the disgrace. Living with another woman in the city wasn't an option, and she couldn't take the risk that someone wouldn't hurt Gabi as a result. She didn't fear the Guardia as Gabi's nana had, but she feared her own people. Would Gabi leave her nana? Thinking about it was spoiling the view, and the day would be short enough.

"And now, there are two people in my life who are important," Gabi said. She tapped Aisha lightly on the nose, lifted her chin, and kissed her tenderly.

A flash of anxiety distracted Aisha from the kiss, and she looked around.

"No one is going to pay attention to us, Aisha." Gabi held her hand.

Aisha took a deep breath, leaned against her, and stared out to sea. "Would you travel the world with me?"

"Despite my dislike of public transport, yes, I would."

Aisha turned to Gabi, her imagination running wild. "We could go to America."

Gabi stroked the hair from her face and stared at her. "You could dance in Mexico."

Aisha laughed. "And Australia."

"I've never thought about Australia. I'd like to go to India. I met a man at the market here, and he told me about his family in Kashmir. We could go anywhere."

"We have roots in India. Many generations back."

"You have to visit England. You'd love Nana's farm."

They walked along the shoreline, and Aisha took their dreams and locked them in her heart and felt richer for them. They would do all these things together and much more. Gabi had said so. She would make money dancing and teaching, and Gabi would sell her jewellery, and they would be happy together. She picked up a tiny shell that the sea had cast aside and wondered what journey it had taken to get here. She looked towards the horizon and pondered what it would feel like to be on a boat, sailing away from here, from her family and the life she'd known. She looked at Gabi and the tug to be with her was stronger, though her heart ached for all that she would leave behind.

"Shall we swim?" Gabi asked.

"I don't know how."

"Would you like me to teach you?"

Aisha's stomach fluttered, and she laughed. The sea would be deep, and she worried about what lurked beneath the surface. The couple who had been basking in the sun were now splashing about with the water up to their waist. They looked like they were having fun. Fear gave way to excitement. "Maybe," she said.

They headed back to the spot on the beach they'd claimed as theirs, and Gabi handed Aisha a bathing costume. "I didn't know if you had one," she said. "I'm ready."

Heat expanded in Aisha's chest as she thought about getting changed in the open, even though she couldn't be seen by other people. She inhaled deeply, wrapped a towel around herself, and removed her skirt.

Gabi watched her and grinned while searching blindly for something in the rucksack. "Would you like me to hold the towel in case it—"

Aisha gasped as the towel fell to the sand. She grabbed it quickly and wrapped it around her lower half again. Her heart raced.

Gabi laughed. "I'm enjoying the view, and no one else can see us."

Aisha held the towel in one hand and removed her knickers. She stepped through the leg holes of the costume but couldn't put it on without revealing herself. Whether anyone else was looking or not, there was comfort in having a shield around her.

"Here," Gabi said and took the ends of the towel. She stood in front of Aisha and held the towel around Aisha's back to protect her from the eyes of the sea.

Aisha wrestled the elastic material over her lower half. Gabi's perfume, proximity, and steady gaze made the task even more challenging, and her breaths became shallow and fast, and her heart raced.

Gabi pulled the towel towards her, bringing their bodies together.

Aisha's breath faltered with the desire she saw reflected in Gabi's eyes. Her kiss was firm and deep, and Aisha wrapped her arms around Gabi's neck. The towel fell again, but she didn't care. She might dream of being with Gabi, but if she only had this day with her, she wanted to understand what it was to enjoy the freedom to love someone openly. Delight expanded inside her. It was as vast and deep as the ocean and the sky above it, and seemingly indestructible. The euphoric feeling was the reason for her heart to beat and her soul's purpose. Without *this*, she would float like an empty vessel tossed around at sea, aimlessly grabbing snippets of fulfilment through her work but always feeling incomplete. This was love. And this was the life she wanted.

"I don't want to stop kissing you," Gabi whispered.

The warmth against Aisha's ear sent a shiver down her neck that spoke to her core in a language she now knew intimately. "Then don't," she said and allowed Gabi to coax her to lie down on the matting. She opened her legs a little so that Gabi could lay on top of her and connect with her.

She'd never imagined not being able to get enough of someone. The deeper Gabi kissed her, and the more completely Gabi's body covered hers in warmth, the more she craved her intimate touch. She groaned at the sensation that spiralled low in her stomach when Gabi caressed her covered breast, and she arched as Gabi tweaked her nipple. Tiny sparks of electricity and heat moved through her in waves and still, it wasn't enough.

She held Gabi's waist and tugged her closer, arched into her, and kissed her harder. The sweet salty taste more delicious than wine. "I want you," she whispered, intoxicated.

Gabi unbuttoned Aisha's blouse to halfway as she kissed her, and when she lifted the cup of her bra and took Aisha's nipple into her mouth, Aisha put her hand at the back of Gabi's head and pressed her closer, urging her to take more. Another shower of stars, another surge of heat burning at her sex, and Aisha tensed and gasped as the feeling eclipsed all her senses. Gabi kissed her tenderly while gentle waves rolled through her, and still she wanted more. "Will it always be like this?" she asked.

Gabi lay on her front now, resting on her elbows, and smiled. "It can be."

Aisha lay on her side and ran her fingers across the back of Gabi's neck. She loved stroking her short hair, the way the hairs sprang back though her fingers, and tracing the shape of her head. "But people change. Things like this, good things, come to an end." She was sure that was the case because so many poems were about loss, and death, and longing. It was just the bad things, like waiting for her parents to accept that she wasn't going to marry, that seemed to persist.

Gabi faced Aisha. "People change, and we can change together, and we can deal with stuff together. You said that I could do anything if I wanted. Well, anything is possible if we want it enough."

"You're so beautiful." She loved Gabi even more for the way she blushed and lowered her head a little. "I could lay here with you all day."

Gabi smiled. "We have all day."

Aisha sat up. "After you teach me how to swim."

Gabi laughed. "Okay, that may not happen in a day."

Aisha stood. "We'll have to come back again. For as many days as it takes." She could dream.

"Deal," Gabi said.

As Gabi headed towards the sea, Aisha thought of other things she'd rather be doing with her than learning to swim. Maybe later, as the sun set and they gazed at the stars under the cover of darkness. Maybe then she would be even more adventurous, and she wouldn't rush back for the last bus home.

23.

G<small>ABI STUDIED HERSELF IN</small> the mirror. She looked older, though she wasn't really. Maybe it was just that she felt older, and in a good way. Spending time with Aisha, she'd realised two things. One, that she really did love her, and two, the scale of challenge they faced to be together was bigger than she had realised. She hadn't talked to Aisha yet, but she would have to soon, because snatching moments whenever Aisha came to the city, whenever she could escape from her mama, wouldn't be enough for Gabi.

Gabi had stayed out of sight for the band's Saturday evening performances, because Aisha had asked her to. But she'd watched from a distance. Aisha worked around the clock, whereas apart from working in Matías's workshop, which she thoroughly enjoyed, Gabi's days ticked by slowly. She'd asked Aisha to go out with her again, to Màlaga or to the theatre, but Aisha had said it would be tricky. Getting home late after their beach day hadn't gone down well with her mama, and she needed to tread carefully. It was an impossible situation, caught between the devil and the deep blue sea.

And now she had to go to the bloody fiesta in Sacromonte and face Aisha's mama and family. Gabi's stomach churned. She wanted to like Aisha's parents for Aisha's sake, but she didn't, and there was only one thing that would change her opinion of them: accepting Aisha for who she was.

She tucked her shirt into the waist of her trousers, then untucked it and straightened it. In or out? She settled for in, neater and less modern. She rearranged her hair now that the gel had dried and tugged at it to give it a bit more height, hoping that if it looked longer on top, Aisha's mama wouldn't judge her too harshly. The hedgehog look wasn't working, so she tried to soften it and ended up with something messier but softer.

She rubbed her palms down her jeans' legs and inhaled to calm her thumping pulse. She felt watched already, and it was terrifying. Having to keep her distance from Aisha and avoid any physical contact would be painful. She would have to be careful how she looked at her, hide her smile, and not speak to her for too long because their feelings for each other would be like a beacon to Aisha's mama. She would be on edge all evening, because how could she not be?

"Are you ready, Gabriela? I don't want to be late."

They could drive to the beach and back and still not be late, and despite her concerns about facing Aisha's family, Gabi wanted to see Aisha. Though why they had to take the bloody bus again was beyond Gabi. "I'm coming." After one last flick at her hair, she headed into the living room.

Nana held Gabi's arms and looked her up and down. "You look stunning, cariño."

Nana wore a new lilac blouse and a black skirt that finished below her knees. She looked every bit like a flamenco dancer, albeit older than the average one. She picked up a cake box and handed it to Gabi.

"What's this?"

"A flan. I made it with oranges from Pablo's garden. You need to keep it upright."

"No pressure." Juggling a large cake box that weighed a good few pounds while being tossed around on the bus was far from a relaxing way to start an evening that Gabi was already screwed up about. "Why don't we take a taxi?"

"Because I like the bus. Anyway, we have a taxi booked to come home." She picked up her new matching lilac handbag and her cane and headed out the door. "Come on, Gabriela, or we'll miss the bus."

Thankfully, the aroma in the bus was less intense, or it might have curdled Nana's flan. Nana sat with her cane between her legs and her hands clasped around the top of it, as she always did. Gabi rested the box on her lap. The chill warmed, and she thought the flan might disintegrate in her lap, so she held it up, and within a few minutes, her forearms started to burn. Sweat beaded her brow, and her stomach knotted. "So, how is Pablo?" she asked, hoping a distracting conversation might alleviate her increasing discomfort.

"Such a kind man. He lost his wife recently. I think he's enjoying the company. We have a mutual love of nature. Do you know how many bird varieties there are here?"

"That's nice." Gabi stared out the window while Nana continued talking about the birds, their markings, their migration and nesting habits, and their diet. She spotted a bird standing on a boulder at the side of the road. It looked a lot like a robin with its reddish-brown chest but also like a finch with its stripped head and brown wings. It flew away, and Gabi wondered how she could fly away with Aisha.

The closer they got to the small white houses on the hillside, the tighter Gabi's stomach twisted. She would try to hold on to the excitement of spending an evening around Aisha and not let it be overshadowed by her increasing anxiety. Aisha had tried to be reassuring, but Gabi saw her concern. It hadn't been easy for Gabi having one parent who disapproved of her choices. Having two would be impossibly hard, and a whole village, terrifying.

By the time they got off the bus, Gabi was about ready to throw the flan the rest of the way up the hill. She'd stopped counting the bicep curls at two hundred. She rested it on the wall, shook out the tension, and picked the box back up. The muscles in her arms complained.

Nana set off towards the caves, wielding her cane enthusiastically. Gabi warmed inside. Nana had not only left England behind, but she also appeared to have shed a few years since they'd arrived in Granada. And now, she was going back to the place that held her fondest memories.

"There she is," Nana said and approached Aisha with open arms.

Gabi smiled, thankful for the box to occupy her hands, and Aisha stepped up and kissed her cheeks. Heat flared through her, and she looked around the street to avoid eye contact.

The strumming of a guitar accompanied the spitting log fire, and the roasting meat above it circulated a spicy aroma. Gas lights lined the street, and they flickered as the sun cast reds and oranges across the side of the hill. A chill slid down Gabi's spine in the warm air, and when a wailing cry pierced the sky around them, the hairs on her arms and neck rose.

"Ah, the call," Nana said.

"What is it?"

"It is the cante jondo, traditional flamenco singing, cariño. Real flamenco."

It sounded like cats squealing. The call quieted, and the fierce sound of guitars assaulted Gabi's ears.

"And that's the response," Nana said.

Gabi had never seen Nana so excited.

"How wonderful, Gabriela. Be sure to enjoy every moment. It's a memory you won't want to forget."

Gabi looked at Aisha and half-smiled. She fumbled with the box as she handed it over. "Nana's flan. For your mama," she said.

Aisha's gaze lingered on Gabi for a fraction longer than Gabi thought safe. She looked towards the comfort of Nana, her bodyguard for the evening, and wrapped her arms around herself.

"Come and meet Mama and Papa."

Gabi struggled to take a deep breath as they followed Aisha into the house. It was bigger than she'd expected having seen Matías's place, and the air was cool. It smelled of fresh baking and sweet fruit. She tried not to look at Aisha when Aisha introduced her to her mama but felt her steady gaze. "Thank you for inviting us." She tentatively leaned towards Pilar and kissed her on the cheeks. She hoped Pilar didn't feel as awkward as she did and was thankful that the introductions were over quickly.

Nana had a way of charming even the hardest of hearts, and she was doing her thing with Pilar. Aisha's mama slipped into easy conversation with Nana over tapas on the table, and Gabi overheard them talking about Aisha's abuela and how the elders were all very interested to meet Nana. She breathed a sigh of relief.

A young girl strode into the room from the back of the cave. She smiled and introduced herself as Conchita. Gabi understood why Aisha thought she was too young to be married. An older man appeared from the back of the house and didn't smile as he approached. He nodded as he welcomed them.

"Papa, this is Estrella and her granddaughter, Gabi."

Gabi felt his stern gaze as a direct criticism of her short haircut, which he couldn't seem to draw his eyes from. She found him intimidating, though if she'd passed him in the street, she wouldn't give him a second glance. He picked up a large joint of raw meat dressed in herbs and, excusing himself, headed out the front door. Gabi didn't like him, just as she thought she wouldn't.

"Estrella, we have sherry, if you'd like?" Aisha said.

Nana smiled. "Thank you, that would be lovely."

"Would you like wine or beer, Gabi?"

Gabi opted for the red because Aisha was drinking it, and she inhaled deeply when they took their drinks outside. A trickle of sweat slid down her back, and she scratched where it tickled. She never liked the discomfort of strained formality, and that wasn't aided one jot by the secret she had to keep. The atmosphere had become even more tense with the glare Conchita had levied at Aisha while she'd poured their drinks. Maybe it was just her imagination, but Conchita had stared at Gabi too while only briefly glancing at Nana.

"I feel privileged to be here," Nana said to Pilar. "Thank you so much for inviting us to your home. I remember when…"

Gabi stopped listening and watched Conchita disappear further up the street to the other side of the fire where her father attended to the meat and closer to the source of the music. Gabi recognised the man from the band approaching, all white teeth and shining black hair. She'd come to dislike him intensely since he'd dominated Aisha in the bar and she'd discovered he had married Aisha's first love. That edgy feeling returned. She watched the smile slide from Aisha's face and hated him even more. Nana came to her side, and Gabi calmed a little.

"Good evening, ladies," he said. He held out his hand to Nana. "Nicolás Reyes. I hope you have your dancing shoes on this evening."

Nana tapped her block heels with her cane. "I always travel prepared," she said.

Nicolás laughed. "Then perhaps you will do me the honour." He held out his arm.

Fuck off.

Nana shooed him off with her cane. "I need someone a little more in tune with my pace and rhythm."

Well done, Nana.

He laughed again and turned to Aisha. "Shall we dance?"

Aisha put down her glass and followed him. The hairs rose on Gabi's neck. She headed towards the music, and Aisha and Nicolás were greeted with a loud cheer. Pilar joined Nana, and they took a seat at a table close by. Nana had a pair of castanets in one hand and her sherry in the other. The now familiar strumming of the guitar and fast and furious clapping set the mood for the dance, and Aisha started tapping her heels.

Gabi became transfixed, and her heart swelled with love and pride. Yes, Aisha's feet moved quickly, but when she held her skirt up and revealed her thigh, Gabi was left with the memory of her tongue on Aisha's tender flesh, and Aisha's strong legs moving rhythmically against Gabi, driving her to near ecstasy. She sipped her drink to wet her mouth. Aisha glanced at her, and her heart thundered. Gabi looked towards Nana and

Pilar, who was watching her. She took a deep breath, turned back to the dance, and immediately caught Aisha smiling at her. It was a smile that conveyed their shared desire. Gabi turned and walked away.

She headed towards Nana and stood at her side with her back to Pilar. She glanced around the crowd to avoid fixing her attention on Aisha, whose father chatted to another man as they cooked. Conchita talked to another man whose height was no match for hers, though she herself wasn't tall. He had an impish appearance, and she assumed he was her intended husband. She spotted Matías and waved. He raised his hand and started towards her, and her tension eased.

"Nana, this is Matías, the man from the market who I'm working for."

"Working with," Matías said. "Your granddaughter is very talented," he said.

The smile dropped from Nana's face, and she opened her mouth as she stared beyond him. She lifted her chin, squinted, and shook her head. "Juan?"

Matías turned his head. "You know my father?" he asked.

"Juan Altamira?" Nana said.

"Papa." Matías waved his father over.

Nana stood and covered her mouth with her hand.

"Estrella?" Juan approached. His smile grew, and he opened his arms. "Estrella Flores." He held her shoulders and looked at her. "Is it really you?"

Gabi closed her mouth. *Holy fucking shit.* This was the man Nana had fallen in love with almost sixty years ago. Her heart raced watching Nana's hand tremble as she greeted Juan, and Gabi had to swallow hard to stop from crying.

A cheer signalling the end of the dance filtered into Gabi's awareness. She watched Nana wipe the tears from her cheeks and embrace Juan, and Gabi's heart ached for them both. Nana kept touching his arm, and he took her hand and kissed it. He treated her as a perfect gentleman would, and Gabi felt Aisha's absence. She saw her heading towards them and smiled, then turned to see Pilar staring at her.

Nana turned to Gabi. "Cariño, Gabriela."

Gabi turned her attention to Juan.

"Juan, this is Gabriela, my granddaughter."

His smile was warm and sincere. He held his hand to his heart. "How lovely to meet you," he said. He opened his arms to Gabi and kissed her cheeks. He smelled of cigarettes, and wine, and sandalwood. There was something else—not a smell but more a feeling that she couldn't define. It touched her. "You look just like your nana."

"Except for her eyes," Nana said.

Aisha came to Gabi's side.

"This is Juan," Gabi said.

"Yes, Matías's papa," Aisha said.

"Superb dancing, Aisha," Juan said. "You get better every time I see you."

"How do you two know each other?" Matías asked.

Juan and Nana looked at each other with soft smiles and an unwavering gaze. Their fondness shone like a beacon, no doubt triggered by a recollection of the times they had once shared and the love that hadn't been extinguished by the years of separation. She checked where Pilar's attention was before smiling at Aisha.

"How long ago?" Juan asked Nana.

"Fifty-six years, give or take a few months," Nana said.

They stared at each other, smiling.

Juan was handsome but shorter than Gabi had imagined. He had greying hair and a gentle energy that effused kindness and contentment. He didn't strike her as the rogue Nana had described, but then he was at least as old as Nana, so he'd probably had to clip his wings. His eyes were sapphire blue, like Matías's, and he seemed to take in his surroundings with the same zest for life that Gabi saw in Nana. As he chatted to Nana, he laughed, and they looked as if time had stood still, and everything that had happened in the intervening years had been lived out in an alternative reality.

Nana's laughter melted Gabi's heart. She watched them touch hands from time to time, while she stood apart from Aisha and felt the unfairness of it all. Nana drank sherry, Juan red wine. He smoked a thin cigarette slowly and chatted without pausing for breath. And when he offered Nana his hand and they danced together, they moved as one, with grace and elegance, as if they'd always been this way.

"Would you like to walk with me?" Aisha asked.

Gabi glanced around. She couldn't see Pilar. Her heart thundered, and she looked around the group.

"Everyone is busy."

Gabi locked eyes with Aisha. The memory of her touch ignited her desire to escape this group of people and spend time with Aisha alone, doing nothing. Even just stargazing would be preferable to the pressure of Pilar's watchful guard.

Aisha led them across the field, deeper into the darkness, and the terrain was uneven. Around the back of a small stone construction, a feed-house of some kind, Aisha stopped and looked back. The streetlights cast light into the night over the roof of the feed house. They couldn't see the source of the music that echoed softly, distant from them now. The shrill of the cicadas and rustling from the bushes caught her attention, and she hoped there weren't any snakes in the undergrowth. Away from the street, the stars were brighter against the cloudless sky, and the warm air was fragrant with herbs, and sunflowers, and a hint of lavender. Aisha coaxed Gabi to lean against the cool stone.

"I've missed you tonight," she said and kissed Gabi hard.

The wine was strong on her breath, and she slurred a little. Gabi kissed her mouth and her neck and whispered into her ear. "I missed you too."

Aisha ran her thumb across Gabi's lips, and Gabi kissed it. "I want to make love with you," Aisha said.

Gabi shook her head, and the throb between her legs intensified. "It's too risky."

Aisha stared at her. She appeared emboldened by the wine or maybe the occasion. Or maybe it was just that Gabi was holding back. If they were anywhere else, Gabi would have undressed Aisha already. She was getting harder to resist, but what if they got caught?

Aisha ran her hand along the back of Gabi's head and drew her into a lingering kiss that challenged Gabi's conscience. Aisha pushed her back against the wall and unbuttoned her jeans. Gabi should be sensible and object. They should take a slow walk back to the party and talk to different people and guard their feelings. Gabi should go home, adjust to the events of the evening, take in Nana's delight and the repressed environment in which Aisha lived. It had been an odd night.

But Gabi couldn't do that. She couldn't just walk back to the party, not with this deep need. She wanted Aisha in a way she'd never wanted anyone. She kissed Aisha, tasted her, explored her with tenderness and whispered a groan as Aisha discovered her wetness. She struggled to support her own weight as Aisha slipped her fingers deep inside her and moved with the gentle rhythm of a lazy tide. She peaked too soon and was left feeling empty. Illicit moments behind an animal feed shed would never be enough, and she didn't want to hide her love. She wanted to fall asleep with Aisha in her arms and wake her with kisses. She wanted to see the world with her. She loved her, and anything other than being together would break Gabi's heart.

"Your mama is suspicious," Gabi said as they made their way slowly back across the field.

"She's nosy," Aisha said.

Aisha touched Gabi's hand and Gabi pulled away. Aisha was drunk and behaving like she didn't care when Gabi knew she did. "We have to be careful. Someone could see us."

"Not this far out, they won't," Aisha said, and linked arms with Gabi and tugged her close.

They ambled in silence, Gabi's frustration growing as she mulled over the hopelessness of their situation. Sacromonte was like stepping back in time a hundred years. "What are we going to do?" she asked.

"Run away," Aisha said and laughed.

Gabi slid her hand down Aisha's back. "That would be a bit extreme."

Aisha stopped walking. "Would you?"

"Run away with you?"

Gabi nodded, though her stomach tightened. "If that's what you want to do," she said, though she hadn't sounded convincing.

She looked towards the lights where the party was in full swing, to where her Nana had been reunited with the love of her life. They had looked like they belonged together, even after all the years that had passed. She had no idea what Nana might plan to do now, but leaving Nana tugged at her heart. Aisha's papa, Nicolás, and Conchita had looked at Gabi as if she were something they might scrape off their shoes after working in the field, and it didn't take much to imagine their concerns would grow with any length of time that she and Aisha spent together. What she knew was that she was in love with Aisha and wanted to live a normal life with her, and that would never be possible in Sacromonte. The scenario was loaded with unanswered questions and had the potential to deliver heartache and suffering. There was nothing simple about the option of running away.

"Why do you hesitate?"

Gabi's mind lingered on one question, and it took all her resolve to control the swell of emotion that backed her thought. "What would you do if we left and then at some point, broke up?"

Aisha shook her head. "I love you. I don't want to be with anyone else."

"I know. That's why I'm asking."

Aisha held her head in her hand. "Why do you talk of breaking up?"

"Because I'm not good at relationships. And I would feel responsible for making you consider a decision that would take you away from your family."

Aisha stumbled as she tried to maintain her balance. "I've never been attracted to men, Gabi. I've never been with a woman because that isn't an option for me. I'm breaking our laws because I have to follow my heart." She pinched the bridge of her nose and when she looked at Gabi, the moonlight revealed her wet cheeks. "I would never ask you if I wasn't clear about how I feel. I can't carry on living in a community that won't respect who I am. What we share is more than I ever imagined it could be. It scares me, but I don't think of us breaking up. I think of being together. I deserve to be happy, and I am when I'm with you."

"And if us being together means that you lose your family?"

Aisha shook her head and wiped her cheeks. She turned away and took two paces, turned back, and took another two paces. "I love them so much."

Gabi lowered her head and kicked at the dirt. Was Aisha ready to leave her family and give up everything she had just for her? And if Aisha didn't settle once they'd left and realised she'd made a mistake, it would have destroyed everything good in Aisha's life. It would destroy them. Maybe Gabi was scared. Maybe she wasn't ready. "You don't know what being in a relationship is like, let alone with someone like me."

Aisha shook her head. "Please don't do that, Gabi."

Gabi looked away. "What?"

"Don't tell me who to love. I have had enough of being told who and what is right for me. I don't need it from you too."

Gabi's stomach lurched. She pulled Aisha into her arms. "I'm sorry," Gabi whispered. The reassuring warmth of Aisha and the scent of their love making turned Gabi's thoughts upside down and turned her insides out. Fear did strange things, she thought—love did too. How could she walk away and leave Aisha with these people who called themselves family? But there was something else to consider. If they ran away together now, how would that impact Nana and Juan? Gabi's stomach twisted as alarming thoughts pinged loudly.

Aisha eased away from Gabi and stared at her. The tears had dried, and she looked as if she'd suddenly sobered up. "Why do you think so little of yourself?"

The blow winded Gabi. Aisha was right. She had always thought more of her girlfriends than she had of herself. Her first proper girlfriend, Lillian, had ended their relationship because she'd said Gabi was needy. And although Gabi had thought the comment strange, it had screwed with her head. She'd gone into the next relationship trying not to be that person and was accused of not caring. In truth, Karin had been a rebound mistake after Lillian. Finally, there was Shay, and she'd been so far up her own arse, she didn't see Gabi as anything other than someone who provided a bed for the night, and it was an easy way to avoid paying rent. The bottom line was Gabi thought she was lousy at relationships, and she'd got enough evidence to prove it. "I get needy when I love someone," she said.

Aisha frowned. "What does that mean?"

Gabi reflected. "Wanting to be with them all the time. Wanting to share stuff all the time. Going out together and giving gifts. Adoring and spoiling her because she's the only thing in my life that matters. Never wanting to be away from her."

Aisha took Gabi's hand and brought it to her lips. "That's not needy. That's loving someone. I want that. I want that with you."

Gabi's throat tightened, and her eyes burned. Tears welled, and she wiped them away. She felt like the eighteen-year-old she'd been when Lillian had accused her, exposed and very lonely. "Someone told me that I was needy."

Aisha cupped Gabi's cheek and kissed her. "Well, they were wrong."

Aisha's lips were soft and warm, her touch tender and caressing, and Gabi felt no shame in needing her and feeling needed by her.

She looked towards the lights, the music, and stepped away a little. "I love you. Leaving here without you would break my heart, but I would do that if it meant you were safe."

Aisha shook her head. "I don't want safe. I want to feel my heart beating with love."

"And your family?"

"I want to be with you. That's my choice."

Gabi couldn't be sure it wasn't the drink that had done the talking, and if there was any running away going to happen, it needed a lot more planning and time. And she had Nana to consider. It was a mindfuck that she didn't have the first clue how to process. "And what about when you start missing them so badly it hurts?" She was pushing Aisha because this wasn't a decision they could take lightly.

Aisha squeezed her hands together. She looked towards the party and the land around them. "I don't know about the future. But I have to leave. Staying here will destroy me."

Aisha was right, and it would crucify Gabi if she'd had to live in this community. But Aisha's love of her family was so strong. Maybe Aisha wouldn't realise what she missed until it was too late. Gabi wanted to be with her, and she didn't want to leave Nana alone. It was too much to process and not a conversation to be had while drunk. "Come to the café tomorrow, and we can talk about it."

Aisha stared at Gabi. "I will."

Gabi kissed her and her heart melted. "Come on, let's get back before your mama sends out the hunters."

Aisha laughed.

Gabi couldn't quite make out the woman in the darkness as they approached the houses just short of the main party and shortened her stride. She looked back across the field and couldn't make out exactly where they'd just walked from, apart from recognising the silhouette of the small outbuilding a short distance away. She released a sigh when Aisha's sister stepped out of the shadows and greeted them.

Conchita addressed Aisha. "Where have you been?"

"We went for a walk. The stars are so bright tonight. It's a beautiful evening."

Aisha brushed against Gabi's arm, and Gabi felt Conchita's gaze zero in on the contact between them. The smell of their lovemaking hung in the air, and she hoped Conchita was too naïve to know it. Heat flooded her, and she surreptitiously checked the buttons on her jeans while creating a space between her and Aisha.

"Mama has been looking for you," Conchita said.

Gabi's stomach lurched.

Aisha shrugged. "What does she want?"

"I don't know."

As they approached the party, Pilar greeted them, gesticulating wildly and smiling as if she'd just won the lotto. Gabi thought she'd glared at her briefly, but she couldn't be sure in the darkness.

"Nicolás, she's here." Pilar waved him over, brimming with excitement.

"Aisha, come dance with me. Everyone wants us to dance," Nicolás said.

Gabi's hate for him centred in her chest, and she clenched her hands and shifted them to her back. He grabbed Aisha's hand and led her towards the crowd.

Aisha glanced towards Gabi and mouthed, "Sorry."

Gabi, aware that Pilar was staring at her with a grin that conveyed triumph, nodded. The lights of the approaching taxi caught Gabi's eye, probably not soon enough for Aisha's mama who she was sure would have gladly seen the back of Gabi earlier if it hadn't been for Nana being so wonderful. They would have to go soon, and that would be a blessing. Gabi didn't want to come back here. She didn't want to see Aisha's family or Nicolás ever again. She glanced around but couldn't see Nana.

The wailing call pierced through the night, shrill and as fierce as the dance that would follow, and then the guitar fired up, and then the music stopped.

"Attention, everyone." Nicolás waved his arms in the air to bring a hush to the clapping.

Aisha stood at his side and smiled as she looked around.

"Thank you. I have something I would like to say."

Gabi watched Pilar as she nodded, her hands clasped in front of her, her smile sickening. The way Gabi's stomach turned and the chill that crept down her spine told her that something was wrong. Something bad was going to happen.

"Aisha and I are getting engaged."

"Fuck." Gabi turned away and started to walk down the street.

There was cheering and clapping, and the clicking of castanets rained down on her in a vicious assault. Her dreams, *their* dreams, tumbled like a string of dominos, and the ache in her heart that would have had her scream out, "No," would have taken her to her knees had she let it. She stumbled over the conversation they'd just had about running away, and it stuck in her throat. Her chest was so tight she thought she was going to suffocate.

"Gabriela, wait for me. Gabriela."

She slowed her pace without looking back.

Nana linked her arm through Gabi's. "I don't want to talk about it," Gabi said.

"Later, cariño. Later."

Never, Gabi thought.

24.

AISHA HAD NEVER KNOWN a pain in her head this violent or acid that felt as though it blistered her throat. Nicolás's announcement of their engagement hadn't been a nightmare. She wished it had, and as the memory carved out its place deeper inside her mind, her heart pumped slower and weaker.

Her mama's exuberance and the way she had watched Gabi's reaction to the news had provoked her anger into a quality of rage that Aisha had struggled to suppress to not disgrace her family. The numbing emptiness had rendered her silent for the rest of the evening, the congratulations and celebrations in their honour falling on her deaf ears and crushed heart.

Gabi had disappeared before she'd had the chance to explain. And with everyone's eyes on her and Nicolás after his proclamation, Aisha hadn't been able to run to Gabi without causing a massive scene. She hadn't needed to see Gabi to know how she felt, Aisha felt it too. She had to talk to her.

She sipped at a glass of water, and it tried to come back up. The claustrophobic feeling inside the house was made more overbearing by her mama's enthusiasm for a second wedding in the spring. Aisha locked eyes with Conchita. Conchita didn't smile, and Aisha hoped her sister could see the pain in her heart.

"I need some air." Aisha picked up the basket and headed out the front door and across the field.

The empty basket hung low from her limp arms. She squinted to focus, though the sun cast its light evenly and softly. The feeling in her throat became thicker, and her heartbeat burrowed into it with a slow, thudding rhythm. Her vision blurred. Her eyes grew wet. Tears slipped onto her cheeks as she walked towards the feed shed where she and Gabi had enjoyed each other. If she could turn back time, she should have run away last night before this cruel trick had been played out, but Gabi had been right about her not being ready to leave her family. The agony of real love and thinking she might not be able to hold onto it was much worse than when she'd just dreamed of love.

She pulled the carrots from the ground and put them in the basket, and three lettuce and half a dozen tomatoes.

"Aisha. Aisha."

His voice, an unwelcome intrusion, numbed her. She walked towards the green beans, and he called her name again. "Leave me alone."

He approached from behind and swept the basket from her. He took her hand and twirled her around. "You look radiant. I need to get you an engagement ring that sparkles as brightly as your eyes."

She pulled free of his hand. Her head spun, and nausea thrust its way up from her stomach. She snatched the basket from him. She would rather pick onions than listen to his infuriating rapture. The vegetable refused to budge from the soil, and she cursed it silently, cursed herself for being weak, knowing he hovered behind her waiting for her to fail so he could rescue her.

He tugged at the stem effortlessly and scooped it from the ground, knocked the soil from it, and threw it into the basket. "Sit with me for a while, under the tree," he said.

"I have work to do."

"Your mama said you have time."

Aisha clenched her teeth and glared towards the house. Her mama waved from the doorway, deepening the veil of disgust that Aisha wore to protect her heart from their rejection. She turned away and sat under the tree. Sitting a while would give her time for her head and stomach to settle, and as soon as he'd said his piece, perhaps he would leave her alone. Nicolás pressed his thigh against hers, and the scent of him clawed in her throat. She shifted a couple of inches away. He moved with her.

"We should make plans," he said.

"I'm not ready to make plans."

He crouched in front of her and held her hand. "Let's talk about where we will live."

She pulled her hand free and picked at the soil.

"There is a place for sale up the hill. It is small, but I have enough money saved for a deposit. It's not too far from your parents. We will settle well there."

Aisha squeezed a lump of dry earth and crumbled it to grains, though not as fine as the warm sand that had slipped through her fingers at the beach. The memory of the day taunted her with its promises, and she let the coarse grains slide from her palm. She looked towards the house, the fields they worked in, and the hills where he spoke of buying a home for them and for their family. He fidgeted at her side, rubbed his hands together, and sighed heavily, failing to hide his impatience with her indifference. Had she really thought she could run away with Gabi? "I don't want to live there."

He leaned forward, his breath as stale as hers after the night, and rubbed his clenched fist into the palm of his hand. "Where then? Where do you want to live?"

She shook her head and stared into the basket. The carrots were vibrant while his talk of the future was suffocating. She stared towards the house. Maybe her parents would understand if only she could talk to them. Shouldn't she at least give them a chance to see her in love, to know that love as she knew it? Maybe they would respect her decision not to marry, if only she could summon the courage to talk to them.

She imagined standing in front of her parents in the living room, her mama sat in the chair, her papa stood at her mama's side. Both would stare at her with a look of growing concern as she struggled to find the words she'd rehearsed a thousand times. "Mama, Papa, there's something I need to tell you." The quiver in her voice would betray her fears, and she would become their prey. The slaughter would be quick, but she would take the pain with her and live with it if it freed her, knowing she had tried.

"What is it, Aisha? You can talk to us," Mama would say.

No, she couldn't. Not about her love. But she had to because she needed her mama's blessing.

"I—" She would falter, because how could she not?

Hearing what she had to say, her papa would grow in stature and press his hand firmly on her mama's shoulder. Her mama would press herself into the back of the chair, retreating as far from her disgusting daughter as possible. She would cross her arms and avoid eye contact, because how could she look at her daughter after this? She had brought the worst disgrace of all to their family, and that was unforgivable. If she'd told them she was pregnant, they would have looked on her more favourably, brought forward the wedding date, and then danced in celebration. This news would cause them to narrow their eyes, and as her words registered fully, their faces would infuse with rage. They would not accept her. And that made the truth what it was. She wasn't ready to face their rejection, to walk away having broken their hearts and turned their world upside down.

They would blame Gabi no matter what Aisha said, and Gabi would have to leave Granada to stay safe. Something as grave as this would never be considered just a family matter. It was an affront to the community, their history, and their ancestors before them, and aside from what it would mean for Aisha once the dust had settled, as it had for Old María, she couldn't risk harm coming to Gabi.

Her agitated mind was trying to protect her broken heart, getting her to think twice about the consequences of running away, and yet, she had to follow her heart. She loved Gabi. She wanted to believe in their dreams of seeing the world and growing old together. She had to speak to Gabi.

"You see, you can't even answer a simple question."

Nicolás jolted her from her thoughts. "I don't know." She turned towards him. "Sometimes I just want to be far away from here."

He shook his head and wiped her cheek.

She froze. The silent tears continued, and now that she was aware of them, she felt foolish and defenceless accepting his kindness. Her distress seemed to soften his demeanour towards her. He put his arm around her shoulder and coaxed her to lean against him. Her stomach churned. His muscles weren't soft like

Gabi's, and he held her too strongly, coveting her rather than comforting her, but he was familiar and warm, and though she was clear she didn't want to marry him, she was confused about everything else.

"I wanted to leave here when Esme died," Nicolás said.

She pulled away. She'd often wondered if her feelings for Esme would always be reflected in his eyes. But as she watched him now, they weren't, and his grief was his own.

"I know, as best friends, you were probably closer to her than me in some ways. She missed you after we married, when you became absorbed by your dreams of being somewhere else." He smiled ruefully. "I'm not criticising you for having an imagination, Aisha. It's what makes you the best dancer in Granada. Esme was the centre of my universe then, and when she wasn't at my side, the biggest part of me became lost. My heart died when she and our baby did."

He became that man again, consumed by his loss, his jaw tight, and his eyes empty with the despair that came from feeling helpless. It was the feeling Aisha had lived with since realising she was different.

"My heart is filled with you now. I know you will never love me as I love you. Something blocks your heart. You've always been that way." He looked to the sky, his Adam's apple rising and falling. "Don't make me out to be a fool, Aisha. I care for you, and one day I hope you will let me make you happy."

This conversation felt so wrong, and the words tightened like a noose around her neck. "You think it's that simple?"

"Why not?"

"Love, I mean. Do you think that one person can learn to let another make them happy, and that will be enough? Don't you think that kind of happiness is a product of two hearts connecting unconsciously and unforced. Not through an arrangement sold to us by our laws. Laws that cast out people who think differently."

He scratched his head.

"Do you not think that love is something so special, that it cannot be defined, that it passes through people, between them, and around them? It doesn't bend to our will, Nicolás, it directs it. Love is all that matters. Without it, we are empty vessels cast out into an ocean too vast for us to navigate."

"You are a dreamer with your head in the clouds. You think life is what you read and sing, a canto that fills your head with illusions and makes you crazy inside. I've watched you change. I've watched you lose yourself to these wild dreams."

"I was lost without them. I'm finding myself because of them. And this love I speak of is no illusion. It's as real as the sun, and the sky, and the air that we breathe. Maybe you had that with Esme. I know I can never have it with you."

He scratched his head harder and took a deeper breath. His face contorted. "I am happy with you."

"You talk as though I'm something to be owned. How is that love?"

He shook his head. "I don't understand you. I will provide everything you need. A house, food on the table, children. I will keep you safe, and you will not want for anything. We will be comfortable."

She shook her head. "I don't want comfortable. I want love, Nicolás. I want my heart to sing with joy. I want to feel alive with everything we think and do. I want to share the same interests. I want to talk and laugh."

225

"We have the same interests."

"We dance together."

"And that's not enough?"

"Not without love, no. It's not enough."

He nodded. "I get it. It's still too soon for you. Spring is a long way off." He sighed and ran his fingers through his hair.

"It will always be too soon for me, Nicolás. I'm never going to want the house up the hill, or the children, or the safety of a man at my side. I would rather—"

"Rather what?"

She couldn't reveal her heart to him, though she would love to send him away with his tail between his legs. That time would come. "I would rather take my chances and travel the world."

He stood and started walking towards the houses, then stopped. "You know, maybe you should just go. And when you see that life isn't greener." He motioned to the distance. "In a month or maybe two, if you last that long, don't think I will still be here waiting for you."

Aisha stood and put her hands on her hips. "You know, I think I will." He stepped towards her. His stale breath brushed her cheek, and the line of his jaw became more pronounced. He could scare her, but she wouldn't back down.

"I'll let you tell your parents, and they can find you another man to marry." He turned away.

"Don't threaten me."

"I hear Pedro is still looking for a wife," he said and stormed off.

She watched him go, and the trembling inside grew stronger, because he was right. If it wasn't him, her parents would find someone else. He could and would move on, as he had after Esme. He would be vindicated by her desertion of him. She couldn't change who she was. And having been with Gabi in the most intimate ways and tasted the reality as so much more than she'd dreamed of, she wouldn't betray her or them. She leaned back against the tree, closed her eyes, and inhaled deeply. "Verde que te quiero verde. Verde viento. Verdes ramas." The grass was greener, and she would see it. The excitement that came when she thought about Gabi gave way to fear again, swifter than the sun dried the rain in summer, as she considered how she might start a conversation with her mama and papa.

25.

"CARIÑO COME AND SIT down. There is a nice breakfast. I can make you eggs if you like."

"I'm not hungry." Gabi had struggled to eat anything since discovering that Aisha was engaged to the greasy-haired, flashy fuckwit that she now hated with a vengeance. As the week had passed, with that tick, tock feeling she'd had as a child, she'd become more convinced that the engagement hadn't been what Aisha wanted.

Gabi had wandered around the streets for hours in a trance, earlier in the week, sat in the coffee shop Aisha had taken her to, and even visited the Alhambra on the bus. Suffering the stench on the bus had been awful that day, and she'd walked along the river in the vain hope of seeing Aisha. All those hours had reminded her of what she missed and drinking herself into a stupor helped blot out the reality for long enough to get some sleep. But the mornings threw light on the truth, and that brought tears and confusion.

She'd walked past the group on Saturday, hoping to get a moment to speak to Aisha alone. There had been something different in the way Aisha had danced. Still with passion but distanced from the crowd and her movements tighter, angrier. The onlookers cheered and clapped loudly. They wouldn't have noticed the subtlety that Gabi had. Gabi hadn't been able to connect with the music and watching *him* guarding Aisha closely had fuelled her wrath, so she'd slipped away through the crowd before either of them could catch sight of her.

She'd berated herself for not trying to find a way to get to Aisha, but how could she set herself up for further rejection when her heart was raw? She could hardly front up to Aisha with that smarmy bastard listening to their conversation. He would pick up on the strain between her and Aisha, she was sure. He would relay everything back to Pilar the Hun, and she didn't want to cause Aisha any more grief than she already had. She had no idea what the Hun might be capable of, but her gut and the way Pilar had looked at Gabi told her that she'd do almost anything to make sure Aisha got married. It wasn't a mother's love, it was matriarchal control, and it left a bitter taste in her mouth and an uneasy feeling in her stomach that had vied with the daily hangover ever since.

"I'm not asking you, Gabriela. Sit down."

Gabi sat and felt like an inconsolable child that had lost its favourite toy and become petulant. She deserved to voice her moodiness. Who wouldn't under the circumstances?

Nana stood. "Drink the juice. It's Pablo's oranges, and they are excelente."

Gabi didn't give a fuck about the oranges. She sipped, and the juice chilled her mouth. She expected acid and found sweet, and it was pleasant. Her head throbbed, as it had all week. A regular feature of her greeting the day, and she hated herself for how quickly she'd reverted to her old drinking habit to drown out what she couldn't deal with. One custom she had changed was the one-night stands. Sex with any other woman wasn't on the cards while she felt the way she did, though she had been approached at the bars she'd frequented. One woman, she couldn't even remember what she looked like, had sat at Gabi's table, and Gabi had quickly excused herself to avoid conversation, preferring to wallow in her anguish alone. That's how she knew her heart was broken, and it's how she knew she wasn't finished with Aisha.

"I'll make eggs," Nana said.

Gabi was over the shock now, just pissed off and very, very sad. She held back the tears as Nana cooked. But her eyes had become like the bloody fountains, spouting water day and night whenever she thought about Aisha, which was pretty much all her waking hours. Aisha had been the best thing that had ever happened to her. She recalled their first missed meeting at the fountain. She knew why Aisha hadn't come back for her this time, when Aisha knew exactly where to find her. Because she couldn't get away. She was virtually a prisoner within her own community.

Gabi had taken the bus to Aisha's house yesterday in a fit of needing to do something to stop the pain of uncertainty ripping her apart. She had no plan. She'd watched from a distance and saw Aisha sitting next to Nicolás under the tree in the field. Pilar the Hun waved and smiled at them. He put his arm around Aisha. She pulled away. Gabi couldn't read Aisha's confusing body language, but she'd realised that she couldn't just turn up at Aisha's house. It wouldn't be a warm welcome. And what would she do? Take flowers and congratulate Aisha on her engagement? Take a ring and ask her to run away as Aisha had asked her to before *he* stepped in and blasted Gabi's happy bubble to smithereens. Fuckwit.

Nana returned with two dishes of eggs, crispy bacon, spicy salsa, and guacamole. She sat and gazed at Gabi. "Cariño, what are we going to do?"

Gabi picked up the fork, prodded the salty bacon and ate it. "I don't know."

Nana cut open an egg and spilled the yolk onto the salsa. She collected a small morsel of everything onto her fork and ate it. "Excelente." She ate another mouthful and dabbed the corners of her lips with a serviette. "There's something I need to tell you, Gabriela, and I'm not sure if you're ready to hear it, but I won't rest until you know the truth, and I hope it might help you with your own situation."

"You're going to stay here, aren't you? I don't blame you. You have Juan, why would you go back? I have to leave, Nana."

"We will come to your point in a moment, if that's okay. Yes, I have decided to stay, but there's something else." She cleared her throat and sipped her juice. "Juan is your real grandpa."

Gabi choked on the salsa, and it burned like hell. She put down her fork and took a slug of juice. She tried to listen.

"Pregnant. Sex before marriage. Gitano laws. Punishable by death."

Silence.

"What?" Gabi said.

Nana laughed.

Clearly Gabi had missed something.

"Gabriela, cariño, you didn't think I was a prude, did you?" Nana sighed and stared into space. "It was wonderful and reckless. But when you're young and in love, you don't think like that, do you?"

It dawned on Gabi that Nana had been talking about her experience with Juan, which was a relief, because the death bit was particularly disturbing. Her thoughts took her to the beach with Aisha and what had become their last moments together behind the feed shed. Thrill had great power over laws. She went back to Nana's opening point because the other words had become a jumbled reflection of her own scenario, and she didn't like the way that felt. "So, Grandpa in England isn't Grandpa?"

"No. He knew our son wasn't his. He took on the role because it came with a good lifestyle. It got him away from the front line, and my father rewarded him financially. We never spoke about the pregnancy again."

"Did Juan know?"

Nana ate a morsel of bread slowly. "I told him yesterday. I've seen him every day and we've talked a lot. Juan and I had never kept secrets from each other. I wanted him to know you, and you, him."

"And what about Dad?" It was odd that he mattered now, but he did. There had been too many secrets, and this was important news. His real father was alive.

"Hm." She sipped her orange. "I want to talk to you about that, because I can't think clearly."

"Surely he should know?"

"That's what my mind tells me. But how will this change anything for him for the better?"

"Maybe something would click. Maybe he'd want to get to know his real father."

"He adored and idolised Miguel as if he was a king. He even turned out more like him than either me or Juan." She laughed, and it sounded strained. "Strange, I know. What you're not aware of is that your dad had a nervous breakdown after Miguel died. I'm worried that finding out the man he loved so passionately, a man he modelled himself on, isn't his father would do more harm than good. He will be very angry. The news could crucify him."

Miguel was just a name on a gravestone and pictures in an album to Gabi. She struggled to process that Juan was her real grandpa, and he was alive and well, and now he and Nana were going to be together. Headfuck didn't come close to describing it. She wasn't thinking clearly either. "What does Juan want? It's his son."

"He would like to see him, but only if it's right for Hugo."

She ran her fingers through her hair and held her head. "I don't know what's for the best."

"Hm, exactly, Gabriela. We can't know what's best, because we can't follow two different courses of action at the same time."

Gabi thought about Aisha. Aisha was stuck between loving her family and loving Gabi. She couldn't know any more than Gabi did whether leaving Sacromonte was the best thing for her, and Aisha had so much more to lose and yet she was willing to risk it all for Gabi. Aisha's mind would be telling her to stay within the safety and security of what she knew, but her heart would be telling her to flee for love. And Gabi should be there for her to support her rather than worrying about a future— them breaking up—that might not happen.

"Did you ever stop loving Juan?"

"No, Gabriela. But if I hadn't left Spain when I did, I would have been killed during the war alongside my parents. Assuming the Guardia hadn't got to Juan and me first. How could I have had an illegitimate child here? We would have had to run away, and that would have meant a certain death."

Gabi couldn't face the eggs. "It's like that for Aisha and me."

Nana nodded. "She has the freedom to leave, but without her parents' blessing, that privilege comes at a big cost."

"We couldn't live here."

Nana chewed on a mouthful of egg. "Even with their blessing, Gypsy laws will not allow her to stay. She will have to go, and her name will not be spoken of again."

"It's shit."

"That brings me to the other thing I wanted to talk to you about."

Gabi couldn't stop thinking about Aisha, couldn't stop the deepening ache in her heart.

"Gabriela."

"Sorry, yes."

"The farmhouse is in a trust fund in your name. There is an allowance of twenty thousand pounds a year which will cover the upkeep of the place should you wish to keep it, and twenty thousand pounds for you to choose what to do with."

If Gabi couldn't be with Aisha, she didn't want to live at the farmhouse without Nana. "I can't—"

Nana raised her hand. "I'm too old to listen to your objections. The rest of my assets you will inherit when I die."

"What about Dad?"

"Hugo will be fine. He agreed to the fund after your mum died, and he doesn't need anything that I can give him."

"Even knowing that his dad isn't who he thought he was?" Gabi asked.

Nana sighed. "It's not easy, is it?"

Gabi shook her head. Her dad should know, but it wasn't for her to tell him, and he wasn't her main concern right now. Nana was. "Will you be safe here, with Juan?"

"Yes, cariño. He has his house and I have the apartment. I am not the daughter of a senior guard commander anymore. We can enjoy each other's company for the years we might have together."

"What about Pablo?"

"We are just friends. There would never have been anything more for either of us. He loved his wife too much, and I hadn't let go of Juan."

Thoughts of leaving without Nana brought a lump to her throat, and she struggled to swallow past it. She rubbed her eyes to stop the tears. "I don't want to be in England if you're here. I'm happy for you and Juan, but I would miss you too much. And I can't stay here if Aisha marries him. I can't see her with him."

"Do you think that's what she really wants?"

Gabi noted the tremble in her hand as she sipped the juice. "My heart says no, but my head is confused."

Nana smiled. "Then you need to find out." She patted Gabi's hand and then held it. "I'm sure you'll find a way." She leaned back in the seat.

Gabi would find a way. She couldn't just walk up to Aisha's front door, but there was the school, the one place she could go where they could talk for a short while.

"Would you like to visit your grandpa?" Nana asked.

Nana's happiness cloaked the ache in Gabi's heart. "Yes." She still couldn't work out where Juan fitted into her life, and her feelings, but with time, maybe that would change. "So, what are you going to do about Dad?" she asked.

Nana sighed. "I need to think it through. It's something I can't take back once I've said it. And it's something I need to do in person."

"He has a right to know?"

"Maybe, cariño." Nana finished her juice. "It's not that simple. Would you be able to cope with me not telling him just yet?"

"Can I be the keeper of secrets?" Gabi shook her head. She wasn't planning to see him any time soon, and if Nana wasn't going back to England, she couldn't imagine when, if ever, she might see him again.

Nana frowned. "Yes, I suppose. I've never thought of myself as someone who keeps secrets so much as judging when the time is right to pass on information. Hearts are fragile, and as you know, it's not a nice experience when they break."

"I can let you be the judge of when it's the right time," Gabi said.

Nana patted Gabi's arm. "Thank you, cariño." She picked up her plate and started towards the kitchen. "By the way, Matías was asking after you since you didn't go to the workshop last week. I'm sure your uncle would enjoy your company, and maybe you could pop into Juan's for a cup of tea."

An uncle and a grandpa, who'd have thought it? It went some way to explaining her connection with Matías and their mutual love of making jewellery. It would make their business relationship more interesting. Weird didn't describe how she felt. At least she wasn't as alone in the world as she'd imagined. She needed to let this new reality settle, because despite having just found them, she would be leaving them all behind. She followed Nana into the kitchen and drew her into a hug. "Thank you. For everything. I'm going to the school to talk to Aisha. No matter what happens, I have to leave here. I just hope she will come with me."

Nana stroked Gabi's cheek and smiled. "I know, Gabriela. And I'm not too old to travel yet, so don't think you're free of me just yet."

Gabi smiled, though the tears burned the back of her eyes. She kissed Nana on the cheek. "I'll leave on Friday morning," she said, her voice broken.

Nana's eyes glassed over, and she wiped a tear that had strayed onto her cheek. "So soon."

Gabi lowered her head. Seeing Nana cry would set her off, and she had to be strong. "I can't stay if she rejects me."

"She won't."

Gabi hoped Nana's confidence wasn't misplaced. "If she wants to come with me, then the sooner we leave the better, no?"

Nana patted Gabi's arm. "Yes, true. Well, we'd better find you a good hotel. Màlaga's not too far," she said.

Gabi kissed her on the forehead. She held her tightly and prayed she wouldn't be leaving Granada alone. "I'm going to miss you."

"Not for long, you won't. Besides, I'll come to Màlaga for a short break with Juan."

Gabi laughed. "I'd like that."

26.

Aisha had cried herself to sleep every night, and the days had passed slower than the shadow of death approached. Her heart weighed so heavily, she feared it would crush the life out of her entirely. She'd found little solace in drawing the abstract image of Gabi that had previously helped her hold on to possibilities. Her tears had transformed it from a work of love to a token of grief.

She'd tried to pluck up the courage to speak to her parents, but there was never a good time with her mama consumed by Conchita's wedding plans and her papa's determination to spend as little time in the house as possible.

She'd let Gabi down, and that was the worst feeling of all.

The list of jobs that needed her attention daily had gotten longer, forcing her to stay closer to home. She'd been tasked with helping the elders with simple things that they'd previously been perfectly capable of doing themselves, taking food and supplies to the farthest places in the hills, which she first had to cook, or gather and prepare. The elders accosted her for hours with their tales of family and the importance of traditions, especially in times of hardship and crisis. It was a conspiracy, an intervention, she was sure of it. She'd had enough.

She'd thought she'd seen Gabi on Saturday night walking past where they were dancing. She'd lost her rhythm because her ears had thundered with her heartbeat instead of the music. When she'd looked up and Gabi had gone, she wondered whether she was already losing her mind. She was fast heading down the path that Old María had been driven down. It was the most evil of all betrayals to be isolated from love by the people who professed to love her the most.

She watched her mama scrubbing dirt from the vegetables, the light stoop in her stance that had appeared, and the silver that streaked her dark hair. She looked tired, worn down no doubt. Why did Aisha care? Why was it so hard to talk to her and so hard to walk away?

She remembered sitting at the table as a young child, drawing on the back of a piece of paper that the meat from the market had been wrapped in. In the creases, the charcoal had made a pattern that resembled the crops growing in the field. Mama had set it against the kitchen wall, pinned there by the salt cellar, until one day the picture wasn't there anymore. Mama had told her stories as she'd cooked, and she'd explained how recipes worked, and Aisha had learned to measure the flour and knead the dough. She'd learned how to bake bread and cakes, how to create different flavours with herbs and spices, and most importantly, how to please Mama.

She had been subjected to the facts of life lesson while sat at that table too. Her mama had gutted a catfish as she'd talked, and Aisha had never understood how Mama could speak of love and how to make a baby in the same sentence. She'd come away knowing she never wanted to have children of her own. That night, she'd recited Lorca's poems until she'd fallen asleep, and she knew love was something more than her mama's interpretation.

There was the time when Aisha had been so sick that she'd believed she was going to die. She hadn't minded that too much, because she would be with her abuela, her papa's mama. Mama had said that time stands still on the other side, so you don't feel the loss. She'd liked that idea. The cloth had felt like ice against her skin, and she'd shivered for days until one day, the sun touched her face with warmth. Mama had always been there when she'd opened her eyes, smiling at her and stroking her hair, feeding her soup and water.

When Aisha started to bleed every month, her mama's attitude hardened. She became more fixated on marriage and children, and Aisha felt sorry for her, because she felt there was more to life, and it had saddened her that Mama couldn't see that.

Aisha swallowed past the lump in her throat and headed for the door.

"Where are you going?"

The sharpness in Mama's tone jolted Ashe. "To the fish market." What was another lie in the stream that covered her tracks?

Mama cut the carrots with stiff movements. "Conchita has gone to get the fish already."

"That's my job."

Mama turned slowly, put her hand on her hip and leaned forward, casting a shadow on Aisha that was darker than the one she already felt consumed by.

"You weren't up in time."

That wasn't true. "You sent me to Señor Pérez."

"His needs are greater than yours. You've become obsessed with going to the city." She pointed to her temple. "It's turned your head."

"That's rubbish."

Mama took a pace towards Aisha and slapped her across the face.

240

Aisha held her cheek, lifted her chin, and gritted her teeth. The sting caused her eyes to water, but she refused to let her mama see her tears. "Te odio," she said under her breath but loud enough to be heard.

"You don't know the meaning of hate. But that is the insolence I am talking about. It will make you as crazy as Old María."

Aisha gesticulated around the room. "This is driving me crazy. Can you not see that?"

Mama went back to cutting the carrots. "You have no idea how good your life is here. You think the world out there will treat you better? That you will dance for more money? That you will have richer food lining your greedy stomach?"

"I will have love."

The whites of her Mama's eyes made her look wild, and the way she screwed up her face gave the appearance of reeling in agony. Except there was a fierceness where there would have been meekness had Mama been truly suffering. Anger this brutal was frightening. Aisha tensed.

"You have people here who love you, and you reject them."

Nicolás had spoken to her about their argument. She bit her lip to stop herself from screaming.

"You show no respect for anyone."

She threw her hands in the air. "And where is the respect for me and what I need?"

"Need. Need." Mama put down the knife. She took a pace towards Aisha, and Aisha cowered and took a pace backwards. "I'm not going to hurt you, Aisha."

Aisha glared and unclenched her jaw. "You already did."

Mama lowered her head. "I didn't mean to hit you."

"I'm not talking about a slap. The physical pain is easy to take. Have you ever had your heart crushed?"

Mama picked up the knife and hovered it above the chopping board. "You have no idea what love is, Aisha. And I will hear no more of this. You are marrying Nicolás, or you will marry Pedro. You decide which one you love more, and then you tell me. You are making a fool of this family, and it must stop now."

"I am not marrying either of them."

"You think I don't know you've been lying to me while you've been sneaking around with that girl? I don't want to know what goes on in your head."

Aisha froze. "How can you do this to your daughter? You think this is love?"

"Yes, Aisha, this is the toughest kind of love. A mama who looks out for her children. We help each other make the right decisions for our families and our people. It is what makes us stronger."

Aisha shook her head. True Gypsies were the ones who ostracised those who dared to speak for changes to their laws. No, she wasn't going to conform. "It makes me weaker. It's killing me."

"Don't be pathetic. You have no idea how our ancestors had to fight, the government, the systems, the Guardia just to survive. You would have us throw away our laws and standards just so you can live in some fanciful way that you do not even understand?"

"I won't marry."

"You will, and there is nothing more to be said about it. If you choose Pedro, I will get your father to speak to Nicolás, but neither will be happy. This is the only choice you have now. It is my fault. I gave you too much space with the dancing. Your papa said we should have guided you, that your spirit was too strong for you to know how to use it wisely. I thought you were capable, but I was wrong." She shook her head.

"I will leave," Aisha said.

"Nunca. That is not possible. Now, grow up, Aisha. I've had enough of pandering to your whim."

"I hate you with all my heart," Aisha muttered and marched towards the door.

"Where are you going?"

"The school." The children wouldn't mind her showing up earlier today. "I am going away from here to be with the children. I'm going to help them to believe they can use their minds to dream of a future they can grab hold of, and that they will have choices when they grow up, because this way, these laws, cannot crucify the next generation."

"Conchita has a final dress fitting later, and everyone will be here. Don't be late back."

Aisha slammed the door shut before her mama said another word and ran down the hill. She stopped outside the playground, out of breath, her vision distorted, her heart pumping as hard and fast as the tears that streaked her cheeks. She took deep breaths until the trees and fields became sharp and bright, and the sun warmed her skin, and she had the strength to face the optimistic faces of the children in the playground.

"Aisha, Aisha."

She smiled weakly at Marta as she ran towards her. Marta had been scarred for life by her drunken father, an accident, he

243

claimed. Her smile would light up the sky at night and her curiosity deserved so much more than the lack of prospects living here would give her. She stroked her hair and hugged her closely.

Marta looked beyond Aisha. "Is Gabi here?"

Aisha cleared her throat. "No. She's busy."

"When is she coming again?"

"I don't know, cariño."

"Why are you sad?"

Aisha wiped the tears from her cheeks and put on the best smile she could. She lifted Marta into her arms. "Because I'm happy to see you today." She sat on the ground and tipped out the beads and thread. "Now, what shall we make?"

Marta picked out red and orange beads and a gold-coloured cord and started threading them in an alternate pattern.

Aisha watched her tiny hands at work. The beads twisted out of her grip as she tried to slot them onto the string, but her persistence won out. Marta's smile grew with each small success, and after she added the final bead, she looked up at Aisha and her smile faded.

"She's not coming back to see us, is she?"

Aisha's lips trembled as she spoke, and the sadness welled in her eyes. She stroked Marta's cheek and forced a smile. "I don't think she can."

"Why?"

Aisha sighed deeply, and Marta frowned at her.

"Is she a tourist?"

Aisha shook her head. "Not really."

"Was she your friend?"

Aisha nodded.

"I want a friend like Gabi," Marta said. "Why don't you make her a bracelet?"

Aisha kissed her head and collected up green and blue beads and a white string. "I can't stay too long. My sister is getting married soon, and I have to help with her dress."

"I don't want to get married," Marta said.

Aisha threaded two green beads. "Me neither," she said.

"But you're engaged to Nicolás."

"Can you keep a secret?" Aisha leaned closer to Marta.

Marta nodded and threaded a gold bead. She smiled as she stared at the almost complete bracelet.

"I don't want to marry him," Aisha said.

Marta picked up another bead and shrugged. "Then don't." She slotted the bead and held the two ends of the bracelet together, and a clasp, and held them up to Aisha. Marta looked beyond Aisha and squealed. She jumped to her feet. "Gabi, Gabi."

Aisha gasped.

"Can you fix this for me?" Marta asked and held up the bracelet.

Gabi ruffled her hair and fixed the clasp. "There you go. And I've got something else for you."

The other children ran towards Gabi as she walked towards Aisha. They sat in a circle, all the children staring intently at Gabi.

An unease crept through Aisha's racing heart, making it thunder.

"I have a legitimate reason for being here," Gabi whispered.

"What's legitimate?" Marta asked.

Aisha laughed.

Gabi smiled and turned her attention to the children. "You gave me some jewellery to sell, right?"

The children nodded and their smiles broadened.

"Well, I have something for you." Gabi handed each child a five-hundred peseta note.

Aisha smiled at the peals of laughter and whispered expressions of disbelief as the children inspected their money. They would never have seen anything like it, and she was pretty sure it had been subsidised by Gabi's own purse. She loved her more for that.

The children stood, one after the other, led by Marta, and hugged Gabi.

"How about we get some drinks?" Gabi said.

Some children said yes, others were already in deep discussion about what they were going to do with the money. Gabi stood and walked at Aisha's side into the building.

Aisha shut the door behind them and leaned against it. She stroked Gabi's cheek. "I'm so sorry I hurt you," she said. She couldn't hold back the tears and trembled as she sobbed.

"Do you want to marry him?" Gabi asked.

Aisha shook her head even before Gabi had finished the question. "I told you I'm not going to marry any man."

"I just wanted to check, because—"

"Because he sprang it on me to control me. It's what happens, and I'm sorry he did that. He knows I'm not going to marry him. I've tried to talk to Mama, but she doesn't want to listen. I want to be with you."

Gabi kissed her.

"I have tried so many times to get to you since, but—"

Gabi pressed her finger to Aisha's lips and stopped her speaking. "It's okay. I didn't believe you wanted to marry him. I stropped for a while, because there was so much going on with you, with Nana, and Juan. I tried to get to you. I watched you with him in the field but couldn't face your mama. I saw you dancing on Saturday, but he was too close." She stroked Aisha's hair and cupped her cheek as she stared at her. "I love you. I've missed you."

Aisha leaned into Gabi, and Gabi wrapped her arms around her. Everything was perfect, and anything was possible. Why then did she have this unnerving feeling in her gut? "Where will we go? What will we do?"

Gabi held her tightly. The fast beat of Gabi's heart, her warmth against Aisha's cheek, and the woody scent of Gabi's perfume was like silk to her skin on a summer's day. Still, the unnerving feeling persisted.

"You know English elms come from England?" Gabi asked.

Aisha laughed. "I had guessed, yes."

"I think you'd like Devon, and the countryside, and the farm, though it's wet and cold. We could grow stuff."

Aisha eased back and pressed her finger to Gabi's lips. "I don't need things to be the same as here. I want them to be different."

Gabi smiled. "Good. I'm not the best gardener."

"I like the idea of going to England and seeing your home. And I want to travel the world with you. I want to sing, and dance, and sell jewellery. I want to help young children know that they have choices, that they can have ambition and achieve their dreams, and show them not to be afraid of what has gone before but to take it and become stronger because of it. But most of all, I want to be with you. Forever."

"And ever," Gabi said.

Aisha frowned. "I don't have a passport."

Gabi laughed. "We can stay in Spain until we get you one."

Aisha smiled. Gabi kissed her, and it was gentle, and soft, and sweet, and she felt the essence of what it meant to be alive return. She kissed Gabi back and wondered if the elms in England were as green as they were around the Alhambra. The somersaults in her stomach tossed around her fears and her wants, and she imagined it would be like that until they settled somewhere, until she was free of the hold her family had on her.

She thought of Old María, and Marta, and Nana, and the many others who she'd never known who had led her to this moment. Without them, and without Lorca's promise of love, words that she'd committed to her heart, she might not have the strength to walk away.

"We can't stay here," Aisha said.

Gabi held her. "I know."

Aisha nodded.

"What about your family?"

Aisha bit her lip. "I want to leave with their blessing, if I can."

Gabi lowered her head.

"I want them to know, so they don't worry about me."

Gabi kissed her forehead. "You can't know how they will respond until they do, I guess."

"Maybe we could stay here, if they were okay with it." Aisha didn't know why she'd said that. If she moved in with Gabi and Nana, if that were even possible, they wouldn't be able to wander around the city together. Aisha wouldn't be able to dance with the group.

"Is that what you want?"

Aisha lowered her head. "I want to be free."

"Then we can't stay here." Gabi pulled Aisha into her arms and hugged her.

"I love you," Aisha whispered.

"Is that enough?" Gabi asked.

Aisha eased out of the embrace and wiped her eyes. "Yes."

"I know how impossible this is for you."

Aisha found it hard to swallow. Her heart raced, and she went dizzy. "I'm scared," she said.

"I am too." She kissed Aisha. "I'm leaving Granada on Friday morning. I can't just be a friend to you. Do you understand? I want to be with you as a lover. I would marry you if we could."

Aisha wiped the tears from her cheeks. "Mama keeps stopping me from coming into town. It's as though she knows I'm trying to get to see you."

"I'll be at Matías's workshop tomorrow afternoon until five. If you can get there, then we can go to the apartment together."

Aisha nodded and kissed her. The workshop was close to home. She didn't know if the tears were of sadness, joy, or relief, or a combination of all three. The feeling of lightness that made her suddenly invincible was overwhelming. Whatever it took, she would be there tomorrow, and she would never return home.

27.

"WE CAN HELP YOU get the documentation you need for Aisha," Juan said.

Gabi nodded. "Thanks."

"The hotel is booked for three weeks," Nana said. "It's not the best in Màlaga because it's peak season, so it's a little further out of the main city—"

"It'll be perfect," Gabi said. Her hands trembled, and she rubbed them together.

They drank herbal tea, and Nana smiled. The tea didn't settle too well in Gabi's fizzing stomach. Gabi stared into her grandpa's eyes and saw her own in the shape and colour. She saw her dad's too, and the resemblance implied a connection that she felt in the warmth in her heart. His kindness and compassion softened the tension.

"If I had been able to, I would have left with Estrella," he said softly.

Nana held his hand. "I would have risked it," she said.

She listened to his story, time moving too slowly, and caught up on the years between Nana's leaving Spain and returning. How he'd married and had a family and how he'd always wondered about Nana. His wife had died some years ago. His daughter, Ana María, had left Spain to marry an American who had swept her off her feet. There was no lack of love in his expression as he talked, and he glowed with pride as he showed photos of his three grandchildren. The two teenage boys, one carrying a football, stood on one side of their father, and one younger girl, just out of nappies, held his hand on the other side. All wore the same broad smile and had the same straight white teeth. He'd not met them but had received a birthday card every year and a phone call from time to time. The man at Ana María's side wasn't like the men here. He was tall, and blond, and broad shouldered. Like his children, he looked happy.

"When is Aisha coming?" Juan asked.

His memory must be affected by the years because she'd told him twice already. "Before five."

"Good, good. And you have a taxi booked."

"Yes, tomorrow lunch time."

Nana had insisted they get a taxi rather than navigate the railway and bus systems. It was going to be quicker and only marginally more expensive. Gabi's stomach did a spin thinking about it all.

"I hope you'll come back," he said. "Aisha's family are old fashioned, and I'm ashamed to say homosexuality isn't tolerated within the Gypsy community. We like to think we are above all that when we are not. But things will change."

Gabi scratched her palm with her thumb.

Juan smiled. "I am happy for you, Gabi. Aisha has a beautiful soul, and the love you share will get you through anything." He smiled at Nana.

She left them together and walked across the road to Matías's workshop. He was bent over something he was polishing. He slid it to one side and wiped his hands on a cloth.

"I'm glad you came back," he said and smiled.

"Hi, uncle?" she said.

He laughed. "Yes, it seems so."

"Secrets, eh?"

"They are big currency here." He stood and offered her the seat at the table. "What will you make?" he asked.

"I don't know." She turned and stared at him. "Can I ask you a question?"

He blushed.

"You don't have to answer it, if it's too personal."

He nodded.

"Your sister has a family, but you've got no pictures of them in your house. You've just got one of her. Why?"

He lifted his chin and pinched his lips together. "We fell out when she said she was leaving here, and we have never spoken since." He cleared his throat. "I was young and arrogant, and I told her she was making a mistake. She was older than me, but I was fiercely protective of her. I felt responsible for her, but she left with Papa's blessing, and for a long while, I didn't understand why he would give her up so easily."

He stared at her silently for a while, longer than was comfortable, and she imagined a debate going on in his head. "But you do now?"

He inhaled and released the air through his nose. His cheek twitched. "I fell in love," he said. He smiled and stood taller. "That changed how I saw things."

Gabi frowned. "You didn't marry?"

He shook his head. "Like Aisha, that option isn't available to me."

Gabi couldn't think of the right thing to say. She blew out a puff of air and shook her head. How many lives had been destroyed by these laws?

"I didn't have the courage to leave."

"Do you wish you had?"

252

"Sometimes, yes."

"That's shit."

"Sometimes, yes." He laughed. "It was a long time ago. I chose to stay. He decided to leave."

"He was Gitano?"

Matías smiled. "I knew if I left here, I would never be able to return even though Papa gave us his blessing. I didn't have Ana María's spirit. I didn't trust that his love for me would last a lifetime. And I enjoyed the security of this community. Maybe I am weak."

Gabi widened her eyes. "That's not weak, Matías. It's a sacrifice. There's a difference. The Gitano way is formidable, and the people so protective of your laws. I'm not sure I would have been able to leave."

He stepped towards her, opened his arms, and they hugged.

"Aisha and I are leaving," she said.

He nodded. "I knew it would come to this. Aisha is stronger than us both," he said.

Gabi smiled. "It's a lot to give up, isn't it?"

"It was too much for me."

Gabi didn't feel as certain as she would have liked that Aisha was strong enough to walk away from her family. Nothing would be settled until five o'clock came, and they were heading to the apartment.

"When are you leaving?"

"Tomorrow. She's coming here this afternoon."

He shook his head. "I'm sad. I have enjoyed your company."

Gabi turned away as heat crept through her. She looked towards the door, thinking of Nana and Juan. "I don't want Nana to be blamed."

"There is wisdom in parts here, Gabi, thank God. Sadly, Aisha's family are very traditional, and that wisdom doesn't extend to our way of life." He pursed his lips and dipped his head. "I imagine there will be a few years of pain until the rumblings die down but eventually, they will. The situation for Estrella and Papa is easier. They will be fine."

Gabi hoped he was right. "Maybe you can come and see us," she said.

Matías laughed. "Maybe." He picked up one of the spiral necklaces that Gabi had made and handed it to her. "Wherever you find yourself, I hope you will make jewellery like this."

She smiled as she recalled the number of times she'd cursed while learning to make the spirals. Linking two of them together had been even more of a challenge, but the result had been worth it. The necklace had a snake-like appearance with the silver coiled around a black leather lace chain. "You didn't sell it?"

"I could have sold it a thousand times over."

"A thousand times over, and we'd be rich."

"True, but I think it would make a wonderful gift for someone special, don't you?"

Gabi's heart expanded, and her hand trembled as she held the delicate piece in her palm. "We could still work together," she said. "I'll set up a business and sell your jewellery."

He held out his hand, and she took it. "That's a deal."

She kissed his cheek. "Thanks, uncle."

He laughed. "You are welcome, niece. It's been great meeting you." He stared at her and sighed. "You must create, Gabi. It's who you are. Promise me that much."

Gabi nodded.

"Now, I have to head into town. Supplier meetings until late this evening." He started towards the door. "I would like to take you tomorrow. Wherever you want to go."

Gabi frowned.

He shrugged. "It would feel good to help you, unless—"

"I'd like that," Gabi said and hugged him.

He nodded. "I'll come by the apartment. What time?"

"Midday."

He nodded.

She sat at the table, and his words of encouragement for her craft settled inside her like they'd always meant to be there. She picked up a piece of metal and worked it slowly, easing the shape from abstract to concrete. An imperial eagle, native to the region, started to evolve. Its strong wings spread wide, and its small sharp beak curved downwards. It was a symbol of power. It would be her gift to him.

28.

As AISHA HAD SAID goodbye to Marta at the school, she'd wondered if Marta had sensed she wasn't coming back. Marta had clung to her and squeezed her tightly, and the spark in her eyes had dimmed as her smile faded. Aisha hoped one day that Marta would find her way out of this place and vowed to help her in some way. Leaving those she loved without being able to say goodbye had to be the worst feeling in the world.

The twisting in her gut had stayed with her as she'd made her way on from the school to the dress fitting with the other women from the village. She'd followed her mama's instructions to the letter. As she'd sat and listened to them, she studied them all, the elders with their opinions, her mama controlling everything, and Conchita, who looked at her differently now. She'd smiled at the appropriate times while feeling strangled by the whole affair. She hadn't challenged their hideous choices for her sister and politely agreed with everything they'd suggested to the point that the air had become thick with an unbearable tension and silence that cut sharper than the scissors they'd used to shape the cloth. She hadn't cared for their thoughts, their judgements, or their criticisms. They couldn't hurt her anymore because in her mind, she'd already left.

But then she'd woken this morning with her stomach in knots, and when she'd climbed out of bed, her heart raced, and she felt nauseous.

It raced now as she tried to act normally, but she picked at her breakfast and couldn't give any attention to the conversation between Mama and Conchita. She took the basket of fresh vegetables and bread and headed up the hill to Señor Perez's house. She enjoyed the sun on her back and pondered where she and Gabi would be by tomorrow evening, how the scenery would have changed, and how sandy the beach would be. What would they eat for lunch? And what would it feel like to sleep in a hotel bed with Gabi? Something didn't feel right, and she couldn't put her finger on it.

It had been a fleeting visit because the old man snatched the basket from her, mumbled his thanks, gave her an empty basket in return, and shut the door quickly and firmly in her face. "Have a nice day," she'd said and taken a leisurely stroll back down the hill.

Overwhelmed by a combination of excitement and loss as she made her way home, she didn't know what it was that made her legs weak and her head light. She sat on a boulder at the side of the path and took in the hills. This beautiful landscape that made her heart ache and caused her to hesitate now had planted its seed of doubt a long time ago. She had nurtured the land and breathed in its offer of clear, clean air in return for her toil. This place had been her guide and had listened patiently to her dreams and her woes, and she would miss the whisper of the wind, and the promises of the fertile earth that directed her now to Old María's house from a sense of camaraderie in spirit, possibly.

Old María welcomed her in and closed the door quickly behind them. She stared with wide eyes, though it wasn't clear at what. "Is Franco still in power?" she asked.

Aisha wondered when the old woman had lost track of time. If she thought Franco was in power, she must live in fear of persecution. She clasped her hand to the ache in her chest. "No, María."

The old woman peeked through the small grubby window to the outside. "Fuck the Guardia," she said.

Aisha cleared a thick layer of dust from the kitchen surface and made them mint tea.

Old María handed her a black and white photograph torn in half down the middle, the image faded. The woman in the picture had a serious expression and a piercing stare. "Did Carmen get out? Did you see her? Please tell me she is well?"

"Yes," Aisha said. Carmen must have been Old María's lover.

The old woman made the sign of a cross at her chest. "Thank God." She settled in the chair and wiped her eyes. "I should have tried harder, but my leg was so bad, I couldn't keep up with her."

Aisha shuddered at the chill as she imagined María's suffering and the years she had lived without the woman she loved. "She said to say she loves you very much."

Old María nodded. "Are the guards still here?"

"No, they've retreated back to the city."

"Did Carmen get away?"

Aisha held María's bony hand. "She did. She's safe. She's going to write."

"Can't read," María said. "She's the smart one."

"Would you like me to get a letter to her?"

María looked up and a sparkle shone through the glassy surface of her eyes. "Can you? Is it safe?"

Aisha wondered if she was raising false hopes but with the state of the old woman's mind, it was more likely that she would forget the conversation before morning. "Yes. I can," she said.

"Do what?" Old María asked. She got up and went to the window. "Did Carmen get out?"

She sat back down, and they drank tea, and then, like the sun slipping over the horizon and easing in the night, she closed her eyes. The corners of her mouth turned down, and her cheeks sagged. Aisha studied her closely to check she was still breathing and crept out the door with a heavy heart.

She smiled at her mama as she put the empty basket on the table. "Let me help," she said and started cutting vegetables for the soup they would eat for lunch.

"It's good to see you happy," Mama said.

"I am happy." She stared into Mama's eyes, and guilt pricked her conscience. She wanted to tell her that she was in love and walk away with her blessing.

She could leave a note, but Aisha knew what it felt like to not be able to share grief openly. If she told them, they could cry together, appreciate each other's loss, and she could leave knowing she had done her best by them. "I want to talk to you about something," she said.

Her mama narrowed her eyes. "You're not going to give me bad news now, are you? Just because I've said you look happy." She laughed.

Aisha bit back the words. Now wasn't the right time. She vowed to say them before she left but not before lunch. "I thought I'd go and see Matías this afternoon. He said he'd like to make my wedding rings."

259

Mama stirred the pot. "Not this afternoon, Aisha. We are going to the city. I told you at breakfast, but I think you were too dreamy to hear."

Aisha froze. "No. I can't."

Mama jolted and glared at her.

"Sorry, I didn't mean to shout. I was just excited to go and talk to him."

"Maybe you can go when we get back, but there's a lot to do. Conchita is coming with us. She wants you to help her choose the flowers for her wedding. We have an appointment with the florist at two, and we need to get cloth for the bridesmaids' dresses."

Aisha's heart thundered, and the words descended on a spiralling loop of despair to her stomach. This couldn't be happening. She couldn't think straight. She should tell Mama she was gay and leave now. "I need to—"

"How was Señor Perez?" Mama asked.

"Alive," Aisha said.

Mama laughed. "Grumpy today, no doubt. He always complains on a Wednesday."

"Mama, I need to talk to you."

"Not now, Aisha, please. I need to concentrate on lunch, and then we must get the bus into town. Now, go and find your sister. She's in the field. We'll talk later."

Lunch had been hard to swallow, and the journey into town on the bus had taken forever. Aisha had stared out the window as they'd passed Matías's workshop hoping for a glimpse of Matías or Gabi, though what good would that do if she couldn't get a message to Gabi? The ache in her heart deepened as she caught sight of the closed workshop door and the absence of

260

Matías's van. Conchita's voice grated on her nerves. She wanted to scream but clenched her jaw instead.

The florist greeted them, orbited by pollen that moved in sync with her movements. She had a red nose and carried a handkerchief in her hand. "Come through," she said and sniffed into the handkerchief.

Aisha trailed her mama and sister into a darker, cooler room, and inhaled the sweet smell of freesias. Buckets of flowers were scattered around the space, purple asters, deep chocolate cosmos, sunflowers, blue thistles, and white dahlias. The soft, cream-coloured anemone with its dark centre caught her eye. Majestic in its elegance, it was perfect for a wedding.

"Please sit. I will arrange for tea. There are magazines if you'd like to start looking through them. Flowers are listed by availability throughout the year, and there are pictures in case you're not familiar with them. Yours is a September wedding?"

She looked towards Aisha, and Aisha shook her head and pointed at Conchita.

"A perfect time for many flowers. Now, about that tea." She left the room.

Conchita picked up a magazine and started leafing through it. "What colours do you think?"

"Everything goes with white," Aisha said.

Mama smiled. "Some colours go better than others, even with white, Aisha."

"What's your favourite colour?" Aisha asked.

"Orange or yellow."

"Chrysanthemums, sunflowers, yarrow. Freesias smell wonderful."

"But García prefers blue."

Aisha closed her eyes. This was going to take forever. "Thistles come in blue." Fitting she thought. "Asters too."

It was just gone half past two when the woman returned. "Do we have any ideas?" she asked.

"It's very confusing," Conchita said.

Aisha shook her head. What she was going through was confusing. Choosing a few flowers for a wedding couldn't get any easier. "Go with a mix of orange, yellow, and blue."

"It needs to match the table of course," the woman said.

"We have gold for the table."

The flower woman smiled, though her nose twitched. Aisha would never have chosen gold for the table either. It was too heavy, along with the meringue style dress and heavy lace veil that they'd chosen for Conchita.

Three o'clock came and went, and tension crept into her shoulders. She needed to get the bus by half past four to get to the workshop for five, and they still had the dress material to buy. "What do you think, Conchita? Freesias are sweet smelling, and you could have a colourful display for the table along with thistles for height and asters or cosmos to add deeper colour. They would make great buttonholes and a lovely bouquet for you."

"I don't know. Mama, what do you think?"

"I think dahlias and chrysanthemums would complement the table perfectly."

Aisha stood. She needed a break from the excruciating pain of sitting and of a conversation going nowhere when she should be going somewhere. "Is there a toilet I could use, please?"

"Of course." The woman pointed. "I'll go and make more tea," she said.

Aisha breathed deeply. They were never going to make it back for five, and while she'd been slowly stewing, it had dawned on her that her mama had planned to keep her away from the workshop today, knowing Gabi worked there on Wednesday afternoons. She returned to the back room of the shop.

"I need to go," Conchita said and headed to the toilet.

"I need to talk to you," Aisha said to Mama.

"Aisha, not n—"

"Yes, now. Mama—"

"Aisha, no—"

"Yes." She turned away to not look at her mama's pathetic flailing objection. "I'm in love with Gabi, and nothing you do or say is going to change that." She turned back.

Mama stared wide-eyed and grew paler as she gasped and gasped some more. She had her hand at her throat. She looked as if she were trying to say something but struggled with her words. She grabbed at her stomach and bent over, groaning, and sweat beaded on her forehead.

A moment of confusion gave way to panic. This wasn't an objection. There was something wrong, something bad happening to Mama. Mama slumped forward and fell to the floor.

"Mama. Please. Mama, forgive me." Aisha ran to her. Her eyes were closed, and she had stopped breathing. Aisha ran through to the front of the shop and told the woman to call for an ambulance. She ran back as Conchita returned from the toilet. Conchita screamed, and Aisha slapped her across the face. "Get some water," she said.

She felt for a pulse and found none. She started compressions on her mama's chest. "Come on, Mama, please." She pounded hard and fast, counted, and watched for a breath.

Conchita returned with the water.

"Now, sit and drink it," she said, "And keep calm. I think she's had a heart attack."

Conchita started to whimper. The woman from the shop came through, gasped, and put her hand to her mouth.

"Did you call the ambulance?" Aisha asked.

"Yes, yes. Oh, my dear. What has happened?"

"She collapsed suddenly."

"You shouted at her," Conchita said.

"I didn't shout at her."

"I heard you. I heard what you said. You're selfish and cruel."

Aisha pumped her mama's chest, the burning in her own biting at the back of her throat and down her arms. "Come on, Mama."

"Like you care," Conchita said.

"If I didn't care, I would have left here years ago. Grow up."

Conchita started sobbing, and the woman left and returned with a box of tissues.

The sirens came, and Aisha willed them closer. She closed her eyes and counted to keep her focused, to keep her going through the pain that gripped her arms. She heard voices, and someone pulling her off her mama. Her initial resistance weakened as she became aware of the medical services. She moved away and sat with her back to the wall. Someone covered her in a blanket, and she realised she was trembling and cold. Tears streamed down her cheeks as the men attending her mama attached wires and fired shocks through her mama's limp body, before they carried her away on a stretcher.

"San Juan De Dios Hospital," the florist said.

Conchita and Aisha followed in a taxi. Aisha couldn't look at her sister.

"I'm sorry I said those things," Conchita said.

"I'm tired," Aisha said.

They travelled in silence and waited in the hospital waiting room in silence. Six o'clock came and went, and then seven o'clock, and Aisha's heart ached for Gabi. Exhaustion slowed her mind. Knowing she couldn't leave the hospital until she had confirmation that mama was going to be okay numbed her emotions. "Go home, Conchita. You need to tell Papa what's happened. I'll stay here until we find out more."

29.

Gabi's sense of déjà vu kicked in at five thirty, and she walked up to Aisha's house to find the front door closed. She didn't linger in case Nicolás or Aisha's papa saw her. She wandered back to the workshop confused and sat crossed legged against the wall that bordered the road facing Matías's house.

Had Aisha told her parents? Had she changed her mind?

She didn't know which was scarier.

Gabi hadn't had to tell her dad, because he was never at home long enough for it to make a difference. Nana had known, probably before Gabi had worked out her own body, and had broken the news to him. Nana had hugged her and confirmed Gabi's thoughts. Love wasn't defined by rules, it was a gift of the heart, and Gabi was free to love who she wanted to love. Nana had also said that not every girl wanted to be kissed and that next time, Gabi should ask before acting on her feelings. She couldn't imagine having to have that coming out conversation now, and with parents whose attitudes were a hundred times worse than her dad's had been. Aisha didn't have anyone to support her. She hadn't had anyone to talk to her whole life.

She sighed and looked up and down the road, feeling Aisha's pain acutely. She wouldn't blame her if she had changed her mind. Buses passed every half hour, and the people inside stared at her as if she were something out of a freak show. She must have looked it, slumped against a wall crying. She closed her eyes to lose track of time. She would wait for as long as it took, until the morning if she had to.

Seven thirty came and went. At around eight, she stood and strolled a few paces to unstiffen her legs and back, and she massaged her numb bum. Maybe she had to face the fact that Aisha wasn't coming. She wandered back to her house but stayed twenty feet away. Light filtered through the small window, but the door remained shut. Should she knock just in case Aisha had told them and they'd done something to her? She quashed the ridiculous thought, though part of her wouldn't put it past them. The door opened, and Aisha's papa came out of the house. He looked hurried and was heading straight towards her. She ducked for cover, and he walked straight past.

Gabi peered out to see Conchita in the doorway. She could speak to Conchita, couldn't she? She waited until Aisha's papa was out of view and ran. "Conchita."

Conchita backed into the house.

"Please, Conchita. Where's Aisha?"

Conchita shook her head, keeping the door between her and Gabi.

"Please. Just tell me she's safe."

Conchita nodded.

"Look. I'm not going to hurt her, or you, or anyone."

Conchita shook her head.

Gabi tried to see inside the house.

Conchita inched the door further closed. "She's not here," Conchita said.

"Please, where is she? I'm leaving and want to say goodbye."

"San Juan De Dios hospital," she said and closed the door.

Gabi's heart thundered, and her stomach churned. She ran, knowing it would be almost another thirty minutes before a bus was headed into the city.

Her lungs felt like they were going to explode. She slowed to a fast walk and stuck out her thumb to three vehicles that passed. The bus sailed past her heading up the hill, but it would still be a while for it to come down. Hopefully it would stop, though she couldn't see a stop sign anywhere.

She looked towards the beeping horn and saw a blue van heading towards her. Matías. What a sight for sore eyes.

He pulled the car over and leaned out of the window. "What are you doing still here?"

Gabi ran around to the passenger side and got in the car. "Aisha's been taken to hospital," she said. "San Juan." Before she'd finished the sentence, he'd turned the van around and was heading down the hill.

"What happened?"

"I don't know. I was waiting, and she didn't show up.

He put his foot down, only slowing for the tightest bends and once they hit the city traffic. "Do you want me to wait for you?" he asked, pulling up outside the hospital.

"No, it's okay. I don't know how long this will take."

Gabi headed towards the hospital main entrance and stopped at the sound of her name being called. "Aisha." She ran to a bench seat in a small recreation area outside the hospital. Tears streaked Aisha's face, and her eyes looked puffy and sore. Gabi sat next to her and put her arm around her shoulders. "Thank God. I was so worried it was you."

"She had a heart attack. It's all my fault." Aisha sobbed.

Gabi stroked her hair and kissed her head. Aisha pulled away and looked around. "It's not your fault," Gabi said and clasped her hands in her lap.

Aisha shook her head. "I told her I was in love with you, and she collapsed."

Gabi took a deep breath and released it slowly. Her hands trembled. "What have the doctors said?"

"She's sedated, and they're doing tests. She keeps drifting in and out of sleep." Aisha started crying and shaking her head. "Papa's with her. They told me to go. They want nothing to do with me."

Gabi screamed silently, clenched her fists, and gritted her teeth. The cruelty was beyond her understanding. She put her arm around Aisha and drew her close. "I'm so sorry."

"All I asked for was their blessing, and they couldn't give it to me." Aisha tensed in Gabi's arms but didn't pull back. "Is that too much to ask for from your parents?"

Her raised voice caused people passing to look at them. Gabi knew Aisha needed to let the anger out, to let go, to be able to move on. She held her tightly as she shouted and sobbed.

"Why, Gabi? Why? I don't understand. What did I do that was so wrong?"

"You didn't do anything wrong. You're just unlucky to be born into a family whose faith and laws have devastating consequences. For them, for you, for everyone. No one wins."

"That's not love, is it?"

"No. It's abuse. Not that they would see it that way. Love comes from the heart, not rules."

Aisha stared at Gabi. "What we have is love, isn't it?"

Gabi held Aisha and kissed her head. "Yes. I will love you forever."

Aisha leaned into Gabi's shoulder.

Gabi glanced around. "I went to your house. Conchita told me you were here."

"How was she?"

"Frosty."

"I'm sorry."

Gabi shrugged. "I wasn't expecting anything else." They sat quietly for a while. "Are you okay?" Gabi asked. It was a dumb question, but what else could she say? She stroked Aisha's face and stared into her bloodshot eyes and wished more than anything she could take away the pain.

"I will be," Aisha said.

"Shall we go?"

Aisha nodded and they hired a taxi from the ones waiting in the rank outside the hospital.

"Do you want to pick up your things?" Gabi asked.

Aisha shook her head. "I never want to go back. I don't want to be reminded of them. I want to forget they exist."

Gabi appreciated the sentiment, but Aisha wasn't thinking clearly and once the heat of emotion had subsided, she would be left with regrets. Gabi didn't want that for Aisha, or for them. "Aisha."

Aisha stared out of the window.

"Aisha."

"What?"

"I know you're angry and hurt, but you won't always feel that way. You love them, and that's not going to change."

Aisha stared at Gabi with a blank expression that Gabi had never seen before. "I don't care if she dies," she said.

Gabi didn't believe she meant it. They travelled to Gabi's in silence. Aisha needed time to think things through before they left Granada. She had to know that her mama was okay, or if not, that she had the opportunity to pay her last respects. She might not realise it right now, but Gabi did. And she wouldn't let them leave until Aisha had calmed down.

Gabi tucked her up in bed and went to the living room. She explained everything to Nana over a large vodka Coke.

"I need another sherry, Gabriela," Nana said and topped up her glass. "I can't believe that Pilar would do this. If I was twenty years younger, I'd knock some sense into the woman."

Gabi shook her head. "It's cruel and heartless."

They stared towards the river. Reds and pinks rose from behind the hills and cast a lighter hue across the opposing landscape. It was as if someone had dusted the treetops with pink candyfloss. Gabi handed over the rectangular box she'd wrapped in fine silver paper and a red bow.

Nana smiled. "What is this?"

"Open it. I made it, and I'd like you to have it."

Nana carefully unwrapped the gift and opened the box. She lifted the spiral necklace and stared at it. "It's the most beautiful thing I've ever seen, Gabriela." She looked up, her eyes glassy, and her lip trembling. She placed the jewellery carefully back in the box.

"I'll miss you," Gabi said.

Nana cleared her throat and took a sip of her third sherry. "I'll miss you," she said.

Gabi bit her lip and wiped her eyes. Nana took her hand and held it. The warmth brought the tears on in floods.

"Everything will be fine, Gabriela."

"I'm scared."

"Cariño, you're ready for this. You've found someone who makes your heart sing. Isn't it wonderful?"

Gabi nodded.

"I'm a little scared to not have you here, but you're not my nursemaid, and you have such a rich life ahead of you. It's time to do something special and being a little anxious is normal."

"I hope so."

"Trust me."

Gabi did. She excused herself after her second drink and went to the bedroom. She undressed, got into the bed, and spooned around Aisha. She murmured, and Gabi held her tightly. It wasn't the way she'd planned for them to spend their first night together, but it was even more special and intimate for the sadness and suffering Aisha had endured. Gabi couldn't love her enough, and she fell asleep, not wanting to let her go.

30.

GABI LED AISHA INTO the hotel room, pulled her into her arms, and kissed her. "Are you okay?" she asked for what felt like the hundredth time in the two hours it had taken them to get to Màlaga.

Aisha ran her fingers through Gabi's hair. "I'm fine." Her smile broadened. "Thank you for making me stay until Mama was discharged."

"I'm glad we waited." Gabi had enjoyed spending a few extra days with Nana too. It had made leaving a fraction easier, though they'd all shed a tear as Matías drove them away. She wrapped her arms around Aisha's waist and tugged her closer. "As long as you're good. That's all that matters to me."

Aisha kissed Gabi on the nose. She eased out of Gabi's hold and walked around the room. She gazed out the window that overlooked the golf course. "This is amazing."

Gabi picked up the mobile phone she'd bought just before leaving Granada and called Nana. Aisha came to her and kissed her.

"Gabriela," Nana said.

Gabi eased out of the kiss. "How did you know it was me?"

"No one else has my number."

Gabi laughed. "We arrived safely." She took Aisha's hand and squeezed it.

"Is Matías on his way back?"

"Yes."

"Good. Tell him to drive safely."

"He's already left."

"Ah, yes. Of course."

Gabi tugged Aisha to her, and they listened together. "So, what are you up to?"

"Juan and I are going for lunch with Pablo."

"Sounds fun."

"It will be. His pomegranates are huge this season, and you should see his mangos."

"I think I'll stick to peaches," Gabi said, and Aisha giggled.

"Well, they're absolutely delicious. Make a fine punch too. We're going to pick some this afternoon. It's too early for peaches, Gabriela."

Gabi was distracted by the warmth of Aisha's kisses to her ear and down her neck. "Gotta go, Nana. I'll call soon."

"Well, I might not be in. I've got a full schedule for the next two weeks."

Gabi cleared her throat as a surge of desire shot through to her core. "And we've got some exploring to do."

"Make sure you put on sun lotion when you're out."

Gabi laughed. She ended the call and kissed Aisha. "What were you thinking?"

"About peaches or exploring?"

Gabi raised her eyebrows. "Exploring." She unbuttoned Aisha's blouse and kissed the top of her breasts. "These are my favourite peaches," she said.

The knock at the door made Aisha jump. Gabi kissed her and went to answer it. The concierge grinned at her as she took in the trolley, an ice bucket, and a selection of tapas.

"We didn't order anything."

"This is with the compliments of the man who dropped you off. He also asked that we give you these." He handed over two small boxes and an envelope.

Gabi took the gifts as he wheeled the trolley in.

"Would you like me to open the champagne, Miss Sánchez?"

Gabi looked at Aisha and Aisha nodded. Gabi tipped him and after the door shut, she laid the boxes and the envelope on the bed. She poured two flutes of champagne and handed one to Aisha.

"It's from Matías," Aisha said. "Read it to me."

Aisha opened one of the boxes and stared at the contents.

Gabi opened the envelope and started to read aloud.

Dear Aisha,

I took the liberty of making your rings, as I promised I would. It was an honour. I hope you both like them. I hope you will wear them after sharing vows in the eyes of God, at some point in time when we are treated as equals, but until then, please put them on and celebrate the love you have for each other every day. You are braver than I was or ever could be. Look after my niece, and make sure she continues to make beautiful jewellery. I will keep an eye on your mama and Estrella. Go and be free.

Matías.

P.S. Tell Gabi, I could have sold the eagle a thousand times over.

Gabi smiled.

275

Aisha opened the second box and set the rings on the bed next to each other. She looked at Gabi. "Will you wear a ring for me?"

Gabi nodded.

Aisha held Gabi's hand and slipped a ring onto her wedding ring finger. "This is a token of my love," she said and kissed her.

Gabi took the other ring and put it on Aisha's wedding ring finger. "I now consider us wife and wife."

Aisha laughed, and Gabi kissed her.

"At least until we get the chance to marry for real."

Aisha nodded. They undressed and sipped champagne.

"I've never made love in a hotel before," Aisha said.

"I know," Gabi said. Aisha stroked the length of Gabi's arm. Gabi inhaled sharply. "I haven't either," she said.

"Really?" Aisha ran her finger down the centre line of Gabi's naked body.

Gabi gasped. "Odd as it might seem, no. You will be my first."

"You're so sexy," Aisha said and moved closer.

Gabi held her tight and inhaled her scent.

"I'm glad you were my first," Aisha whispered.

"And only," Gabi said. "Now we're married."

Aisha bit her ear lobe.

Gabi felt the hair between Aisha's legs, the moistness, and Aisha bit down harder on her lobe. "Feisty, eh?" Gabi whispered hoarsely.

Aisha moved back and stared at Gabi with such intensity, it left her breathless.

"Play nice," Gabi said. "You can't look at me like that without it having a very strange effect on me."

Aisha narrowed her eyes and drew her lip between her teeth. She ran her fingers through Gabi's hair and inhaled deeply. "I don't even know what that means," she said and took Gabi's nipple into her mouth.

Gabi groaned and bucked at the surge of heat that shot through her. Aisha slipped her hand between Gabi's legs, and strength and firmness gave way to softness and tenderness. The fiery sensations that ebbed and flowed between her nipple and her clit were so delicious, it rendered her speechless.

Aisha tumbled her backwards onto the bed and straddled her. Gabi tasted a hint of the sea on her lips. Aisha touched her warm skin, and ripples of ecstasy coursed through her as Aisha entered her.

"I love this feeling." Aisha gasped.

She took Gabi's nipple into her mouth as she made love to her. The thrusts, slow at first, then faster, touched deep inside Gabi. The pressure that her clit ached for came and went, and she craved the feeling again. She pulled Aisha up to her and kissed her hard on the mouth.

Every time Aisha kissed Gabi, moving down her body, Gabi felt it ripple through her core. As Aisha licked her clit, she thought she would explode. Aisha kept kissing her, teasing with her the lightest pressure, driving her wild. She wanted Aisha's sex at her mouth. "Turn around so I can touch you." Aisha moved so they were head to toe.

Gabi held Aisha's waist and closed her mouth around Aisha's clit. She slid her tongue between Aisha's folds and entered her. The silk against her tongue and lips was warm and intoxicating, and she massaged Aisha's clit with her thumb as she explored inside her until Aisha started to tremble.

Gabi stopped kissing her and slipped her fingers inside Aisha. She moved with an easy rhythm that Aisha mirrored with the roll of her hips. Aisha groaned. She felt so good inside, so soft, as she surrendered to Gabi's touch.

Small flashes of electric energy in Gabi's core stole her breath away, and she tensed. The thrusts inside her came faster, and the intensity rose too quickly for her to slow Aisha down. She too surrendered and cried out.

Gabi held Aisha's hips and thrust deeper inside her. Aisha groaned and shook, then fell away and lay on the bed for a few moments, her body quaking.

She laughed and kissed Gabi. "That was awesome."

Gabi kissed her gently and smiled. "Champagne and tapas?"

Aisha raised her eyebrows. "I know what I'd like to do," she said.

Gabi's sex ached in anticipation of what was coming next. "We have all the time in the world," she said.

"And I want to do it now," Aisha said. She got off the bed and returned with the bottle of champagne and their flutes.

"You're going to soak the bed," Gabi said as Aisha tipped a little from her glass onto Gabi's stomach. Aisha licked it off, and Gabi felt the rush of desire.

"I'll be careful." She grinned, took a sip, and lowered herself to Gabi's sex.

"Holy shit." A fizzing sensation created a tingling heat, and she shook uncontrollably and then almost as quickly, became motionless. "Fuck me," she whispered and collapsed back onto the mattress.

"Any time," Aisha said and took another sip of champagne.

Epilogue

Granada, Spain, March 2014.

There were two things they needed to do. Then they could relax for the evening and reminisce a little. Number one, go to the cemetery, and number two, collect Nana's ashes. In that order specifically because Nana didn't want her final place of rest to be the cemetery. She wanted her ashes spread at the base of the small pomegranate tree that had been planted almost twenty years ago next to Matías's workshop. It was where her grandpa's ashes had been scattered just four months earlier, and Matias's too, five years before his father's. They'd missed Nana's funeral because they'd been trekking in the outback in Australia and without a phone signal. Once Gabi had got over the initial sadness, she had managed a wry smile. Nana had probably planned it that way to save Gabi the pain of having to deal with everything. Gabi's dad had done that. He'd been there for Nana when Juan, his true father, had died too. She was glad Nana had found the right time to tell him. She'd been very clear about what was to be done with her ashes, and Gabi wasn't going to let her down at this final hurdle.

Gabi turned the key in the apartment door and was met with the sweet aroma of rose and orange blossom. The vase on the table was empty of water, and the yellow heads that hadn't fallen bowed towards the sunlight. She wondered if Pablo still lived in the big house up the road with the pomegranate orchard and the sweetest oranges in Granada. Probably not. He'd been at least five years older than Nana.

Gabi picked up the vase and took it through to the kitchen. She wandered through to Nana's bedroom. The fuchsia pink dress and matching hat that she'd worn when they travelled here almost twenty years ago hung in her wardrobe, alongside the black dresses that were the custom here. The bed was perfectly made, as if Nana had never slept in it. The butterfly brooch and her favourite heart shaped locket were laid out on the dressing table. It was probably the only time she'd taken that locket off, the night she'd gone to sleep and not woken.

Gabi picked it up and turned it in her hand. She prised it open and smiled at the small chunk of gold, no bigger than a few grains of rice stuck together. Juan had struck gold, and Nana had struck gold in the end too.

Aisha put her arms around Gabi's waist and hugged her. "Are you okay?"

Gabi showed Aisha the nugget inside the locket. "I'm fine. She was happy here."

"Do you think people can die of a broken heart?"

She stroked Aisha's cheek. "I know I could."

Aisha kissed her.

"I want to take flowers," Gabi said.

"We can pick some up at the market."

The market stalls Gabi remembered had changed owners. The old man's rug stall had been replaced by a bohemian-style pottery display. Matías's jewellery stall had been replaced by another. She bought a bunch of pink carnations, red roses, and white lilies, and they made their way, hand in hand, to the cemetery.

It looked bigger, probably because it housed more people now. There were new names on the wall with the little boxes that held the ashes, and the statue that had been in a decrepit state all those years ago hadn't been restored.

She stopped at the Flores family plot and stared at her nana's full name, Estrella Sánchez Flores, engraved beneath the names and dates that marked her parents' short lives. Aisha squeezed Gabi's hand. Gabi laid the flowers down. "She had a long life. A good life."

Aisha wiped tears from her cheek and Gabi drew her closer. "It's still sad."

"Loss always is."

They walked back to the apartment with the urn and sat it on the table on the balcony overlooking the river and out to the Sacromonte hills. She hoped Nana could see them.

Aisha handed her a glass of Rioja, and they made a toast. Aisha looked towards the hills, and Gabi noticed the tremble in her hand as she sipped her drink. She put her arm around her waist and held her close.

"Are you ready to go back there?"

Aisha sighed. "If I don't go now, I never will."

The caves looked the same, a change of door colour here and there, and Matiás's workshop in the field opposite had been well maintained. Gabi felt his warmth and kindness, and Aisha turned her wedding ring with her thumb as they stared at the pomegranate tree.

Gabi poured Nana's ashes around the root and stared at them. Tears filled her eyes and burst onto her cheeks. "I swore I wasn't going to cry," she said.

Aisha wiped her eyes. "It's impossible not to cry with so much love here."

They sniffled together, holding hands, and the sniffles turned to a chuckle, and the chuckle to laughter. Gabi didn't have a clue what she was laughing about, but it was good to laugh here. She took a deep breath. "Are you ready?"

Aisha gazed towards her parents' house. Nana had kept them informed. Her papa had long since died, and her sister had three children and a baby grandchild.

"Yes," she said.

The front door to her mama's house was open, and Aisha glanced across the field. Her mama was picking the crops, her back bent low, her movements a snail's pace. Aisha pressed her hand to her chest.

"I'm right here," Gabi whispered. "If you want to leave, we can."

Aisha shook her head. "It's the right time."

Aisha frowned at the woman who walked towards them with a toddler holding her hand, and then she smiled. Conchita stopped walking and held her hand to her mouth. Gabi felt Aisha's hesitation, and her heart thundered. Conchita let go of the child's hand, ran towards them, and threw herself into Aisha's arms.

Gabi blew out a long breath.

"It's you, it's you," Conchita said.

Conchita's noise alerted Aisha's mama, who looked up and started towards them. The child cried.

"I can't believe it's really you," Conchita said, her eyes wet with tears.

Aisha wiped the tears from her own cheeks.

"Mi amor, Aisha. You came back." Pilar held Aisha's shoulders and looked her up and down. She looked towards Gabi and smiled. "You are welcome to my house."

"Gracias, Pilar," Gabi said. The pride she felt at Aisha's courage spread warmth inside her chest, and she released a long slow breath of relief.

She looked to the hills and across the field to the feed shed, reminded of the night when Aisha had asked her to run away, all that had happened in between, and how much they had missed. There was so much to catch up on now, so much to discover. Aisha was an aunt, and they were welcome. They had family here. They had made the right decision to return, to heal wounds, and they wouldn't look back. Who knew, they might even decide to settle in Granada and maybe her dad would visit them for a holiday.

Gabi took Aisha's hand. "I love you," she whispered.

"I couldn't have done it without you. Any of it. I wouldn't have left and travelled the world if it hadn't been for you. And it's because of you I'm back here now."

Gabi kissed her. "You've changed lives, Aisha. You were always going to do that, my love. And you can carry on doing that here, for your own people. I'm just glad you chose to take this journey with me."

About Emma Nichols

Emma Nichols lives in Corsica with her partner and two children. She served for 12 years in the British Army, studied Psychology, and published several non-fiction books under another name, before dipping her toes into the world of lesbian fiction.

You can contact Emma through her website and social media:

www.emmanicholsauthor.com
www.facebook.com/EmmaNicholsAuthor
www.twitter.com/ENichols_Author

And do please leave a review if you enjoyed this book. Reviews really help independent authors to create visibility for their work.

Thank you.

Other Books by Emma Nichols

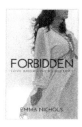   

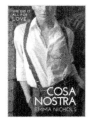   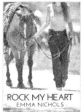

Thanks for reading and supporting my work!
www.emmanicholsauthor.com

Printed in Great Britain
by Amazon